WINGS
OF
FURY

ALSO BY EMILY R. KING

The Evermore Chronicles

Before the Broken Star
Into the Hourglass
Everafter Song

The Hundredth Queen Series

The Hundredth Queen
The Fire Queen
The Rogue Queen
The Warrior Queen

WINGS OF FURY

EMILY R. KING

47NORTH

Published by 47North, Seattle

www.apub.com

Amazon, the Amazon logo, and 47North are trademarks of Amazon.com, Inc., or its affiliates.

ISBN-13: 9781542023733
ISBN-10: 1542023734

Cover design by Ed Bettison

Printed in the United States of America

For Mom.
You wouldn't like me getting a tattoo with your name
on it, so you get this instead:
MY MOM IS A BADASS.
Love you!
(You might want to skip Chapter 16.)

A tale is told that only women know.
For when the men of the Golden Age passed down
Their stories of victory and sacrifice,
They did not think to ask the women theirs.

TITAN HOUSEHOLDS

FIRST HOUSE

Cronus & Rhea

Aeon Palace, Mount Othrys

SECOND HOUSE

Coeus & Phoebe

Sage Tower, Pillar of the North

THIRD HOUSE

Crius & Eurybia

Blue Moon Fortress, Pillar of the South

Fourth House

Hyperion & Theia

Coral Mansion, Pillar of the East

Fifth House

Iapetus & Clymene

Dimmet Stronghold, Pillar of the West

Sixth House

Oceanus & Tethys

Fort Admiral, Location Unknown

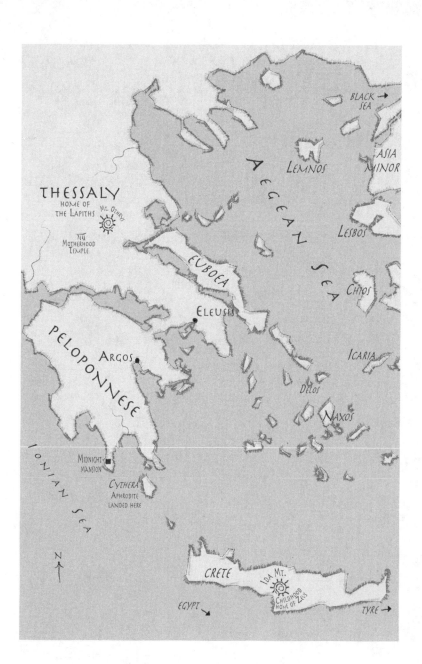

PROLOGUE

My mother told me that men would speak about the Golden Age as a time of peace and happiness for all. Passed-down stories would boast of an era of general ease when the lives of men were blissful, full of abundance, and blessed with spontaneous growth, each man unconstrained in heart and soul. However, the women of our age would tell a very different story.

I thought of my mother's words while the pounding grew louder at the front gates. The vestals hurried into the courtyard, their panic starkly evident in the torchlight.

"They've come for her," said Matron Prosymna.

"What about the children?" asked a vestal.

The matron beckoned us to leave the kitchen, where my two older sisters and I had just finished setting the table for the evening meal.

"Follow me, girls. Quickly." The matron shooed us across the courtyard to the toolshed as though an ox-horned river god were chasing us. "All of you inside. Cleora, keep your sisters out of sight."

"Yes, High Matron," my sister replied.

Cleora, Bronte, and I climbed into the narrow shed and crouched together, me in the middle. At eleven, I was three years younger than Cleora and two years younger than Bronte. The cupboard accommodated us with little room to spare.

The pounding at the gates grew more urgent.

"By order of the First House, open up!" a soldier boomed.

Matron Prosymna shut the shed door, narrowing my view to a slim gap, and strode to the gates. Her vestals formed a line behind her and stood as still as the stone statue of Gaea cradling the world in her full womb, which graced the center of the courtyard. The vestals' white chitons flowed airily to their ankles. Each one's hair was sheared close to her scalp and layered in feathery wisps. The matron's laurel crown, an emblem of her lofty station, was nested in her short gray tresses.

"Veil yourselves," she said.

Each vestal donned her velo. Constructed of stiffened linen painted gold, the modesty masks depicted various beasts and creatures. The velos had no hole for the mouth, just for the eyes; the beak on the matron's peacock mask hid her lips as she spoke.

"We represent Gaea, the Protogenos of the earth, acting in her boundless name with loyalty, virtue, and re—" The banging at the gate interrupted the matron. "Restraint."

My sisters and I tugged down our velos. Like all girls age six or older, we carried our modesty masks with us at all times. We had not taken them off since our mama came home last night from serving in the Aeon Palace and told us to flee our city to the Mother Temple.

The matron squared her shoulders. "Let them in."

Two vestals slid back the iron bar from across the double doors. The gates burst open. Liege men filed in, their shiny breastplates gleaming over knee-length chitons in the torchlight. I moved my head to peer through the gap as nine men spread out to search the courtyard, kitchen, and stables.

I squirmed against my sisters to see better.

"Althea," Cleora hissed. "For once in your life, be still!"

Sitting still was very difficult, but I tried to do as she said.

Matron Prosymna clasped her hands in front of her. "Divine day, General. How may we help you?"

The brutish general, identifiable by his scarlet cloak, slid his gaze from her to the other women. "Where is the handmaid Stavra?"

"She isn't here," the matron replied. "Only us vestals."

"Stavra Lambros!" the general bellowed, his voice echoing off the temple walls. A pair of soldiers returned from the stables and reported to him. He reeled on the matron. "You say Stavra isn't here? Then why is her horse in your stables?"

Matron Prosymna unclasped her hands and gripped them tighter. "Sometimes travelers board their horses—"

The general pushed her into the line of vestals behind her and drew his sword. "Speak the truth, woman. We come in the name of the Almighty, the God of Gods."

The matron trembled, shaken by the reference to our ruler.

"One last chance," the general threatened. "Where is Stavra?"

Matron Prosymna held his stare. The general raised his blade to her chest. Still, she did not speak. He reared his sword back to strike her.

"Decimus!"

Mother stood at the other end of the courtyard. A tall, broad-shouldered woman thwarting propriety by not wearing her velo, Stavra Lambros's charming beauty drew attention everywhere she went. She had warned us Decimus might pursue our family. We had often encountered the general—a bearish, ill-tempered lout with ruddy cheeks that drooped into jowls—while waiting outside the palace gates for Mother to finish her servant duties.

"Seize her," he said.

Two liege men rushed her. Mother pulled a dagger from the folds of her skirt. Decimus waved for his men to stay back.

"This is Gaea's house," Mother said. "My family has sought sanctuary with the Mother of All Gods."

"The elder gods bow to the Titans," Decimus countered. He stepped forward, then again, and again, pausing just outside of her striking range. "You've been summoned by the Almighty. Come with us or forfeit your life."

Mother held her stance of attack, her eyes as bright as licking fire. Decimus snatched her wrist and wrenched her arm over her head. She cried out and released her weapon, and he yanked her against him and lifted his sword to the delicate tendon along her throat. She tilted her chin up and spit. His head reared back, saliva dripping from his lashes.

"Brazen bitch."

He swung down, whacking her over the head with the hilt of his sword. Mother's eyes rolled back as she sagged in his arms.

I gasped softly. Cleora covered my mouth with her hand, pressing my quivering lips. The cupboard stank of urine. Bronte must have wet herself. Matron Prosymna sank to her knees before the general. "Spare her," she begged. "For her children's sake."

Decimus passed Mother's limp body to a liege man. "Put her on my horse."

His subordinate carried my mother out through the gates.

The other liege men harassed the vestals, plucking at their masks and skirts to make them squeal, and stripping three women of their velos. One soldier forcibly kissed a woman while Decimus watched indifferently.

A flame of fury hit me. The God of Gods gave and he took, both in unbridled abundance. As a Titan, and ruler of the First House, he had the whole of the world as his inheritance. But my mama was no one's possession.

I wrenched from Cleora's hold and pushed out of the shed. Bronte shrunk away from the open door while Cleora grabbed for me. I slipped from her grasp and picked up the dagger. The general caught sight of me as I charged him.

My blade grazed his right forearm. He sucked in a cavernous breath, drinking in the whole night sky. Matron Prosymna ran forward to grab me, but Decimus moved faster, and he struck me so hard, I flew into the statue of Gaea and tumbled to her feet.

I landed on my side, short-winded, my velo knocked off. I reached for it, but Decimus stomped down, crushing the stiff linen and pinning my hand to the ground. He pressed his foot harder, unrelenting despite my moan.

"You're Stavra's youngest daughter, Althea."

"Let my mama go."

"You plead for her while I crush your fingers?" He stepped off my hand and inspected me hungrily. "With your dark hair and golden skin, and those lovely wide eyes, your beauty will outmatch your mother's." He raised his voice to the matron. "Has Althea been tagged?"

"Pardon, General?"

"Has another man spoken for her?" he enunciated impatiently.

"Not yet, but—"

"I'll return for her when she's ripened. Don't try to hide her or pull her into your zealot's fold, or I will see that the Almighty learns that you do not display his alpha and omega insignia on your front gate, and he will dismantle this 'temple' brick by brick." Decimus wiped at the cut on his arm, smearing blood onto his finger, then drove his bloody fingertip between my lips. "I'll return for you, kitten."

As he stalked out of the gates, his company marching after him, I scrubbed at my lips and spit in the dirt. Matron Prosymna scurried to my side.

"Althea, you foolish, foolish girl." She glared at my sisters. "You were supposed to watch her!"

"I tried," Cleora replied.

"You failed," the matron snapped.

Bronte's soft weeping rang out from the shed. Cleora comforted our sister despite her own tears. Neither one looked at me.

I pushed to my feet and hobbled to the gates. The liege men retreated into the twilight with our mama slung over Decimus's horse like nothing more than a sack of grain.

Ten months had passed when a pair of soldiers entered my sisters' and my bedchamber in a chorus of heavy breaths and shuffling feet. Their brass uniforms, marked across the chest with the alpha and omega symbols of the First House, glinted in the waxing moonlight. Though the men were both too slender to be Decimus, I tensed.

Bronte and Cleora slept across the chamber on the bed they shared. Since we had no other family to speak of, the vestals had taken us in. Matron Prosymna was a harsh matriarch who allowed little time for anything other than chores. I hadn't danced—my favorite communal activity—since our arrival. Lying nearest to the door on my own smaller cot, I pretended to sleep as the men set a woman down beside me on the thinly stuffed mattress. I couldn't see much except her frail body, then the soldiers shifted back, and a moonbeam grazed her face.

Mama.

The men left in a parade of rushed footsteps. I waited for my mother to speak or move. Very carefully, so as not to startle her, I touched her hand.

"Mama?"

Her breaths deepened and lengthened, and her chest burst with tears. Since her capture, we had prayed morning and night to Gaea for her return. Most women taken by the Almighty were never seen again. A bag of two hundred silver pieces would arrive on their kin's doorstep as though the worth of a soul could be weighed in silver. A mortal soul, that was. The Titans were legions of their own self-worship. Though monsters, they esteemed themselves above the stars.

Mother slid her hand into mine and squeezed. I rolled over to hug her, draping my arm across her waist, and gaped at her swollen belly.

"Mama?" I whispered again, scared now.

"The babe is strong," she rasped. "I cannot hold it much longer. I'll try to stay with you and your sisters. I'll try, but . . ."

But her mortal womb wasn't meant to birth a Titan.

On occasion, women impregnated by the Almighty staggered into the temple for aid. Couplings between a god and mortal always led to procreation. Childbirth came, and with it, tragedy.

Mother grasped her belly, her cheeks puffing as she spoke. "Listen closely, Althea, my shooting star. Gaea gave women many talents. We are strong—stronger than any monster. Weak Titans fear us and try to control that power, but a woman's love is her wings. We can soar high, higher than the gods."

Her belly bunched up, the skin and muscle hardening. She clenched her teeth to quiet the pain, but it found a pathway out of her in an ago-nizing groan.

Vestals rushed into the chamber with extra blankets and a pail of hot water. At their exclamations of alarm, Bronte and Cleora roused and blinked in astonishment. One of the vestals urged them to get up and began ushering all three of us out.

"Althea stays," Mother said, clinging to my hand.

I exchanged wide-eyed glances with my older sisters, then they were pushed into the corridor.

Mother screamed, a feral release of agony. Matron Prosymna and the cook, Acraea, ran in, and I backed away so they could work.

"The babe is coming fast," Acraea said.

"Then we will work faster," replied the matron.

Bearing down, Mother screamed again. I had heard it told that Titan babies entered the world in the same way they lived—with the rage of thunder—but I had never been present for a delivery. In truth, I had never seen any of the monsters up close.

Mama cried out again. I pressed my shoulder blades against the wall, unable to remember the last time I was so still. The chamber smelled of musty sweat and something older, more primal. Mother pushed, but her body worked just as hard against her.

The seconds built to minutes.

Long, long minutes.

The vestals urged her to bear down again, despite the blood . . . and more blood. Mother gave her mightiest scream yet, legs trembling, face scrunched up in torment. Her next was drowned out by a high-pitched wail.

She sank back, her tears of pain dissolving into gentle sobs of relief. The matron cleaned up the babe and lifted it for all to see.

"A girl," she announced.

The baby didn't appear as though she had been sired by a monster. Titans could grow to twenty-five feet tall. The Almighty was the biggest at fifty. Yet Titans were still more human than Gaea's first creations, the Cyclopes or Hecatoncheires—fiends with fifty heads and a hundred hands each. The babe was the same size as a mortal newborn, with all her fingers, toes, and eyes in the correct places. Her only oddity was her thick, curly black hair, which made it look as if she wore a wool hairpiece.

Perhaps she didn't resemble a monster because she was only half of one.

My mama whimpered, and her sweaty face drained of color. The stench of fresh blood trickled into something darker, a sort of decay, flooding my nostrils. The infant let loose another cry. Matron Prosymna passed the babe to Acraea, then she and the other vestals worked on my mama. They spoke nary a word, their lips pinched white.

Mother extended her hand to me. I went to her slowly. Usually, I walked slightly forward on my toes as though I were always one leap away from taking flight, but now my feet dragged across the floor.

My mother gripped my hand with remarkable strength. "Althea, you're not yet grown, but soon you'll be a woman, and with that comes tremendous blessings and burdens."

I could hardly hear her above the wailing infant, so I merely nodded.

"The guild will watch over you. Heed the matron and hearken to the goddess. Don't forget your worth as a woman, Althea. You and your sisters need each other. Vow to me that you will protect them."

"Me, Mama? Shouldn't Cleora or Bronte—?"

"Your destiny is to guide and protect your sisters. Family doesn't abandon family. Do you swear you will watch over them?"

"I swear."

"Good, my shooting star." She patted my hand and let go. "Remember your wings."

Acraea laid the swaddled infant beside my mother and tucked a blanket around them. Mother rested her forehead against the rosy babe's, as she often did with my sisters and me. She said she did so to memorize our smell, our touch, and the shapes of our souls.

Mother hummed her favorite lullaby, a morose melody about Gaea's grief over her monstrous children, trapped in the underworld. The infant suckled at Mama's breast while the matron worked to stem the blood dripping to the floor. Mother finished the lullaby, then laid her head back and shut her eyes. The newborn drifted off in her arms, and they both fell silent.

"Mama?" I asked.

Acraea touched my mother's shoulder and listened for her breathing. The matron raised her bloody hands and swiped at her forehead with the back of one, waiting. After an eternity, Acraea bowed her head.

"Gaea, receive thy daughter," she said, her voice breaking.

Matron Prosymna prayed as well. "Gaea, welcome Stavra beyond the gates of the sun and into the land of dreams."

Tears brimmed in my eyes. How peaceful my mother appeared, like she could have been sleeping—but she was too empty looking, too still.

Matron Prosymna opened the window to let in air. Leaving the infant with her mother, the vestals mopped the floor with rags.

"She was too pretty," said Acraea.

"She should have worn her velo," replied another vestal.

Matron Prosymna nodded gravely. "This is what happens when a woman isn't careful."

I balled my hands into fists. "My mama did nothing wrong! The Almighty did this. He and his bastard."

"Shh," said the matron. "You'll wake the baby."

The infant slept despite the death around her. She was small and fragile now, but she would grow into her birthright. She was an atrocity—half human, half Titan.

Fully a monster.

I scooped her up and ran to the open window. Once there, I didn't know what to do. I only knew that Mama was dead and someone had to pay.

"Put the baby down, Althea," said the matron.

"She killed my mama!"

Matron Prosymna lifted her hands, still stained with my mother's blood. "Stavra is at rest. Let her soul go to the gods in peace."

"The gods don't care what becomes of her soul," I said. "Every day, we prayed for her safe return, yet she's gone."

"Goddess forgive your insolence," the matron hissed. "Quit this ridiculousness and hand over the baby."

"The world needs one less Titan," I replied.

"She's an innocent." The matron patted her chest, over her heart. "What will you do to honor your mother's memory? Will you care for your sisters—*all* of your sisters? Or will you break your promise to Stavra before her body has gone cold?"

I glanced at my mother's body, then out the second-story window. The babe slept fast, her ignorance unfathomable. Didn't she know everything was ruined? Didn't she know that Mama—our mama, *my* mama—was never coming back?

"Who will teach her about your mother?" the matron pressed, gradually crossing the chamber to us. "Who will tell her how brave and strong your mother was?"

The newborn stirred a little and squeaked, like a bunny.

Matron Prosymna paused, just out of arm's reach. "The babe isn't your adversary, Althea. She's your sister. Your family."

I eyed the baby more closely. Her nose was too large for her face. I often complained about the size of my own nose. Bronte and Cleora liked to tease me about its width. The baby's nose was the same shape and had the same proportions as mine. She might have been half Titan, but she was also half mortal.

Half my blood.

Half me.

"You should name her," said the matron.

"Name her?"

"Yes, child. She needs a name."

None of the Titan spawn sired by the Almighty deserved a name. Still, I wondered what my mother might have called her.

Footsteps pounded in the corridor. The door swung open, and three soldiers barged in. The one in the lead—a man with a long, angled face like a rat's—spotted my mother lifeless on the bed, then swung his attention to me.

"Hand over the baby," he said.

The matron stepped in front of us. "She belongs with her family. No one need know she survived. I swear on Gaea's boundless name, none of us will tell a soul."

Ratface stepped closer, swinging his meaty shoulders and gripping his sword. "Save your promises, matron. The babe comes with us."

"You condemn her to death," she replied. "The God of Gods will end her as he has all his children."

"It isn't for us to question the Almighty's will." He shoved the matron out of his way and prowled toward me.

My mother's words cut through my mind. *Protect your sisters.*

I lunged out the open window onto the ledge. Ratface's long arms swiped at me. Light on my toes, I scurried along the sloped rooftop as he climbed out after me.

Holding the newborn tighter, I edged around the corner of the roofline. The courtyard stables ran parallel to the temple. The ledge ahead ended at a gap between two peaks. Unafraid of heights, I stepped across. My ankle turned on a loose roof tile, and I wobbled backward. My bottom hit the sloped roof, and I slid. Air whooshed around me as I landed in a pile of hay.

The baby groused in my arms. I hushed and rocked her.

Bronte and Cleora leaned out the gynaeceum window on the second floor and gaped at me. Ratface searched for a safe path down from the roof. I wriggled out of the hay to the ground, my ankle aching as I limped toward the front gates.

A soldier emerged from the shadows. He was bigger than the others, with a shaven face and wavy dark-brown hair that hung down his back. I paused, waiting for him to draw his sword. His brow pinched.

"Angelos, secure the baby!" Ratface yelled.

The soldier in my way started for me. "Give me the baby and I'll see that you're safe."

"No," I argued.

Angelos opened his arms to take the baby. I jerked away, jostling her awake. Though her eyes were closed, she began to wail. He grabbed for her again. I kicked him in the kneecap and sped past him.

"Run!" Bronte and Cleora shouted in chorus.

I rushed the gates. Two soldiers with swords drawn hurried out of the temple and blocked my pathway.

Ratface gave up on descending the roof and started back through the window. "Get me the baby!" he ordered, then disappeared inside.

The soldiers blocking the front gates prowled forward. I whirled around to find Angelos behind me.

He opened his arms for the infant, his expression solemn. His voice matched his sympathetic eyes. "You must let her go."

The babe howled.

Another soldier reached around me from behind and tried to wrestle her from my grasp. I held on as tightly as possible without hurting her, but he wrenched her away. I beat my fists against his back.

"Let her go!" I cried.

He pushed me hard. My sore ankle turned on its side again, this time with a popping noise, and I fell to the ground in pain.

Ratface stormed out of the temple and saw they had secured their prize. He whistled, and the soldiers mounted up, except Angelos, who lingered beside me. He extended his hand to help me up, but I pushed to my feet, my ankle aching fiercely.

The newborn wailed and wailed.

"She's my sister," I pleaded.

"I'm sorry," he whispered.

"Angelos, we ride!" Ratface called.

Angelos hesitated another moment and then mounted up with the liege men, and they rode out. The infant's wails faded with the thunder of horses' hooves into the jasmine-scented night.

I sank to the ground in tears, my arms limp at my sides.

Mama was gone, and so was my baby sister.

Gone before she even had a name.

1

I carried the full water pails away from the pond and through the dappled woodland. Two hours before daybreak, I had scoured the kitchen and commons floor with scalding water. Now, as the sun crested to the east, my back ached from scrubbing away the soot marks around the hearth on my hands and knees.

The nearby stream roared as snow-water torrents hurtled down the mountainside. In spring, the forest itself rested in a wintry haze, the hamadryads in each tree dozing until dawn dismounted her rosy throne and surrendered to daylight. In the almost seven years that we had lived in these hills, I had come to know the many craggy paths through leafy recesses. I navigated every dip in the ground and ducked from every bough, considerate of the yawning hamadryads. The water sloshed over the edges of the pails and onto my muddy feet. I should have slowed down so as not to waste more, but the handles cut into my palms, and my empty stomach grumbled. Replenishing the water supply was my last morning chore before I could eat.

Travelers headed my direction up the trail, a party of hoplites—poor citizen soldiers, farmers, and artisans who elected to take up weapons in defense of their homeland. The road was too narrow for them and me, so I stepped into the underbrush and bowed my head. My hair fell forward, hiding my unmasked face.

"Divine day," one man said as they passed.

I flinched. His voice did not sound familiar. Still wary, I glanced from the corner of my eye. Once in a while, I met men from the nearby village for a brief romp down by the pond, but I didn't recognize these men.

A very pretty unmasked girl, no older than thirteen, sat with her hands bound in front of their lead rider. An offering for the Almighty, I wagered. She could have been one of their daughters, or a girl sold to them by a poor family. It was hard to say what circumstances led her here, another girl who was worth just two hundred silver pieces.

Though I was supposed to return home already, I waited until the party disappeared up the winding road before hefting the water pails onward.

The temple compound was shrouded in springtime foliage, its outer walls a two-story dormitory that housed all the vestals, their oratory, and their workspaces. Within the courtyard of the U-shaped dormitory—in addition to the kitchen, stables, and outbuildings—stood the actual temple, a modest stone structure with columns on a base of stairs and an ornate precipice. The most recent addition to the courtyard, come five years ago, was a statue of the God of Gods posed naked with his arms at his sides and chin lifted defiantly. It, and the tattered First House flag hung at the front gates, displayed the minimal devotion required of any household in the territory of Thessaly.

My bad ankle throbbed by the time I arrived. After I broke it as a girl, the bone hadn't healed right, often giving me pains when I stood too long or walked too far. A line of vestals exited the temple after offering morning prayers before the statue of Gaea. They had already laid their daily sacrifice of fruit or bread before the statue of the Almighty. He always came first. I mumbled, "Divine day," and kept on for the open-air kitchen.

Acraea kneaded bread dough, with two slaves assisting her. My sisters worked alongside them, Bronte grinding grain and Cleora stoking the fire. They, too, had woken early. Cleora ran the kitchen and hearth, while Bronte swept the quiet halls and tended to the garden. A bundle of freshly picked greens was piled by the washbasin, waiting for Bronte to clean and chop. Our meager breakfast of stale bread, which they nibbled on as they worked, and wine was on the plate and in the chalice we shared. Fewer dishes to wash, Cleora would say. She always found ways to lessen our workload.

I set the pails by the fire, then poured them, one at a time, into the big pots for boiling. Finally, with a moment to be still, I stretched my back.

Cleora stared at the dancing flames. "You're late."

"Or dawn was early," I replied.

Bronte snorted. I joined her at the worktable and reached across her to snag a piece of flatbread from our breakfast plate. She flicked me in the arm.

"Don't forget to pray," she said.

I mumbled a short prayer of thanks and shoved the bread into my mouth. "You're filthy," I said, rubbing a smudge of dirt off Bronte's forehead. Her straight flaxen hair was tangled with bits of rosemary.

She wrinkled her nose at me. "You smell like a sow."

"You smell like an herb."

Acraea laughed at us from where she kneaded dough at the second worktable. She wasn't like the other snobbish vestals who'd joined the Guild of Gaea in their childhood and kept their distance from us. Acraea had taken her vow of virginity later, after running away from an arranged marriage years ago. She brushed her hands on her apron and flung a gunnysack at me.

"Go to Othrys for figs and burgundy olives," she said. "We need them for the bounty bread."

"I said I would help with the mending, and I need to muck out the stalls. It's also my turn to watch the flock." I always had a long list of things to do. Whereas Bronte and Cleora had set chores, I did whatever needed to be done, which was usually what no one else would do. I had been anticipating a day by myself in the fields to practice with my spear and shield away from the matron's disapproving scowls.

"The slaves will take over your household commitments, and Bronte will tend to the sheep," Acraea replied.

"Why doesn't she go to the market and I watch the sheep?" I asked.

"The wild dogs hunted down two lambs yesterday. She's a better archer."

I caught Bronte's small smile. For her, tending to the sheep also meant time away from the overbearing matron.

"We need those ingredients," Acraea added.

The bounty bread was baked for the First House Festival, the anniversary of the Almighty's overthrow of his father, Uranus. The olives and figs, representing the blood that Uranus shed upon the earth, had to be soaked in wine for at least five days before the dough could be prepared. People across the world baked the bread in the God of Gods' honor. The day of celebration wouldn't be the same without it, but I didn't like having my commitments handed off.

Besides, traveling to the city meant that I might run into Decimus. I was always on the watch for him. We all were. At times, I thought he had forgotten me, but the tag burned into the back of my neck wouldn't let me forget *him*.

"Acraea, when do we leave?" I asked, tying back my deep-auburn hair with a piece of string.

"The matron said she's needed here," Cleora replied, meticulously tending the fire.

My eyebrows shot up. "I'm going without a companion?"

"You're eighteen," Acraea said. "That's old enough for a day trip to the city alone."

I often pointed out my age to justify my independence, but I was surprised Cleora would allow this. She didn't like me going to the city at all, let alone by myself. The matron must have insisted. I grabbed the gunnysack. "All right."

Cleora straightened up and finally looked at me. "Where's your velo?"

"Upstairs in our bedchamber."

Her amber eyes flashed. "You went outside unmasked? Were you seen?"

"Nothing happened," I said, sipping from the wine chalice the three of us shared. Cleora snatched my wrist, and I nearly spilled down the front of myself.

"Who saw you?" she asked.

"The hoplites weren't interested in me." I reached for a piece of flatbread with my free hand, but she shifted and blocked my way.

"Take this seriously," she said. "Did they speak to you?"

"Just pleasantries in passing."

"Althea," she groaned. "How many times must I tell you not to leave the compound unmasked? Go fetch your velo. You're not traveling without it."

Cleora's usual bossy overprotectiveness grated on me. Of course, I wouldn't go to the city without my modesty mask. I wasn't dense. "Can I eat first? Gods."

"Watch your tongue," the matron snapped.

Everyone froze except Bronte, who was busy grinding wheat, preoccupied by her own humming. She sang to herself so often that no one found it odd when she didn't respond to Matron Prosymna's appearance in the doorway of the kitchen.

"Do not blasphemy in Gaea's house," said the matron.

The goddess wasn't present to take offense, but I didn't point that out.

"Althea didn't mean anything by it," Cleora said, letting go of my wrist.

"I will hear an apology from your sister," the matron replied.

"Althea?" Cleora prodded.

I refused to meet their gazes. I was not sorry about my slip of the tongue.

"Althea," Bronte said with a kindly singsong in her voice. "You should apologize."

It might have been petulant of me, but my older sisters ordering me about was too much just then. My hands and back still ached from chores, and my stomach grumbled for more food. For nearly seven years, I had toiled hours a day for the guild. At what point would I earn the right to speak without watching my words?

"Perhaps she needs more work to avoid idle time," the matron said.

Eating breakfast was idle time?

"Althea's grateful for all you provide," Cleora replied in a rush. "She hasn't eaten yet, and you know she's grumpy when she's hungry. I'll fetch her velo." She whisked out of the kitchen.

"The rest of you get back to work," Matron Prosymna commanded. "Bronte, shouldn't you be leaving for the fields?"

Bronte glanced at the pile of herbs set aside for her to wash and chop. "Cleora asked me to help here before I—"

"Your sister will manage. You're required elsewhere."

Bronte slowly set down the pestle, then met the matron's stare. My sister hid her disdain so well that sometimes I forgot I wasn't the only one barely tolerating our life in the temple. "Yes, matron," Bronte said with a hint of derision.

Matron Prosymna cast me one last pinch-lipped glare and stormed out.

Acraea returned to kneading the bread, shaking her head. "You know how to liven up a morning, Althea."

Bronte brushed the coarse-ground grains off her hands. "My little sister's stubbornness could raise the Gigantes from the underworld."

"You don't wear your velo to the watering hole either," I shot back.

"*I'm* careful not to be seen, mm-hmm," Bronte teased. "You know how Cleora feels about us leaving the compound."

Cleora hadn't gone outside since our mother was taken. Though she was twenty-one now, and a full-grown woman, it was an unacknowledged courtesy that we never spoke of her self-segregation from the outside world.

Bronte showed the bowl of ground grain to Acraea. "This looks finished."

"It's perfect," Acraea replied.

Bronte ground grain better than anyone else in the compound. She adjusted her gold necklace, frowning. "Should one of us check on Cleora?"

By "one of us," she meant me.

I downed the wine in our cup, then took the last two pieces of flatbread and ate them on my way upstairs.

Cleora was straightening my bedcovers as I arrived. Our small chamber was only just better than the slave quarters, but Cleora had added homey touches: painted violets and yellow crocuses along the base of the plain ceramic walls, polished tile floors, our few belongings displayed beautifully on shelves, our clothes organized and stowed in cedar chests. Our mother's lyre in its wooden case was the showpiece on one shelf, and leaning against the opposite wall was our family loom.

It was cramped quarters for the three of us, but Cleora cared for it well. She was slender yet strong from lifting heavy pots of water and hauling logs to feed the ever-burning fire in the kitchen hearth, and she moved with a measured grace that radiated temperance. She wasn't a dancer—though she played the lyre beautifully—but her internal tempo was steadfast. Watching her work was mesmerizing, like observing the waves of the sea, constant and purposeful.

"I'm sorry," I said.

"Now you apologize?" Cleora pulled at the bedcovers with quick tugs. "The matron only has so much patience."

"She'll forget about it."

We both knew that without Cleora instructing the kitchen slaves or Bronte and I assisting in preparing the food, Matron Prosymna would struggle to feed the fifty or so vestals living here. We had become indispensable, especially Cleora, whose ability to run a household more than compensated for her reluctance to do outside chores.

"I cannot find your velo," she said. "It must be here somewhere . . . Ah, here it is."

She pulled my modesty mask out from under the bed and sat down, facing the window and its view of Mount Othrys. Our former home, the city of Othrys, kneeled at the feet of the mountain peak, strewn around its fringes in the stony foothills. I sat beside Cleora, close enough to smell the almond oil she had dabbed into her wavy red hair.

She offered my mask to me. "I know you dislike wearing your velo, Althea, but don't take it off today."

"I shouldn't have to veil myself every time I step outside."

"You sound like Mama." Cleora sighed.

"Mama was right about a lot of things," I said.

"Perhaps, but we must be grateful for what the gods have given us."

Women weren't doomed to live off scraps of happiness, but I suspected Cleora was concerned about Decimus seeing me in the city. I wouldn't worry her more. "I won't take off my velo."

She tied the strings behind my head. Plumes extended from the eye openings, resembling a mane, or flames, depending on one's interpretation of the exquisite craftsmanship. It had belonged to our mother and, before her, our grandmother.

"Quit moving," Cleora said.

"My nose itches."

"Why can't you ever sit still?"

"I can." I wriggled my nose to scratch it against the inside of my mask, but otherwise, I didn't move.

"Finished." Cleora's finger skimmed the scar on the back of my neck. It had taken four vestals to restrain me—and another four to hold back my sisters—when the matron burned the U-shaped tag into my skin. "Does it still hurt?"

"Only my pride." I rearranged my hair to cover the mark.

"I need to get back to the kitchen. We've got bread to bake."

I glanced sideways at Cleora. Her tired voice and bloodshot eyes worried me. She had slept restlessly last night. She always did around the anniversary of Mother's death. It would be seven years tomorrow. Mother was on all our minds.

"Why don't you lie down?" I said. "I'll tell Acraea not to expect you back until this afternoon."

"The work is good for me. Having order in the house brings me peace." Cleora tipped her forehead against mine. This show of affection had originated at the dawn of time when only Gaea, the Protogenos of the earth, existed and nothing lived on her yet. Uranus, the Protogenos of the sky, rose above her, sapphire blue and set with stars, and he rested his forehead against hers. That union of the primordial gods formed the first family—and family meant everything.

I shifted back. "Would you like anything from the city?"

"Just your safe return. Tell Acraea I'll be right down. And, Althea? I try hard to make this our home. Please keep the peace with the matron."

A hot lump expanded in my throat. I wanted a home of our own, just the three of us, far away from here, but Cleora tried to make this place a refuge. I didn't intend to compromise that for her.

"I'll do better," I said, and slogged back downstairs to the kitchen.

The slaves' regimen for preparing meals was already suffering from Cleora's absence. The girls were loitering about, sipping wine and chatting. The fire in the hearth was dwindling, no additional grain had been ground, and the dough looked as though it had been shaped into loaves by a Cyclops.

Acraea snapped at them to get back to work. "They're worse than sheep," she grumbled. "Where's Cleora?"

"She'll be right down. I'm leaving now."

Acraea passed me a basket with the shopping list, a pouch of coins, and food and water for the day. "Don't forget, the olives must be—"

"Burgundy. I remember."

I reached for an apricot from the basket on the table, and a pebble struck my hand. Bronte chuckled from where she stood outside the window, her bow and arrow slung over her shoulder. I stuck my tongue out at her, and she grinned before heading out to the fields.

Watching her go, I struggled not to envy her the quiet day she had ahead. Somehow, she always managed to find time alone, though, in honesty, she was more bearable to be around after she'd had a day to herself. Bronte would pass the time by singing in our secret cave or napping in the sun while she pondered ideas that she would later discuss with the vestals. She had a mind for philosophy and took interest in the guild's beliefs in Gaea by starting noncontentious debates. Her favorite philosopher was the second-generation Titan Prometheus, the god of forethought. Most philosophers lived in the north, with the House of Coeus, where they studied with the greatest minds in the world, but as a woman, Bronte would never have that opportunity. Just as I could never become a true dancer. Women ran and maintained households. Everything else—particularly the arts and higher thinking—was for men.

I carried my basket of food to the stables. Our donkey had shoved his head through an opening in the fence around his pen to chew on the baby green shoots in the herb garden.

"Don't let Bronte catch you," I said, yanking him back into his pen. "I hope you didn't eat anything poisonous."

A section of the garden was reserved for medicinal purposes. Bronte could tell her plants apart, but, to me, they all looked the same. I strapped the saddlebags to the donkey and climbed on. The donkey would be slower and less comfortable than the matron's mare, but I doubted Prosymna would permit me the favor of borrowing her horse.

Acraea caught me before I left and slipped a bundle into the basket. Up close, I could see the burn mark on her forehead that was usually hidden behind a fringe of gray hair. Conversely, the tag on the back of her neck, given to her as a young girl on behalf of the husband she later ran from, had nearly faded. She discreetly unwrapped the butcher's knife for me to see.

"Keep an eye out for him," she said.

I wanted to reassure her that she didn't need to worry, that the chance I would encounter Decimus was low, but I couldn't. As I rode out of the gates and up the path through the hushed, shadowy woodland, I wished I could have brought my spear and shield as well. Women weren't allowed to carry such defenses.

Taking the kitchen knife out of the basket, I hid it in the folds of my skirt with one hand and gripped the reins with the other. Maidens usually traveled in pairs, but even safety in numbers was an illusion. I would ensure my security with a blade.

2

Taking a detour would shorten my time in the city, but I never traveled east without stopping to see my mother.

At a divide in the road, I dismounted and led the donkey down a footpath between cypress trees and speckled sycamores. Spring had flung itself back into the northeastern region of Thessaly, brightening every bush and tree in brilliant green.

The hamadryads living in the dogwood and mulberry trees studied me as I passed. Their faces blended with the rough bark, their arms twisted into the boughs and bodies winding around the curvy trunks. The woodland spirits were good natured unless disturbed.

I stepped over their roots and ducked from their branches to avoid bothering them. The ground softened to sandy soil, an easier place to bury the dead, as well as prime ground for the olive trees that marked the entrance to the graveyard.

Headstones in the shape of pillars were scattered across the mossy sanctuary. I stopped before two, one shorter than the other, and rested my hand on the tall one.

"Hello, Mama."

Six pairs of wings were etched on the front, which read, FAMILY DOESN'T ABANDON FAMILY. The shorter headstone stood atop an empty grave for our half sister, who hadn't been seen or heard of since the guards ripped her from my arms. Not a day went by that I did not think of her, wonder what my mother would have named her, and picture the life she would have lived.

Though no one was buried there, it hurt my heart to kneel before the vacant grave site and dig, shoveling up dirt by the fistful. After Mother's death, we received an official letter of appreciation and payment for her service to the First House as an honor maiden. The Almighty referred to his captives as honorable, as though their abduction was a noble calling.

The letter I burned.

The pouch of coins I buried.

Now I dusted off the pouch. Years ago, when my sisters and I buried the coin, we promised each other we would only spend it on one thing.

"Mama, I'm getting us out. It's time."

Cleora was too comfortable at the compound, and too committed to the guild. Any longer living there, and she might never leave. But the true impetus was time. Decimus would not wait forever to return for me.

After tying the pouch to my belt, I patted the dirt back into place and covered it with moss to prevent anyone from noticing. Cleora or Bronte would have uttered a prayer for the well-being of our mother's and our half sister's souls, but I gave up on turning to Gaea a long time ago.

I led the donkey past the wide-eyed hamadryads and back to the road. We followed the steep gravel path uphill and around the throat of the mountain.

Sunshine poured down, warming the day. Cool winds blew up from the valley, but the fresh gusts didn't stop my velo from sticking to my face. I nibbled on pieces of cheese beneath it. The mask itched, but I couldn't take it off in case I chanced upon other travelers.

Abductions had increased in recent years. No one stood up to the Almighty, not his five Titan brothers who managed their own households or his wife, Rhea, a Titaness. I hadn't been to Othrys since last autumn, before the rainy season made traveling these vertical roads treacherous, but it was rumored that Rhea spent more of her time at the Blue Moon Fortress in the south with her brother Crius, head of the Third House, than at the Aeon Palace with her husband.

Around the next bend, the Aegean Sea stained the horizon. The glittering expanse of cerulean, dotted with stretches of islands, belonged to the Sixth House. The Titan Oceanus was estranged from his five brothers. His watery realm was the only domain not governed by the First House. Mother once told us that a tribe of women inhabited one of Oceanus's isles, living without stone walls and velos. It sounded like paradise.

Far above me on the mountaintop, manifesting like a shadow in the eventide, the outer wall of Othrys rose into view. I tucked the kitchen knife back into the basket and guided the donkey into the flood of people waiting for admission through the main gates.

A pair of soldiers stood guard, questioning various groups and individuals about their purpose for entering. They stopped mostly women, who needed permission from a male relative to leave their home. I twisted my bare neck around for the guards to see my tag—evidence that a man owned me. Tagged women were viewed as tamed, and less likely to travel without permission.

"Divine day," one guard said, waving me into the city.

I fell in line with the stream of entrants crowding the narrow streets. A thick mix of unwashed flesh, animal excrement, and emptied chamber pots—all baking in the sun—hit my nose like a mallet. Nothing stunk of civilization quite like the city.

Riding farther into Othrys, I entered the colorful market district. Pale plaster huts with red tile roofs were hedged in among lean-tos and patchwork tents. The street teemed with customers bargaining with merchants. Stray dogs and cats sniffed about for scraps. The agora sold everything: baskets of spices piled high and shiny bolts of bright silks, every kind of fresh fish and cured meat, a rainbow of cheeses and produce, vibrant woven rugs, and even children's toys.

I tied the donkey to a post in front of a tavern, collected my things, and set out for the nearest produce booth. The stand was stocked with an array of winter root vegetables, and springtime had reintroduced a bounty of beans, artichokes, spinach, and beetroots. My eye landed on a plate of almond-and-walnut honey pies. Our mother used to bake them for our birthdays. The handheld treats were a family favorite.

An unmasked maiden bumped into my side as she reached for figs.

"Pardon me," I said, my voice trailing off. Her chin, cheeks, and forehead were covered with burn scars. The lattice marks scored into her skin were too precisely patterned to be random.

Carefully—intentionally—this girl had been marred.

Last time Acraea came home from the city, she had mentioned that families performing ritual burnings had increased. Parents were dismayed by the Almighty's abductions of their loveliest daughters, so disfigurement of young women had risen in popularity. Acraea never told me exactly how she escaped with the single burn on her forehead all those years ago, only that Gaea had helped her. Nowadays, men paid a higher bride price for a marred woman than a pretty girl in a velo. Some girls were so afraid of capture or spinsterhood, they mutilated themselves.

"What can I do for you?" barked the merchant.

I snapped into focus. The scarred girl was gone, and my sack was still empty.

"Do you have burgundy olives?" I asked as I began collecting figs.

"All out, but I have these."

Acraea would send gadflies after me if I came home with black olives. I haggled with the merchant over the figs, bringing him down in price enough to purchase two honey pies, then continued on.

I knew my birth city well. Sometimes I missed the scent of goat's milk and fresh verbena in the morning, but I never missed the soldiers, posted on every street corner, watching residents with penetrating stares. They reminded me of Decimus and the night my mother was taken. A pair of soldiers loitered up ahead, so I took a shortcut down an alley to avoid them and exited in front of the Aeon Palace.

All Titans resided in mansions. This was the zenith, the grandest and most impressive godly estate in the world. A dwelling fit for the head of the First House, the God of Gods.

The Aeon Palace could be seen from all across the land. It had been built atop the peak of the mountain range, its shape a smooth continuation of the summit. Constructed upon the precipice of the stony apex, the exterior walls rose steeply into a triangular point, its singular spire impaling the sky. Craggy walls opened to depthless archways and lofty doorways into alcoves. Battlements and ramparts divided the structure into seamless levels, and spacious terraces lined with parapets cut into the structure. A band of clouds ringed the top, partly obscuring the snowy crown where the flag of the First House flew, the Almighty's alpha and omega insignia on a backdrop of blue-and-white stripes. It was said that nobody but the gods could pass through the portal of clouds to the great hall above.

Before me, the gates stood five times taller than any man. Sacrifices of bounty had been set around the entry, baskets full of fruits and cheeses that rotted in the midday sun. Once a week, the refuse collectors threw everything into a wagon and hauled it away for pig slop. The gates creaked as guards pushed them open for soldiers approaching with wagons full of wine barrels. The Almighty dined mostly on nectar and ambrosia, the food of the gods, but he also had a taste for wine.

Through the open gates, I saw two young women lounging under leafy apricot trees. They wore blue, the Almighty's favored color for his honor maidens. No wonder Rhea spent most of her time in the south. Her husband's betrayals were blatant. Or perhaps the honor maidens were only permitted to wander the palace grounds because Rhea wasn't present to throw a jealous fit. According to rumor, somewhere in the city was an unmarked mass grave where the Almighty's honor maidens were buried, most dead under mysterious circumstances. After Rhea left the palace, the frequency of these deaths dropped dramatically.

The honor maidens saw me, saw the open gates, saw their chance at freedom, yet didn't run. The God of Gods didn't need to chain his prisoners. Fear held them.

The gates shut behind the last wagon with a shuddering bang. I waited for the onlookers to disperse, then spit.

Not my god. Not my ruler.

I weaved through the agora, pushing into the rising winds. Merchants rushed to tie down their tents and secure their wares. The mountain skies changed moods faster than Matron Prosymna, but the sudden change in weather wasn't a reason to start home. Storms rattled through the hilltops day and night. At times, Helios, the sun god who rode his golden chariot across the sky each day, became infatuated with the Oceanids, the nymph daughters of Oceanus. A storm would brew over the ocean when Oceanus grew agitated by Helios ogling his daughters, and those winds would eventually make landfall. The gods' choices affected mortals every day, and stars, that was tiresome.

The search for burgundy olives took me back into the agora and all the way across the market district. I gave up on finding any and set out on a personal errand.

On my way, I passed the palaestra, where wrestling was taught and practiced. Men were hard at work training in the open arena. Every two years, teams of the best wrestlers from the First, Second, Third, Fourth, and Fifth Houses gathered here to compete. I knew the basic rules of the game, but women weren't permitted into the palaestra.

I arrived at the fisherman's booth. Buckets of oysters, clams, and mussels were packed around the lean-to, and silver fish hung from the canopy. The wind slapped the sign against the tent: **OCEANUS'S CATCH.**

The fish merchant's face lit up. "Bronte!"

"Close. I'm Althea."

"With your velo on, you look just like your sister."

Bronte and I were both tall, but the similarities stopped there. She had hazel eyes; mine were gray. Her hair was blonde; mine was coppery auburn. "It's good to see you, Proteus."

"What can I get you?" he asked. "I have fresh octopus, caught this morning."

I held down my velo as another gust pushed past us. "I was wondering if you know of anyone selling a boat."

"I'm selling a boat myself. Who's the buyer?"

"Me."

Proteus stepped out from behind his booth to whisper, "Women cannot own property. You know that."

"Then I won't tell anyone I'm a woman."

His belly shook with laughter. "A blind man wouldn't make that mistake."

"What if he was a very kind man who sold the best fish in all of Thessaly?"

Proteus's lips spread wide. "For you, I'll make an exception. I'll leave your name with the harbormaster. Do you sail?"

"Not yet." I passed him the pouch of coins. "Two hundred silver pieces."

"The boat is worth two seventy-five," he said.

My shoulders drooped. I had nothing else of value except Mother's arm cuff. Cleora had inherited our mother's lyre, Bronte her necklace, and me her arm cuff with the lioness heads. They were her most precious possessions, but Mother would never want me to value a bangle above my sisters.

"What's this worth?" I asked, sliding the cuff down my arm.

Proteus gestured for me to stop. "Keep it. I owe your mother and father a favor for helping my daughter a long time ago."

People hardly ever mentioned my father, Tassos. He passed away when I was very young. Cleora and Bronte remembered some things about him, but very little. "What did my parents—?"

"Just a moment." Proteus left to assist an older woman who was grousing about his selection of shellfish.

A gust of wind plucked harder at my velo. I held it down while I waited for Proteus, but the day was growing late, and now I had everything I had come for except the olives. I signaled goodbye to him and started back to the tavern. My whole body hummed, and my steps lightened. *I bought a boat.* I practically danced down the road and to the courtyard ahead where people surrounded a stage. A group of actors was performing a reenactment of *The Fall of Uranus.* They were at the part when the Almighty accepts the adamant sickle from Gaea. The painted ceramic sickle the actor held was a mediocre representation of adamantine, a rare, very hard, lusterless metal. The God of Gods' brothers—Coeus, Crius, Hyperion, and Iapetus—were represented on stage by other actors. Only the sixth brother, Oceanus, who refused to join them in overthrowing their father and was now an outcast because of it, was not depicted.

The actors' masks reflected each Titan brother well: Coeus, the intellectual, in the likeness of an owl; Crius, the seer, covered in stars; Hyperion, the light of heaven, with the face of the sun; and Iapetus, the spear of mortality, in a warrior's helmet. To the delight of the audience, the four brothers held down their father, the sky, from the earthly pillars where they dwelled—north, south, east, and west—while the Almighty swung the sickle and castrated Uranus. He sank to the ground in agony, and the Almighty lifted the sickle over his head. The audience cheered.

My insides coiled into a hard knot. This was how our ruler came to power, through treachery and violence and bloodshed. Eons ago, when this dethroning took place, the Almighty was known by another name, a name no longer spoken. Members of the First House staged reenactments year-round, and while this production was decent, the real play took place during the First House Festival when Titans from all over the world gathered in the city to celebrate the Almighty's triumph. In a fortnight, Othrys would be flooded with visitors come to feast and drink and make merry.

The crowd shifted, and my view of the stage was lost. I pushed past the audience to a white tent I had never seen before, half-hidden in an alley of the ramshackle buildings. The sign out front read, **ORACLE. WHAT WILL FATE BRING YOU?**

The vestals didn't believe in oracles. Matron Prosymna said our fate could only be found in giving our lives in service to Gaea. My mother, though, believed that fate itself directed us. At times, the night of her death was muddled and too painful to recall, while other times, I remembered her words with stark plainness: *Your destiny is to guide and protect your sisters.*

A bearded soldier with long hair ducked out of the oracle's tent. He carried a basket, looked left and right as if checking to see whether anyone saw him, then lumbered away.

Another gust swept around me, yanking at my clothes and velo. I grabbed my mask as the bands loosened, catching it before it slid off. Unable to undo the knot without removing the mask, I tied another to secure it and walked back to the donkey.

As I packed my goods into the saddlebags, another gust pushed my mask askew again. I dropped the sack to catch it, and the figs fell out, plunking around my feet. I bent down to pick them up with one hand, my other on my velo, but a big fist grabbed the figs first and stuffed them back into the sack.

I glanced up. The soldier from the oracle's tent rose to his full height, a good deal taller than me. His wide shoulders tapered to a trim waist and strong legs. A short brown beard covered his sculpted jaw and pointed chin, making it difficult to determine his age, though he was definitely older than me. The soft ends of his hair curled around his ears, framing his face and accentuating his amber eyes. He looked familiar, though I couldn't recall from where.

"Let me help you," he said, stepping behind me.

He untied my mask without permission. The knife was in the saddlebag on the other side of the donkey, too far out of reach. My heart thundered as he retied the strings and backed away. I lowered my hands, my velo securely in place.

"Divine day," he said in farewell as he picked up his basket of burgundy olives.

"Wait. Where did you find those? I've been looking all over. Every merchant I asked is out of them."

His eyes tensed at the corners, then he held out the basket. "Take them. They're yours."

"You don't want them?"

"They were given to me."

"If they were a gift, you should keep them."

His lips lifted coyly. "I think they were meant for you."

I didn't understand what that meant, but if he was giving me the olives, I couldn't refuse. "I'll pay you for them."

"They're a gift, from me to you."

Paying him for a gift would be an insult, so I accepted the basket with a murmured thanks and packed it away.

The soldier's keen gaze darted down the length of me, then back to my face. How did I recognize him? "You should return to your husband," he said.

"I'm not married."

"Then you're betrothed?"

"Oh, I'm never getting married."

"But you're tagged."

My hand darted to the back of my neck, my U-shaped scar.

"I apologize for the overfamiliarity," he said. "I noticed it while I was tying your velo."

Discussing my tag with a soldier was the last thing I wanted to do. "I'm a ward of the Guild of Gaea."

"You're a vestal?"

"No. I live with them."

He gave a confused frown. "You'll never marry, yet you aren't a vestal?"

The sides of my mouth flattened. Those were a woman's only options: surrender to the gods or to a man.

An army officer stepped out of the tavern beside us. At the sight of his ratlike face, I turned away. He was the soldier who'd stolen my half-Titan sister: Brigadier Orrin—Ratface—General Decimus's right-hand man. The back of my neck began to itch. I half expected Decimus to exit the tavern, but no one else came out.

"Theo," the brigadier called. "What are you doing here? I thought you were working."

"I came for a drink after my shift, sir," answered the soldier who had given me the olives—Theo, apparently.

"You should have told me you were coming," Ratface said. "I would have waited. It's been too long since we've shared a cask of wine."

Theo gave an uncomfortable swallow that he covered with a sideways smile. "An oversight on my part," he said. "I understand if you don't have time for one now."

"I do have to get back . . ." Brigadier Orrin slapped him on the back. "But I have time for one more."

Theo cast me a farewell glance over his shoulder, and the two men ambled into the tavern.

I mounted the donkey, my stiff movements unhurried despite my urge to flee, and rode toward the city gates, with one eye on the lookout for Decimus. Only after I was far down the road and away from Othrys did I exhale. And still, the scar on the back of my neck itched.

3

The temple lights shone in the soft late-day sun. I returned the donkey to his pen and hefted the supplies to the kitchen, my back and bottom aching. Dozens of loaves of fresh bread were set out on the corner table, ready to be put in baskets. Acraea was busily straining yogurt at the worktable while the slaves gossiped and pretended to sweep. A group of vestals was just now sitting down to roasted lamb and honey-hearted cups of wine.

The vestals quieted as I entered, took off my velo, and untied my hair. The vestals always ate first, before the slaves. My sisters and I didn't have set mealtimes. Though we sometimes dined with the slaves, we usually waited until all the chores were finished. That's when we could finally convince Cleora to get off her feet for the day. Sometimes Bronte and I would eat first, then perform for Cleora while she dined. I would dance while Bronte sang silly ditties, and Cleora would beam. We saw her happy too seldom.

"Good, you remembered the olives," Acraea said as I unloaded the wares I'd purchased.

"You have no idea how difficult those were to find."

"Really? I suppose I did hear about a hard frost making them scarce."

One of the slaves spoke up. "I heard about that from a maiden at the watering pool. She said Menoetius and Epimetheus got into some sort of argument over which of them had impregnated a woodland nymph. When it was discovered that Epimetheus was the father, Menoetius flew into a rage. The poor nymph fled to an olive grove to hide. Menoetius called down a terrible frost that froze all the trees, and the nymph, to death."

That would have been good to know before I spent hours searching the market.

The sons of Iapetus, second-generation Titans, were often getting into squabbles that affected mankind. Menoetius, known for his rashness, and Epimetheus, known for his thick-headedness, once burned down an entire forest in a wager about which could catch a shooting star and throw it farther.

"Where are Cleora and Bronte?" I asked.

"Bronte hasn't returned from the fields yet," Acraea replied, her attention on the honeycomb she was crushing in a bowl.

"And Cleora?" I asked, scanning the room. None of the vestals would meet my gaze. The slaves were behind on preparations for tomorrow's meals, half the pots still needed scrubbing, and more people had yet to be served supper. Bronte would stay out as long as possible before returning, but Cleora hardly left the kitchen until all the meals were finished and everything was tidy.

"I, ah, believe she's meeting with the matron," Acraea said, drizzling honey over the yogurt.

Cleora would not leave the kitchen unattended at supper hour unless it was important. I thought back to the morning. "Is this about me blaspheming? I apologized." Not to the matron, but Acraea didn't need to know that.

"I don't think so? I believe they're finishing her music lesson."

Acraea's vagueness poked at me. As second-in-command in the kitchen, she always knew where Cleora was and what she was doing. It wasn't hard to keep track of her. She never left the compound.

"It's a little early in the evening for lessons," I noted. And why, if the matron was giving Cleora a lesson, didn't I hear her lyre?

Acraea gripped the side of the mixing bowl, her knuckles paling to white. "Althea, don't do anything rash."

"Why would you say that? I'm not Menoetius, after all."

Acraea waved her sticky hands about, mumbling indecipherably. Something wasn't right.

I started toward the stairs.

"The matron asked not to be disturbed," Acraea called after me.

"During a music lesson?" I walked faster.

"This is what Cleora wants!"

I took the stairs two at a time, yelling so my voice would carry up the stairwell ahead of me. "Cleora, you're needed in the kitchen!"

The gynaeceum where the women weaved and spun, and where the matron gave music lessons, was dark and empty. I marched down the hall to our bedchamber. No one was there either.

The matron's chamber was at the far end of the corridor. I slammed through the door. Cleora lay on the floor in front of the hearth, seemingly unconscious. The matron held a red-hot poker above Cleora's face.

I wrestled the poker from the matron's hand. "What are you doing?" I yelled.

Matron Prosymna's velo hid her face, except her frightened eyes. "Your sister asked for this. She was too afraid to do it herself."

My whole arm shook as I held the fire poker over my head. I scoured my sister's face for damage, but her pale skin was unmarked. "Be grateful you didn't burn her, or I would have had to shove this down your throat."

The matron gulped.

I tossed the poker aside and bent over my sister. "Cleora? Cleora, wake up." Her arms hung from her sides. I shook her, but she didn't stir. "What did you do to her?"

Matron Prosymna lifted her chin, her tone unapologetic. "She asked for a sedative."

"You should have told her no! No to the sedative! No to the burnings!" I regretted putting down the poker. The matron appeared more afraid of me when I held it.

"I told Cleora I would take her to a nurse with experience giving chastity crosses, but you know her fear of leaving the temple."

"Chastity crosses?" My voice broke to a scraggly whisper. "Those horrible scars have a *name*?"

"That's what they call them in the city. Oh, quit judging, Althea. Practices such as these have been around since the beginning of time."

"My mother didn't believe in following practices just because others said they were acceptable. She taught us to think for ourselves."

"You don't know your mother as well as you think you do." The matron shook her head and gave no further explanation.

"Cleora works her hands to the bone for this place, and this is how you reward her? You preach about loyalty, virtue, and restraint, but my mother was more of a follower of Gaea than you'll ever be."

Matron Prosymna removed her velo, uncovering her sharp sneer. "Stavra's teachings were wrong."

"Wrong?" I pointed at my drugged sister. "What you did here was wrong!"

"Cleora lives in fear. You would deny her peace of mind?"

"I would deny her unnecessary pain and a lifetime of regret." I gathered Cleora in my arms and hefted her upper half off the floor. Her lifeless weight sank against me, so I tugged her backward out the door, dragging her feet.

Matron Prosymna followed us to the threshold. "You aren't children anymore. The guild cannot protect you forever."

I threw a daggered glare at her. "Never come near my sister again."

My arms and legs shook as I lugged Cleora down the hall and into our chamber. I lifted her limp body onto her bed, splashed her face with tepid water from the washbasin, and patted her cheeks.

"Althea?" she moaned, waking up and shielding her eyes. "Oh, my head."

"You deserve more than a headache. What were you thinking?"

Cleora sank back into her pillow. "You wouldn't understand."

I kneeled beside the bed and took her hand in mine. "Scarring your face . . . ? Cleora, what would Mama say?"

"Mama might still be with us if she had chastity crosses," Cleora whispered. "I don't want to end up like her."

"You won't."

"You can't guarantee that. Not for me or yourself or Bronte or any other woman."

"Cronus would have to come down off his mountain and fetch you himself," I seethed. "Uranus is more likely to escape Tartarus."

Cleora turned her head away and shut her eyes. "You shouldn't speak the Almighty's name. It brings ill fortune."

"I will *not* be silenced, Cleora." I scowled out the window at the mountain peak, the palace, and the city lights. After he overthrew Uranus, Cronus had demanded that he be referred to as "the Almighty" or "the God of Gods" and forbade the use of the name his mother and father gave him.

I stroked Cleora's hair from her face. "We'll be all right."

"You cannot foresee the future, Althea."

"No, but I . . ." I stopped myself from telling her about the boat, waiting until both my sisters were present. "I cannot guarantee what will happen, but I can tell you what will *not* happen. I vow Cronus will never have you."

Cleora winced again, then rested her head against my shoulder. "I think I'm going to enlist in the guild."

"You want to be a vestal virgin?"

"We both know I have no aspirations to leave the temple. I already abide by their rules. Joining is an option."

Not for me. I wasn't a virgin, and nothing could undo that. Swearing fealty to Gaea required purity and a commitment to live here for the remainder of one's days. Cleora's devotion I could almost understand—she already lived in harmony with the guild and worked hard to contribute—but defacing herself? I could never comprehend that.

I picked up her mask and held it out. "Next time you start thinking about doing something irreversible to yourself, remember you have your velo."

Cleora took her mask. It resembled a creature not often depicted—a bee. Most velos were inherited family heirlooms, but Cleora's came from a craftsman's workshop. Mother said that while she was pregnant, she and Father browsed hundreds of velos before they agreed upon this one for their firstborn. Two small antennae stuck out from above the mask's wide eye holes. The profile was slender, with a pointed chin and a serene expression, a contrast to the serious one I always wore. She never told me why our parents selected it for her. Perhaps she didn't know.

Bronte pushed open the door, peeked inside, and entered. "What happened? The matron is fuming. She told Acraea we should find somewhere else to live."

Cleora covered her eyes, draping her arm across her face, and gave no reply.

"Well . . . ," I started, searching for the proper words. "Cleora mentioned she might become a vestal and live out her days here. I may have reacted strongly."

Bronte lifted one brow. "The matron is furious. Acraea is pleading with her not to throw us out."

"Prosymna has threatened us before," I replied.

"This time, she means it."

"Whose temple is this?" I asked. "Prosymna acts as though she's the goddess in charge."

"Althea," Cleora said faintly. "Don't be disrespectful."

I threw my hands up. "I'll talk with Prosymna."

"No," Bronte replied firmly. "You'll make things worse."

"She won't tell us to leave." I was almost certain about this. I was more certain that Bronte didn't need to hear the truth from me. Cleora should tell her about the chastity crosses.

"Cleora, will you really join the guild?" Bronte asked. "I thought the three of us wanted to leave when the time was right and make a place of our own together."

"I did too," I said.

"I haven't decided yet," Cleora replied, her tone careful.

It seemed to me she had. Perhaps she would change her mind when she heard that we had a way out.

"I have news," I said. Cleora uncovered her eyes, and Bronte straightened attentively. "I bought a boat."

"A boat?" Bronte replied. "How?"

"I paid for it with the coin from Mama's death."

"The blood money?" Bronte said, aghast. "Althea, you're joking."

"I'm not. Don't you see what this means? We can finally leave this place."

Cleora went so still I could not tell if she was breathing.

"And go where?" Bronte asked.

"The southern isles." When Oceanus, the Titan god of the seas, was disowned by his siblings, Cronus agreed to a treaty for trade routes with the other Houses, and for his armada of triremes to sail the seas.

Oceanus's vast territory of oceans and isles became a refuge for runaways and outlaws. The southern islands in the Aegean Sea were the ideal place for us to seek shelter and build our life together, away from Decimus, away from the guild, away from Cronus.

"But none of us know how to sail," Bronte noted.

"We'll hire a guide."

Cleora still had not moved or spoken, but she was breathing.

Bronte chewed her bottom lip. "How much coin do we have left?"

"Proteus set a fair price," I replied. "But seaworthy vessels are expensive."

"How much?" Bronte pressed.

"None."

Cleora dropped her chin to her chest. "Oh, Althea. How would we afford a guide, or supplies for our journey?"

"Or to set up a new *life*?" Bronte added.

"We can do this," I insisted. "Perhaps we could make a trade or sell something. The loom, maybe. I don't imagine we'll haul it with us."

My sisters quieted. With a seaworthy vessel, the possibilities opening up to us were undeniable. A long moment later, Bronte spoke up.

"I have coin set aside."

"You do?" Cleora and I said in unison.

"I stashed it in the instrument case. Under the lyre."

I opened the wooden case. Running my hand over the lyre's shiny turtle shell, careful not to touch the strings, I reached under it and pulled out a heavy pouch. Cleora extended her hand, and I passed it to her. She opened it and peered inside.

"Bronte, how did you . . . ?"

"Sometimes, when it's my turn to tend to the sheep, I go into the village and grind wheat." She gave an awkward half smile, her cheeks reddening. "The older customers like that I sing while I work. Last I counted, I've saved just over a hundred coins. I knew when the time came to go, we would need our own silver."

"Why didn't you tell us?" I asked.

"I knew it would come up one day. As Prometheus says, 'I prepare, for one day my opportunity will come.'"

Bronte's fascination with Prometheus began as a girl. She would dress like a boy and go out to listen to the philosophers quoting the god of forethought during their street-corner debates. She often made a point of walking past a mural in the city of the hulking, bearish-looking god.

Cleora rubbed at her temples. "Can we finish discussing this the day after tomorrow?"

The mood in the chamber shifted to a grim sort of resignation. The next day was the anniversary of our mother's passing.

Bronte kicked off her sandals, then removed Cleora's and lay down beside her. I was hungry—perpetually, it seemed—but I took off my sandals and joined them.

Nighttime tiptoed into the bedchamber and cozied into the corners. Our feet were lined up in a row at the bottom of the bed. They varied in size—as with our noses, mine were the largest—but on the heels of our right feet, we had identical freckles. Bronte called them our sister stars.

"I wouldn't have taken my vows without telling you two first," Cleora whispered.

"Do you really want to become a vestal?" Bronte asked.

"When Mama needed help, she came here for a reason."

Cleora wanted the guild to shield her from the Almighty. Didn't she understand that the vestals could not shield me from Decimus? I could not stay at the temple forever, and yet, I could not imagine my life without both of my sisters . . .

"Mama's the reason why I took to working in the garden," Bronte whispered, her voice melancholy. "She could grow anything."

"Gaea blessed her with bounty," Cleora answered.

I leaned my head against her shoulder. Of the three of us, Cleora had the most conviction in the goddess. Her faith brought her peace, no matter how much our viewpoints differed. I would rather be trapped in a tree like a hamadryad than join any guild where Matron Prosymna was in charge, but I wouldn't rob my sister of that small peace.

We lay together for what felt like an eternity, thoughts tumbling through my mind about Decimus, about our new boat, about my responsibilities. Eventually, I started to get up to check that the slaves had finished the mending, then I remembered that I had gifts.

"Ugh, Althea, lie back down," Cleora said. "I was almost asleep."

"She held still longer than I thought she would," Bronte remarked.

"I got you two something." I rose, pulled the honey pies from my cloak pocket, and handed them one each.

"Where's yours?" Bronte asked.

"I ate mine already," I lied. I only had enough coin to purchase two. "Do you remember Mama's pies? I wish we still had that recipe."

"It was Papa's recipe," Cleora said, her mouth full.

Bronte nodded. "Each year, he made honey pies for Mama's birthday. After he passed away, she made them for our birthdays. They were her favorite." Bronte passed me a third of her pie. "It's yours."

"But—"

Cleora offered me a third of hers too. "Take them," she said.

I accepted the portions and ate them slowly. Honey and crumbs stuck to my lips. I licked them clean, then my fingertips, savoring every last bit. Cleora lay back down with a tired groan. Bronte cuddled her left side, and I nestled against the other. Bronte hummed a lullaby, the song Mother favored most. These private moments were fewer and fewer because of our household duties, but they were my favorite. When the three of us were together, it felt like nothing bad could happen and we could do anything.

After she finished the song, Bronte spoke into the dark, "Which isle would we escape to, Althea?"

Cleora exhaled a drawn-out breath. This was not the time to push her.

I draped my arm across my sisters. "We needn't decide that tonight."

But I had decided.

The time had come to leave Thessaly.

4

Sneaking out of the temple with my spear and shield hadn't gotten easier over the years, but I had gotten better at it. The most difficult part was leaving my bedchamber without waking anyone.

I crept through the dark and set my shield on the roof first, then fed my spear through the window. Cleora and Bronte lay asleep behind me, their breathing quiet. Before we all went to bed, Acraea had spent an hour calming Matron Prosymna, then came to say we were allowed to stay on the condition that I showed the matron more respect. I agreed, but I didn't scrub the kitchen floor before dawn for Prosymna or her goddess. I did it so my sisters and I had somewhere to live.

Stepping onto the roof, I shuffled to the edge and tossed my spear and shield onto the hay below. I hung from the roof, feetfirst, and dropped. After collecting my gear, I crept to the stables. The matron's trusty mare poked her head out of a stall. I fed her some clover and barley, then I saddled her and led her across the courtyard, through the gate off the kitchen. Once outside, I mounted her, and we rode the moonlit trail.

Selene, the second-generation Titan goddess of the moon, shone in her full glory. We reached Othrys in a third of the time it took the donkey. I hid my face behind my shield as we approached the city gates, where a pair of soldiers stood guard. My cloak covered me and my tied-back hair. As long as no one looked too closely, they would assume I was a hoplite.

"Evening," said a guard.

I grunted.

"It's a fine night for a visit to the tavern," said the other.

They waited for my answer. I grunted again, and my voice cracked, sounding like an enthusiastic note of agreement. They laughed and let me pass.

I rode up the dim roadways, past the closed booths of the agora, to the tavern. Drunken men loitered around the open door, where music rang out. My finger tapped with the downbeat. The temptation to stop in and listen to the music over a drink almost made me veer off course, but I kept going.

The palace shed a garish radiance over the ramshackle huts. Soft lamplight glowed from around their closed shutters, deepening the shadows in the alley. Hardly a soul could be seen. I encountered more stray dogs than people, and of the few people whose paths I did cross, none were women.

I retraced my steps to the oracle's tent. Though I was uncertain about the notion of fate, my mother said my destiny was to protect my sisters, and I swore I would. Now, with our freedom almost within reach, I had to know whether or not persuading Cleora and Bronte to leave the guild and sail to the southern isles was the right choice. My mother wasn't around to offer direction, but an oracle might.

No lamplight shone inside the tent, and no noise came from within. My hopes sank. Perhaps not seeking a seer's advice *was* my fate. Perhaps some charlatan looking to swindle me out of coin would dissuade me from following my instincts and leading my sisters to the southern isles.

A faint light flickered on inside the tent, followed by a voice calling out.

"Althea Lambros, we've been expecting you."

My feet locked in place. Of course, an oracle would know I was there—I had come all the way in the middle of the night in search of insight—but my nerves still jumped. Would a charlatan know my name?

No matter what the oracle said, I would do what I thought was right for my family, yet I was curious enough to approach the tent and step inside.

The room was small. A drawn curtain separated the tent into two rooms. A woman faced the entrance, a single candle burning on the table she sat behind. Her wild black hair spilled around her slim, smooth shoulders, and her red dress flowed to the floor, skimming her bare feet. An authentic theater mask of a goat hid her face, its expression frozen in a woeful grimace. The mask had no eye openings, but the mouth had a slash for speaking through. Two horns protruded from the forehead and curved out and up to the sides like crescent moons.

"Welcome." Her throaty voice didn't suit her youthful, glowing skin. "Put down your spear and shield. You don't need them."

Perhaps she *could* see through the mask . . .

I aimed my spear at her as I slowly lowered it to the floor. Showing no alarm, she pointed at the stool across from her. "Please sit."

"Can you see me?"

"Oracles see with more than our eyes, Althea."

"Who told you my name?"

She gestured at the stool again. "Rest."

I withheld my growing curiosity and sat across from her at the table, setting my shield near my dusty feet.

She held up her hands, palms out. "Your hands, please."

"First, my payment." I removed from my pocket the two silver coins I borrowed from Bronte's stash, setting them on the table.

"I require no payment."

"I would prefer that you accept it." Her reading would not feel legitimate without my paying for her services.

"If you insist," she said, picking up the coins. Once she pocketed them, I extended my hands toward hers. She took my wrists in her grip, then her left hand drifted up to my gold arm cuff. "This belonged to Stavra."

"You knew my mother?" The oracle seemed closer to me in age, but it was possible she had met my mother when she was a girl.

"You didn't come here to discuss Stavra," she replied.

"I'm here about an oath I made to her."

"Your oath to watch over your sisters was sworn without your knowing the whole truth. You have much to learn about promises, Althea."

The thin curtain shifted behind her as a shadow passed by. We were not alone.

The oracle released me and started to stand.

"Wait," I said. "I want to lead my sisters to the southern isles. Will we be safe there?"

The oracle sat back down and took my wrists again. "I do see an isle in your future, but I also see darkness. You seek freedom and justice. Both will come at great cost to your family."

"How can I protect my sisters?"

The oracle pulled a spindle of white string from her pocket. "We can tell you about your *moira* through a full reading. But have a care. Such knowledge cannot be unknown."

Moira—fate—was the one cosmic power I would consider listening to.

"I would like a full reading," I said. "But I don't have any more coins."

"You paid enough already." The oracle wound the string around my hands, binding them together. The white thread felt thin and sticky but strong, like a spider's web.

Two more women stepped out from behind the curtain, both with voluminous black hair and theater masks shaped into ominous goat faces. The woman on the right held a pair of silver shears, and the one on the left, a stick.

The oracle finished tying my hands with multiple layers of string, binding them together. At the finish, the spool of string was the same thickness as when she'd started, as though none had been unwound.

"I am Clotho," said the oracle. "These are my sisters, Lachesis and Aisa."

Clotho held up her spindle. Lachesis, the one with the shears, cut loose the line around my hands. The string warmed and glowed against my skin. The last sister, Aisa, unwound my hands slowly, one loop at a time, then laid the string on the table and counted lengths of it with her stick. The sisters lifted the string and stretched it out between them. Clotho and Aisa each held an end, and Lachesis held the middle. The string extended across the width of the tent, longer than I was tall.

An unnatural stillness came over them as the brightness of the string intensified. Their hair shone white in the radiance, and the expressions on their goat masks changed from grimaces to eerie smiles. The sisters spoke in chorus, their voice as one, the pitch low and piercing:

"The time of Cronus's tyranny will end. A clever, brave hero was preserved and hidden among mortals. A Titan child of Cronus and Rhea lives. Find the Boy God. Raise him up, and he will unite all the Houses under one mighty throne. He will erect the greatest palace in the history of the world, where he will reign and rule with thunder and justice."

A vision overtook my mind, palpable as a waking dream.

A god sat in a majestic marble throne, in a great hall atop an unfamiliar mountain peak. Dozens of small white scars riddled his forearms and calves. Another scar, red as the dawn, cut down the side of his flat nose and ended at his upper lip, which was mangled from the deep slash. His eyes, a deep blue so intense one might mistake the tone for black, had deep crinkles at the sides and short, pale lashes. He was not fat, per se, but his muscled form lacked definition, and the weight around his middle outmatched the girth of his chest. Still, I imagined that, when he was younger, women must have found his robust frame irresistible, and he had enjoyed them aplenty. The remnant of that rogue was visible in his high, wide cheekbones and the stern cut of his jaw. His ears stood out at the sides of his head, adding an accessible charm.

But the gods aged slowly.

His wavy silver hair thinned at the back of his head, finer than his thick, wiry beard and chest hair. In one calloused hand, his veins visible under pale, freckled skin, he held a lightning bolt that twinkled as softly as a dying flame.

Hundreds of people kneeled before his mighty throne, their heads bowed in reverence. The god surveyed his subjects, a profound crease between his bushy brows. Such a worry line only developed after years of frowning, yet he did not appear cross. He peered at each of his subjects with empathy, as though he was well aware of their individual trials and woes, their tender hopes and dreams, and he carried the troubles of their hearts in his own, bearing up their needs and desires with a noble attentiveness that could only be born from abiding love.

It was then that I recognized my perspective of the great hall. I wasn't watching from an omnipotent angle, hovering overhead. I was positioned right beside the god, in an adjacent throne. More thrones flanked ours, all occupied by others, though I could not see who. The truth of my position struck me motionless. The people weren't just kneeling to the silver-haired god. They were bowing to us all.

The vision dimmed until I was back in the tent. The three oracles exhaled at once, and the string darkened. Lachesis braced against Aisa, too weakened to stand on her own.

"May the goddess bless you," Lachesis said, then led her sister behind the curtain again.

"I—I don't understand," I stammered, shaking off the final tendrils of the vision. "One of Cronus's children is alive?"

Clotho teetered back to her stool on shaky legs. She leaned forward against the table, bracing against it for support. "The Boy God can be found in the southern isles, on Crete. Just as Cronus defeated his father, so will this boy rise up to defeat his. However, he will not prevail without you."

A sense of understanding pricked my heart. What Clotho warned of was truth. I couldn't explain how I knew, just that I *knew*, with the same certainty that the sun would rise and set on the morrow, that this Boy God was part of my future.

I pressed a hand to my flip-flopping stomach. How had my fate become intertwined with a god's?

"What if I don't help him?" I asked.

"Fate works in mysterious ways. By the hand of faith, we are guided to our destiny. The journey is the trial." Clotho wiped at her sweaty brow, her throat flushed.

"Are you all right?" I asked.

"I will be," she replied shakily. "Reading your future was like gripping a star."

The oracles' process with the string and shears and measuring stick was bewildering, as was their reading. It was true that a Titan could only overthrow another Titan by vanquishing. The gods could not die, for divine ichor—not blood—flowed through their veins. But I still felt the oracles must have misread my destiny.

"Perhaps you and your sisters mistook me for someone else," I said. "Can you unspool another string and look at my future again?"

"You only have one *moira*, Althea. Now listen very closely. A guide will be sent to you, and you will recognize him by his good deeds. Follow him to the Boy God. Help the Boy God rise, or you and your siblings will never know peace. Cronus must not discover that his child lives, or he will stop at nothing to destroy him. Should he succeed, the God of Gods will rule forevermore." Clotho rose from her stool on wobbly knees. "Your sisters are in danger."

"What?"

"There's no time to explain."

I grabbed my spear and shield.

Clotho followed me to the door. "Go quickly!"

As I mounted the mare, I asked, "What do I do if I find the Boy God? What should I tell him?"

Clotho didn't reply.

I glanced over my shoulder at her, but she was gone. Indeed, the whole tent had disappeared. Turning in a circle, I saw no sign that it had ever been here. The oracles, too, had vanished.

A gust blew at me, whirling a piece of string at my face. I snatched it out of the air. The piece of white string, as long as my finger, fluttered in my grasp. It looked remarkably similar to the one Clotho had unraveled from the spool.

Two soldiers nearby began patrolling in my direction. I tucked the string into my pocket and rode for the gates. The guards recognized me from earlier and waved me through. As soon as I was out of their sight, I kicked my heels into the mare's flanks and took off.

5

I rode hard down the rocky pathway. Everything the oracle said about the Boy God fled my mind, replaced by a single thought: *Your sisters are in danger.*

I pushed the mare harder. The wind barreled down the mountain with us, shoving at my back. *Hurry*, the gales seemed to say.

At last, just after midnight, the outline of the temple came into view. The gates stood open. I longed to charge in with my spear and shield held high, but I dismounted in the woods and left my shield tacked to my saddle. The hamadryads dozed around me, their drooping branches sighing up and down. The trusty mare stayed behind as I put on my velo and crept forward.

Five horses without riders stood in the temple courtyard. A soldier guarded them, his back to me. The soldiers must not have been there long. Their horses were sweaty and lathered from their recent trek. No one else was visible. The matron and vestals had either fled or were trapped somewhere under guard. My sisters would have hidden before getting caught. They wouldn't have left without me.

Under the cover of shadows, I slipped inside the courtyard and sneaked toward the *andron*. The liege man with the horses turned toward the open gates—Theo. The soldier from the market who gave me the olives and retied my mask.

I slid past him and inside the *andron*. This chamber was for men's use only, but since no men lived here, the vestals had converted it into storage space. Unused furniture, empty baskets, chests of old clothes, and spare velos had been left in an array of forgotten piles across the room.

Footsteps pounded overhead on the second floor where the bedchambers and gynaeceum were located. Voices carried down through the ladder opening.

"We searched every chamber, sir."

"Search them again," a deep voice replied.

Steps thudded closer. I tucked my spear behind a broken bed frame and climbed into a large woven basket.

The ladder creaked as one of the soldiers came down. Footfalls scuffled across the dirt floor. I held my breath as his steps came nearer. Through a gap in the weaving, I saw two big boots. The soldier circled the room, then the door banged as he exited.

"See anything?" he asked.

"No, sir," Theo answered.

"The Lambros girls are here somewhere. Keep an eye out, Colonel Angelos."

I recognized that name . . . Angelos . . . Of course, Theo was Angelos, one of the liege men present the night my mother died. He had offered me a hand when another soldier had pushed me down. That night had been seared into my memory, but Angelos was seven years older now, with longer hair and a short beard.

I wriggled out of the basket and fetched my spear. Through the window, I glimpsed the soldier beside Angelos, and my empty hand flew to the back of my neck.

Decimus.

I had hoped that with age and perspective, and with the passage of time, he would seem more harmless than my memory of him, but he was still fearsome.

He stood at a formidable height and wore the bulk of his massive, muscled body with tremendous magnitude. Arrogance rang out from his every weighted step and brutal sneer. He commanded attention from those around him, not because he had earned their respect but because his absolute confidence triggered a sort of nervousness. He was not the sort of man who denied himself his desires.

Yet age had frayed him. His hair shimmered with gray, and his deeply tan skin bore wrinkles and dark spots from too much sun. Overall, though, time had been kind to him, unjustly so.

I had to find my sisters.

Gripping my spear tightly, I ascended the ladder to the second floor and tiptoed down the corridor. Loud noises sounded ahead. I sidled up to an open doorway and peered in. A soldier was tearing apart a bedchamber. While he was turned away, I darted past and continued to the gynaeceum.

The unlit chamber appeared empty. Each evening, the vestals gathered to sit and talk and spin and weave. Some nights, they put on performances for each other: music, poetry recitations, or plays. A large wooden chest, normally used for storing theater masks and costumes made out of old clothes, occupied its usual spot in the far corner, but the contents of the chest had been piled outside it. I lifted the lid, and a blade was thrust at my nose.

"Father of stars," Bronte breathed, lowering the kitchen knife. "It's you."

She and Cleora were crammed inside the chest, both of them wearing their velos. We'd discovered this hiding place as children, during visits with our mother. We would pretend to put on performances for big crowds—Cleora playing her lyre, Bronte singing, and me dancing. When it was time to leave, the three of us would fold ourselves inside the chest and hide, giggling, until Mother pretended to "find" us. These days, the chest barely held the two of them.

"Where have you been, Althea?" Bronte asked.

"I'll tell you after we get out of here."

They climbed out one at a time. I expected to find Cleora pale and shaky, but she carried herself with rigid coolness.

"Althea, do you *still* think speaking the Almighty's name doesn't bring ill fortune?" she asked.

"Decimus has returned," I explained.

Cleora's scowl dissolved, and she wrapped her arms around me. "I didn't know. The matron woke us to say liege men had come. We hid straight away. Did Decimus see you?"

"I don't think so."

Bronte peered into the corridor. "This way is clear."

"Soldiers are searching the bedchambers," I said, then checked outside to ensure that no liege men were patrolling the perimeter for escapees. "We should go out the window. I left the matron's mare in the woods. We'll ride to the cave."

Bronte and I looked to Cleora. Her fear of going outside was mighty, but her fear of capture was mightier. She nodded in agreement.

Seven years after our mother's passing, on the very day of the anniversary of her death, we were finally leaving this place.

Somewhere nearby, a woman began to scream. The abject sound grew louder, shriller, more filled with pain. The many faces of the vestals and slaves flew through my mind. I wondered who we were hearing . . . and what they were doing to her.

This is my fault.

The thought repeated itself over and over, drilling into my bones.

Bronte covered her ears and scrunched her eyes closed. The last time I had seen her this distressed was when Mother was captured. Cleora held herself completely still, except for her nostrils, which flared with each rapid breath.

Their terror shook me into action. I climbed onto the roof with my spear. The screaming stopped. Bronte gave a visible shudder, then snapped back into focus and followed me.

Cleora paused at the window. Although her velo was on straight, she adjusted it and fussed with the ties.

"I'll lead the way," I said. "The cave isn't far."

Cleora didn't budge. "I forgot Mother's lyre, and, Bronte, you left your bow and arrow."

"I have a spare bow and arrow in the cave," Bronte said.

Cleora backed away from the window. "Your coin pouch is in the instrument case."

"We'll return for them later," I replied.

Cleora retreated another few steps. "We won't be able to travel very far without silver," she said, then fled the gynaeceum, disappearing out of sight.

"What in the name of Gaea?" Bronte griped.

"She'll be back."

Feeling exposed, we climbed inside the gynaeceum again. The heavy silence pushed down on us as we waited, and the moment seemed to lag on forever.

Doubts began to creep in. Our bedchamber, where we kept the lyre, was just down the corridor. What was taking Cleora so long?

"She hasn't gone out in years," Bronte whispered. "Maybe she can't bring herself to leave."

"She can," I insisted.

"I should go find her."

"Give her a moment." My answer was mostly selfish. I trusted Cleora, but I also didn't want to be left alone.

We remained there, huddled in the dark, mired in our worries. Cleora should have returned by now. *Had* she changed her mind? Or had something happened to her?

A muted cry came from outside.

"Bronte! Althea!"

We poked our heads out the window. Cleora waved from our bedchamber window down the way. She lifted the instrument case to show us.

"I'll meet you outside," she said in another loud whisper.

Below, a soldier patrolled the dirt path between the compound and the woods. We all ducked inside again.

"Lambros sisters!" the soldier shouted, sounding the alarm. "They're on the second floor!"

Bronte and I rushed into the corridor, my spear firm in my grip, and pulled up short. Ratface Brigadier Orrin stood between us and the way to our bedchamber.

We ran the other direction toward the stairwell at the rear of the compound. He barreled after us and snatched Bronte by the hair, swinging her around. She raked her nails across his cheek and yanked herself loose.

Orrin called to his comrades. "They're up—!"

I jammed the spear into his thigh. He staggered sideways against the wall with a low groan. Bronte gaped at us, looking from him to me. My mind went blank. I didn't know what to do next. I had never speared a person before, only rabbits and squirrels.

Orrin gripped his injured leg. "You bitch."

"I would have aimed for your heart," Bronte snarled.

She grabbed the spear, and together we wrenched it out. Orrin sank to the floor, his face pinched in pain and his punctured thigh bleeding.

Bronte tugged at me. "Come on. Cleora must be ahead of us."

I raced after her to the back stairwell, still somewhat dazed.

"Althea Lambros!" Decimus hollered. His voice impaled me. "Don't bother running! I will find you!"

We thudded down the stairs to the kitchen. Acraea stood in the shadows, her back against the wall and an iron pan in her fist.

"Thank Gaea you're all right," she whispered hoarsely. "The soldiers forced the other vestals and slaves into the stables. Go, before they catch you."

"Have you seen Cleora?" Bronte asked.

Acraea shook her head.

"We thought she was in front of us," I said.

"I'll send her your way," Acraea replied. "Go!"

We fled out the back gate and crouched in the trees.

Time slowed again. My legs burned from squatting, and my eyes ached from squinting at every shadow. The compound was too quiet. Cleora should have come out by now. I hoped she hadn't tried to go out the front gate, where Angelos was standing guard.

I caught a glimpse of a shadowed figure as it threw a box out of our bedroom window. The box landed nearby and broke into pieces. Bronte crawled over and held up the shattered pieces of our mother's lyre. My whole chest fell inward. The cracked turtle shell was beyond repair.

Bronte searched the murky undergrowth, then crawled back to me. "The lyre is ruined, but I found my bag of coins."

A scream came from above. Cleora appeared in our bedchamber window with Decimus behind her, his arm wrapped around her chest and a dagger pressed to her cheek. Cleora stared straight ahead, her chin high. Her expression broke me. It wasn't fear or anger or sadness. She looked resigned, as though she always knew this day would come.

"Althea," Decimus called. "Your sister is appealing, but she lacks your feistiness."

Another figure appeared in the gynaeceum window. An archer.

"My work has made it impossible to return for you until now," the general continued calmly, articulately, like he had memorized his speech. "But all these years, Althea, I've only thought of you. Now it's time for you to come home with me."

"Run, Althea!" Cleora cried. "Run—!"

Decimus smothered her mouth with his hand. "Come to me, Althea, and I won't hurt her like you hurt my brother, Orrin."

"They're brothers?" I breathed.

Bronte shook her head, dumbfounded.

Orrin appeared at the threshold of the back gate with Matron Prosymna held against his chest. He stepped over something—someone. My tongue turned rough and dry. Acraea lay sprawled on the floor, a spear sticking straight out of her middle. Orrin bled from his leg, but that didn't prevent him from shuffling forward, his sword against the matron's throat. She was very still, but her back arched against him awkwardly.

"I don't like to be kept waiting, Althea," Decimus bellowed. "I will kill the vestals one by one!"

"Do not fear, daughters," Matron Prosymna said loudly. "The Mother of All Gods is with us. Believe in Gaea's boundless glory."

"Silence her," Decimus ordered.

Orrin drew his blade across the matron's throat, as quick as a lightning strike. She folded forward out of his arms and fell to the ground in a heap.

Bronte started to go to her, but I held her back. Matron Prosymna could not have survived an injury like that, nor could Acraea, and we couldn't risk being spotted by the archer. My pulse boomed in my ears. Acraea and the matron deserved better than martyrdom.

Cleora squirmed against Decimus, her mouth still covered. He pressed his blade more firmly against her cheek until she quit moving.

"Althea!" he cried louder. "Come to me, or I'll give your sister to the Almighty!"

"This isn't supposed to happen," I whispered. "It's supposed to be me."

"You cannot reason with him," Bronte replied. "He'll say anything to draw you out."

"He's come for me. I can negotiate for her release."

Orrin limped back inside the kitchen. Above, Decimus and Cleora disappeared from the window, as did the archer. I rose to go inside, but Bronte pulled me back down.

"What's to say Decimus will let go of Cleora once he has you?" she hissed. "Surrendering is too risky. He's likely to seize you both."

"I swore to Cleora that Cronus would never have her."

"I cannot let you go," Bronte said, her voice frenzied with panic. "Decimus will say anything to draw you in. He cannot be trusted."

I vowed to our mother that I would protect my sisters, yet to help Cleora, I would have to leave Bronte. How could I choose one over the other?

The sweet voices of muses filled my mind, or outside my head; I couldn't tell where they were coming from, only that the voices surrounded me.

Find the Boy God.

A warmth built at my side, near my hip. I peeked in my pocket. The string from the oracles' tent glowed as white as a lump of dying coal.

Bronte monitored the temple. "They'll be after us soon. We must go."

"Family doesn't abandon family," I said through gritted teeth, my vision blurred from tears.

She gripped my shoulders. "We'll get Cleora back."

I glanced at the matron's crumpled body. Cronus wouldn't care that his liege men had slain a devout follower of Gaea. He had no respect for the elder gods, or for mortals, only for his own greatness.

"We have to go," Bronte pressed.

Years ago, after the tag was burned into the back of my neck, I convinced my sisters to agree that if I were taken by Decimus, they wouldn't risk themselves to try to save me. They were to let me go. To make our agreement equal, I committed to the same terms. Leaving without Cleora was the only thing to do. I knew it, and I loathed myself for it.

I whistled for the mare. A moment later, she trotted out of the woods. Bronte launched herself into the saddle, and I mounted behind her. She clicked her tongue, and we took off into the trees.

In no time, we heard the sound of riders in pursuit. Bronte directed the mare around a crag and under a shady overhang deep in the woods. The soldiers galloped past us. I pressed my cheek against her shoulder, our heartbeats banging between us, and waited until they were gone, then we backtracked south. Every step we took away from the temple— from Cleora—felt like a jab to the soul.

We reached the steep, rocky hillside below our cave and hid the mare in a copse of hazelnut trees. The moon's silvery light glazed the echoing hills and wooded valleys. Bronte and I scaled the rock wall cautiously, mindful of the steeper parts. The cave entrance was set above the tree line, facing the temple and highway.

Bronte fetched her bow and arrow from the cave, and we sat on the ledge overlooking the treetops. Hooting owls and buzzing insects filled the silence. Though their horses were too far away to hear, we observed the liege men as they rode off, Cleora bound and gagged behind Decimus on his steed. Cronus's prisoners rarely got away healthy and whole. Getting her back would be next to impossible.

I pressed my palm against the cool, stony ground, seeking a connection to the earth. *Why, Gaea? Why Cleora?*

This wasn't a prayer—it was an accusation. The only time I acknowledged the goddess anymore was when she failed those who believed in her.

I didn't expect an answer, yet something warmed against my hip. I fished the string out of my pocket; the tiny thread glowed in the moonlight. Had the string come from the oracles or another power? Where, or whom, did the oracles draw their divinations from?

Their counsel had firmly taken root in my mind. The clearest part was their assertion that Cronus would fall, and that my help was needed to bring to pass his destruction.

I fastened the string around my finger, tying it into a ring. Challenging Cronus, and triumphing, would require strength that I didn't possess. In order to get Cleora back, I would need the aid of a formidable ally, someone powerful enough to dethrone the God of Gods.

I needed a Titan.

6

The goddess of the dawn, Eos, reigned briefly compared with her brother, Helios, the god of the sun, or their sister, Selene, the goddess of the moon. But Eos's short display of power was transcendent. The goddess of the dawn was the bridge between night and day, a doorway into the soul of all creation and an ethereal glimpse into the transitions of eternity.

Dawn was my favorite moment of the day. It was an invitation to seize any opportunities that the day might bring. But today, this divine promise of hope could not rouse me from my gloom.

Bronte exited the cave and joined me on the overhang, her bow and quiver of arrows over her shoulder. The sky cast a dreamy, rosy light across the forestland before us. I straightened from my hunched position, my eyes bleary and puffy from crying off and on for hours.

"You've been out here all night," she said. "Come in and sleep."

"The soldiers might return."

"I'll keep a lookout."

Bronte lifted me to my feet and shuffled me inside where a campfire warmed the small cave. Over the years, we had turned this cold, dark enclosure into a cozy hideaway, complete with a pot for boiling water, ceramic plates, wooden cups, several full waterskins, and bedrolls.

I lay down on the bedroll nearest the fire and nestled into the warm wool. Sleep came quickly. I dozed until full daylight streamed into the cave, lighting up my face and waking me.

Bronte kneeled by the fire, picking leaves off a branch of ironwort and humming to herself. A pot of water boiled in the flames.

I pushed myself up onto my elbows. "How long was I asleep?"

"I don't know exactly. It's early afternoon." She passed me a bowl of hazelnuts that she had lightly toasted, then dropped a bundle of the ironwort into the boiling water and stirred it in to steep the tea. Bronte had a talent for foraging successfully year-round, as well as hunting game in this forest's wild hills.

"When do you think it's safe to return to the temple?" she asked.

"I don't think it was ever safe."

She chewed the stem of a linden flower, so the white-and-yellow star blooms stuck out of the corner of her mouth. "Where did you go last night?"

"I visited an oracle in the city. Rather, there were three oracles."

Bronte pulled the flower out of her mouth. "Why would you do that?"

"I had questions about the future."

"Yes, that's why people visit an oracle," she replied wryly. "What sort of questions?"

"I asked about leaving Thessaly and starting over elsewhere."

She jolted backward a little.

"Does that surprise you?" I asked.

"I suppose it shouldn't since you bought that boat, but neither you nor Cleora mentioned your intentions to start over elsewhere until yesterday. I knew we might leave eventually, but I thought I was the only one prepared to go."

"Why would you think that?"

Bronte pushed her blonde hair off her face thoughtfully, her hands calloused from endless hours of grinding grain. "I saved coin so we could afford to leave Thessaly. You and Cleora didn't show much interest."

"I didn't want to upset Cleora by talking about it," I replied.

Bronte gave a chagrined nod. We had both hidden our unhappiness for our sister's sake. "What did the oracles tell you?"

I weighed my words carefully, uncertain how much hope to give her. The truth was probably the precise dose of optimism we needed. "They said a child of Cronus lives."

Bronte's mouth dropped open. "Cronus would never let one of his children survive. He swallowed them so they couldn't grow up and overthrow him, like he did with his father."

"The oracles believe that a Boy God lives, and that he will rebel against Cronus."

Bronte slowly took the pot off the fire. "What does this Boy God have to do with our leaving Thessaly?"

"The oracles said he wouldn't succeed without us."

Bronte almost spilled the pot of water as she set it down. "They expect *us* to help a Titan? And not just any Titan—a son of Cronus?"

I popped a hazelnut into my mouth and spoke while chewing. "No honor maiden has escaped Cronus, but with a Titan on our side, we might be able to get Cleora out."

"Did the oracles tell you anything else?" Bronte asked.

They did warn that, should I fail, Cronus would rule, unchallenged and forevermore, but I wouldn't burden Bronte with that. We had just one purpose: to prevent Cleora from meeting the same fate as our mother.

"The Boy God is on the southern isle of Crete," I said. "The oracles want us to find him."

"And you'll listen to them?" She smiled humorlessly. "You hardly listen to anyone, including Cleora and me."

"I listen. Whether I obey you or not . . ."

Bronte laughed dryly. "I thought you didn't believe in the gods or fate."

I shook my head. "I trust Mama, and Mama always said Cronus would rue the day he betrayed Gaea. He has to fall somehow."

Bronte dipped the wooden cups into the pot of tea, filling them, and handed one to me. "On the night Mama passed away, I saw something outside our bedchamber window that I never told a soul about." Her quiet voice quivered uneasily. "A black-winged creature was perched on the roof and staring in at us. I buried my head in a pillow, and when I looked again, the creature had gone. I didn't see it again—until last night. This time, there were three of them, all armed with brass-studded scourges. I think they were the Erinyes."

Gooseflesh scuttled up my arms. The infernal goddesses sought vengeance on oath breakers. "Why were the Erinyes there?"

"I don't know. Looking for an oath breaker?"

Twice had I sworn a vow of honor—once to my mother the night she died, and once to Cleora yesterday. The Erinyes wouldn't have come for me since I was actively working to fulfill my oaths, would they?

A shadow fell across the entrance to the cave. Bronte and I launched to our feet. I grabbed my spear, and she lifted a branch from the fire like a torch, a faster defense than cocking an arrow in her bow. The daylight obscured our intruder until he stepped into the dim light.

Colonel Angelos raised his empty hands. "I'm unarmed."

His mistake. I jabbed at him, knocking him in the chest with my spear, hard enough to pierce the thin cloth he wore. "How did you find us?"

"I saw Bronte foraging in the woods, and I followed her."

I cast a slantwise look at my sister, who grimaced sheepishly.

"I'm alone," he said. "But Decimus will return to the temple and search the area soon."

"You came to warn us?"

"I came to join you." Colonel Angelos kept his hands raised as he stared down the end of my spear. "I visited an oracle yesterday. Three of them, actually. They told me to find the Lambros sisters."

"Why?" Bronte demanded.

"It's hard to explain. They did something unusual with a string and my hands . . ."

"You sound mad," she countered.

"I saw him leave the oracles' tent yesterday," I said quietly. "The oracles did something similar to me, with a string, when they did my reading."

He nodded twice in succession. "Soon after I left, I spotted you in the agora, outside the tavern. Didn't you wonder where I got the olives?"

My mouth went dry.

"The oracles insisted that I accept them," he continued. "They said a good deed would lead me 'to the light aligned with my fate.'"

The oracles had told me a guide would be sent to me, and I would recognize him by his good deeds, and they had told me that *after* Angelos had given me the olives. Had they sent him to me *before* I had decided to visit them?

"This is ridiculous," Bronte said. "Why would the oracles send you to us? We've never even met you."

"Colonel Angelos was at the temple the night Mama died," I explained, my voice low.

Bronte waved the burning branch at him again, like she would at a stray mutt. "Then why are we even talking to this fool?"

A fair question. No man in the party of soldiers who'd taken our baby sister, and then handed her over to the Almighty for slaughter, deserved our time.

Colonel Angelos lowered his hands. "When I was a boy, my mother and I were captured by a slave ship and sold in auction to the Aeon Palace. I worked on several triremes in the royal armada as a deckhand until I was twelve, and grew twice the size of the boys my age. Decimus drafted me into the army, and I swore servitude to the Almighty."

"Breaking an oath to the throne is punishable by death," I said. "You could lose your life just for coming here."

"My mother is unwell." Angelos cranked his jaw, repressing the emotion welling in his eyes. "She's worked too hard for too long. I found a tavern owner who agreed to acquire her and take her in for easier work, but my mother won't leave the palace as long as I'm there. As you said, my oath binds me. The oracles said there's a way for me to retract it, but I must help you travel to Crete."

"How did you know about Crete?" Bronte asked.

"The oracles told me that too. Crete is near my birthplace, Kasos. I haven't been that far south since I was a boy, but I sailed all over the Aegean Sea while I was in the royal armada. Oceanus's territory is treacherous to those who aren't familiar with it. The sea itself is moody and merciless. The god of the sea cares not what mortals do as long as they don't interfere with his family of Oceanids. Thus, the lawlessness of his realm is ideal for drifters and slave masters."

Bronte waved the burning branch at him again, her eyes narrowed. "Why do you think we would ever accept help from you?"

"The oracles told me that a child of the Almighty lives and will rebel against his father."

"And you believe them," I stated.

His gaze probed me. "Don't you also wish it to be true?"

I let his question hang. It was none of his concern what I did or didn't hope for. Besides, Theo Angelos could not be the guide that fate was to send us. He served Cronus. No good deed could undo his oath to that tyrant.

"I've served the Almighty a long while," Angelos said. "He has done horrific things in the name of his throne."

"As have his soldiers," I countered. "Now run back to the palace before your brothers-in-arms notice you're missing."

Angelos steeled himself against my glare. "You cannot fight fate, Althea Lambros."

"You have nothing to do with my fate."

His amber gaze flowed down me like warm honey. "You are exactly how the oracles described: an unmatchable light."

Bronte jabbed the torch at him, close enough that he flinched. "You have no idea who she is, or what either of us is capable of. Get out."

"I'll go," Angelos said, retreating a step. "May Gaea be with you."

"She won't be," I retorted.

Frowning, he bowed his head and marched out.

Bronte shuffled forward to the entrance of the cave and peered outside. "The nerve! He's lucky I didn't burn off his nose." She dropped the branch back into the fire.

"He did get one thing right," I said. "We need to go to Crete."

"We aren't seafarers."

"Like I said, we'll hire a guide." I twisted the string tied around my finger, hoping we would find our true guide. Angelos was a lifelong soldier, sworn to obey the God of Gods. Sending him away had been the right thing to do.

Deep voices sounded outside, one louder than the other. I hurried to the entrance of the cave and stopped to listen. Angelos's voice carried up from the lower forest on the opposite side of the bluff where we'd left the mare.

"I searched up there already," he said.

"Did you?" replied another man. Decimus. "Isn't it odd that you rode ahead of us and didn't mention where you were going."

"I thought the Lambros sisters would be an easy find, sir."

"Don't forget I tagged the youngest one."

"I haven't, sir."

Bronte joined me at the mouth of the cave. While I had been listening, she had smothered the fire, armed herself with her bow and arrows, and packed a satchel with supplies.

"How close are they?" she whispered.

"Wait here."

I crawled to the ledge. The liege men wore shimmering helmets with horsehair plumes, making them visible in the woods. Decimus and Angelos stood under the shelter of the tree canopy with Orrin. A bandage wrapped Orrin's upper thigh. Two more soldiers cased the area, circling closer to our mare.

Bronte cocked an arrow in her bow and aimed at Decimus.

"Don't," I whispered. "You do that, and they'll all be after us." Her shot wasn't guaranteed either. They were too sheltered by the trees. The risk of missing wasn't worth wasting one of her arrows.

"Sir," Angelos said, his voice barely reaching us. "Should we search the temple one more time? The sisters may have returned there."

My quick breaths rang in my ears. I had assumed he'd led Decimus to us. But was he trying to help us instead?

"Orrin?" Decimus called. "Take your men to the Mother Temple. The rest of us will finish here before joining you."

Orrin and two more men mounted their horses and rode west for the temple, disappearing into the woods. Angelos and Decimus moved farther away from the bluff, away from our mare.

Now was the time to move.

Bronte put away her bow and arrow, and we climbed down the ridge slowly, holding on to tree roots, careful not to knock over loose rocks. Right before the bottom, at the steepest part, I slipped forward a little and caught myself. The hamadryads in the hazelnut trees surveyed us suspiciously. They didn't communicate with words—their roots stretched low into the ground and spread out across the forest floor, giving them the ability to feel vibrations around them—but I could sense we were irritating them by pulling on their roots.

I reached the ground and brushed myself off. Bronte jumped the last stretch, landing beside me.

Angelos and Decimus had fallen out of sight, but every once in a while, the snap of branches made the hamadryads flinch. The mare sensed their agitation and flicked her tail. I petted her side, calming her, as Bronte lifted herself into the saddle.

The sound of galloping horses caused us to pause. Orrin and the two soldiers, who had supposedly left for the temple, charged at us. I leaped into the saddle behind my sister and kicked the mare's flanks with my heels. We rode a short distance, then yanked back on the reins. Decimus and Angelos blocked our path. Bronte led the horse in a circle, searching for a way out, but the cliff extended behind us, and the other liege men, each on their own horse, could easily chase the two of us down on our mare.

Decimus turned his sword on Angelos. The general's right forearm bore the scar of the wound I'd given him all those years ago. "You must think me a fool."

"Sir?" Angelos asked.

"You rode ahead to warn them."

Angelos backed up toward the bluff.

Decimus bellowed something about loyalty while my sister and I rode back closer to the cliff.

"What now?" I asked.

"We abandon the horse and go up to the cave, then back down the north side of the bluff on foot. They cannot reach that thicker section of the forest on horseback."

Bronte knew the woodland better than me. I trusted her plan.

We leaped off the mare and began to climb. The steepest part of the cliff, at the bottom, was tricky. Only one section was safe to go up, so Bronte led the way. As she scrambled upward, a large rock began to pull away from the wall and fall toward me. I jumped down, and it sailed past me, hitting the ground.

Bronte waited for me above.

"Keep going!" I started to climb again, but the safe path was no longer stable. I reached for a secure place to hold and pull myself up. It was too far above my head to grab.

Bronte made it above the treetops. I glanced behind me to find Angelos backed up to the wall below me. Decimus, Orrin, and the four other soldiers had dismounted from their horses and now crowded around us.

"This is your fault," I said, skidding down beside Angelos. "You led them here."

"This has nothing to do with your stabbing Orrin, or Decimus's tag?" Angelos retorted, his eyes fixed on the men. "How skilled are you with that spear?"

"Good enough."

I pulled my shield off the saddle and slid it onto my left arm, then raised the spear with my right. In doing so, I bumped into a tree. The hamadryad pushed back at me with her branches, sweeping me forward. The movement spooked our mare, which reared up and took off into the woods. I bent my knees in a fighting stance and faced Decimus.

"Althea." Decimus chuckled. "You've more courage than your sister. Cleora shed tears all the way to the palace and fell to her knees before the Almighty." He laughed louder, his thick belly straining against the cloth. "When he touched her, she soiled herself."

I growled and took a charged step forward.

Angelos cut in front of me, blocking my way.

Decimus's laughter cut off. "Theo, when did you last see your mother?"

"Do not mention my mother," Angelos spit, so venomously that a shiver coursed down my spine.

"A master may speak of his slaves," Decimus replied. Angelos's brow creased ever so slightly. "You don't know? The palace slave master sold your mother to me this morning. He said she has at least one, maybe two, good years left in her, though my slaves don't last as long as other people's."

Angelos's stare turned deadly.

Decimus signaled to his soldiers. "Bring me the Lambros sisters. Orrin, fetch the other one before she gets too far."

Orrin mounted and rode off around the bluff. The four remaining soldiers started for us. Angelos and I backed up toward the cliff wall.

"How are you with that sword?" I asked, my clipped voice revealing my nerves.

"Good enough."

He raised his sword and charged. Before I could throw my spear, he cut the arm off the first soldier. The second rounded on him with a battle cry, and Angelos sliced him down the center, then dropped to his knees and cut through the thighs of the third. The fourth soldier landed on him. I jabbed forward, stabbing him in the side. While the man was pinned, Angelos swiveled around and sank his sword through the soldier's chest.

With an eye on Decimus, Angelos yanked out his blade and then my spearhead. The soldier dropped to the ground beside the one missing an arm. Angelos slammed his sword straight through the one-armed man's heart, ending him, then raised his bloody blade to the general.

"Althea," Bronte called from above, beckoning to me from the ledge. She had an arrow cocked in her bow. "Come on!"

Angelos and Decimus approached each other, swords at the ready. Decimus was massive, but Angelos was big too, both broad shouldered and jacketed with brawn. I glanced back at Bronte, but she had gone. I thought she would cover me while I ascended, but something—or someone—must have drawn her away.

Decimus and Angelos were locked in combat. Iron clashed with iron. Angelos's back foot hit a gnarled tree root, and he lurched to the side. Decimus leaped forward and threw him against a tree, his blade against Angelos's throat.

I stepped over to the hamadryad beside me. "Sorry about this," I said, and drove the end of my spear into her trunk.

A rumbling quake rent the air. I pulled my spear out and then drove it into the next tree, and the next. One by one, the rumbling grew louder. Branches swayed and swatted at me so hard they knocked me on my back. Roots closed in around my wrist, wrenching away my spear. I wrestled my weapon back and got up, ducking another blow from a bough.

Other branches batted at Decimus, throwing him aside. More boughs swept at Angelos and struck him to the ground. He wrenched himself free from their spindly grasp while I chose another path up the ridge.

Sharp rocks cut into my palms, and my footing gave way more than once, but little by little, I climbed to the top. Bronte wasn't on the ledge. I ran into the cave, but she wasn't there either. Angelos ascended to the ridge, breathing hard, his sweaty hair wild about his blood-speckled face. He saw me alone and marched to the other side of the ledge.

I joined him and looked down. On an outcropping below, Orrin yanked Bronte by the hair as she kicked at him. Her hunting bow was crushed on the ground beside them, and her quiver of arrows was scattered about.

Angelos leaped off the ledge and landed on the outcropping. Orrin threw Bronte aside and struck at Angelos with his sword. Before I could jump down too, a hand grabbed the back of my head, spun me around, and threw me. I fell straight forward, hitting the ground hard enough to jar my chin. Stars filled my vision. I rolled onto my back and blinked up at Decimus.

He snatched my ankle and dragged me until I was under him, trapping my legs between his thighs. He pushed my arms to the ground, and his mouth landed on mine. I bucked and slammed my head into his.

Decimus sat up straight, his nose bleeding. "Damn you."

He slapped me hard, sending me sideways. My jaw popped and my eye felt close to bursting. He landed on me again, restraining me, and ran his finger through the blood streaming from his nose. Then he painted it across my lips.

"This is my oath," he seethed. "You are mine, Althea Lambros. In all your days, you will cling to me or you will cling to no one. Let the Erinyes have me should I fail to make you my woman forevermore."

Ice filled me. The taste of his blood in my mouth stained my insides like a frosty brand.

I rolled over and retched.

Decimus stroked my head, his voice deceptively gentle. "Your rebelliousness is in the past now. You'll come with me and wear your velo. No other man shall look upon your face again."

I picked up a handful of gravel, speckled with my blood and vomit. "All right. I'll come with you."

He kissed my forehead, blood wetting his lips and teeth.

I flung the stones at his eyes, and he reared back with a roar. I rolled out from under him and staggered to my feet, then picked up my spear and drove it through his shoulder.

He stumbled back. I leaned into him, pinning him.

"Bitch," he hissed.

I leaned deeper into the spear, pushing his pain into his flesh.

Behind him, Bronte pulled herself up onto the ledge. Blood covered her front, and she held a single bloodied arrow in her hand like a knife.

Decimus grabbed the spear where it entered his shoulder, and with a strength I expected only from a god, he pushed against me. My heels skidded over the gravel. I shoved back with my full body weight and my full temper. The spear sank even deeper into his flesh. Decimus cried out and pushed harder. Dizzy and aching, I tried to hold my ground, but he yanked the spear out of his shoulder and rose with it in hand.

"I'll take out one of your eyes for that," he snarled.

Bronte ran up behind him and stabbed him in the side with the arrow. As he arched back in pain, she picked up a large rock and smashed it over his head. Decimus went stock-still, then his eyes sank closed and he toppled to the ground.

I teetered on my feet. My sister slipped her arm around my waist, her movements surprisingly swift and steady. The blood must not have been hers. We shuffled to the path and started down the cliff, sliding on our bottoms for the last steep section.

A few of the hamadryads, still upset, swatted at us with their branches. We weaved around them to the soldiers' horses. Only two of the four remained, and we each mounted one.

Angelos appeared on the ledge above, his chest heaving and his bloody sword shining in the sunlight. Orrin attacked him from behind, then the two men disappeared from sight. I clicked my tongue, and my horse took off.

Bronte rode hard, passing me to take the lead. We tore through the woods down the pathways she knew well. My face and head ached fiercely. My jaw felt out of place, and my left eye was so swollen that I could hardly see out of it. Once we were well away from the soldiers, Bronte slowed. I matched her pace, thinking she wanted to talk, then noticed she was favoring her bloody side.

"You *are* hurt," I said.

"The cut is shallow. Angelos intercepted Orrin's strike and threw him off me." She didn't say it, but any deeper and it would have been a death blow. "Perhaps we should rethink having Angelos as our guide. He has experience, and he isn't asking for payment."

"But, Bronte, he *took* our little sister."

Bronte pulled back on the reins, halting, and I did the same. "You're not the only one who misses her," she said, her voice strained. "Sometimes, in private, I sing the lullaby Mother sang to all four of us, and I think of what might have been had our half sister been spared. But if we're going to take a chance on someone, shouldn't it be on someone sent by fate?"

"Do you really believe fate sent him?" I hadn't told her what the oracles had said about sending us a guide.

"How else could he have known about the Boy God?" she posed. "Prometheus says, 'Fate leads those who listen and drags those who resist.'"

I touched the string around my finger. *You will recognize him by his good deeds.* Angelos had certainly proved himself beyond giving away a basket of olives, and I wanted to believe what he had told us about his meeting with the oracles. If Cronus really had a living son who could dethrone him, I wanted that, too, for my sisters and for every woman in Thessaly.

"We'll turn around," I said. "But if we don't spot him right away, we leave."

We rode swiftly back to the bluff. The entire time I wondered if we were wasting our time. As we arrived, Angelos was sliding down the steepest part of the cliff. At the bottom, he brushed himself off and stalked over to us.

"Where's Decimus?" I inquired, scanning above.

"Last I saw, Orrin was trying to rouse him to consciousness. I would rather not wait around for them to rally."

"Still interested in being our guide?" Bronte asked.

"I'm interested in helping my mother. Should that entail leading you to Crete, so be it."

"Taking you on as our guide doesn't mean we trust you," Bronte hedged.

"Nor does it mean I trust the two of you."

"I also don't like you," I muttered.

"I cannot return that sentiment."

His slight smile caught me off guard. "I don't care either way," I said tersely, then nodded at my saddle, motioning for him to mount up.

Angelos vaulted into the saddle behind me. "You care what I think, just a little."

"Let's hope your sense of direction is better than your intuition about women." I leaned back into him as he chuckled, then I snapped the reins, and we rode for the sea.

7

A salty wind barreled down the road that cut between the whitewashed stone huts, rousing me from my exhaustion. The seaside village consisted of housing for merchants and boat builders and, of course, taverns for the fishermen and sailors that came and went from the docks.

I dismounted and stretched my lower back in front of an open-air tavern full of customers. Angelos got down after me. Trying not to touch him more than necessary had made our two-hour journey to the seashore highly uncomfortable.

Bronte slid off her horse, her blood-stained chiton hidden under her cloak, and adjusted her velo. I had always admired her modesty mask. Its double serpent heads met at the forehead, and their long bodies wrapped down the sides of her face. The tails met at her chin, completing our father's family crest. The mask itself had belonged to his mother, our grandmother, whom we never met. Bronte's velo was the only possession we had from our father's family. She was given it at birth, a tradition. Girls were born, and immediately they were made to cover themselves. It was hard to imagine our lives could be different.

"The harbormaster is keeping our boat for us," I said. "Do you know where we might find him, Angelos?"

"Theo," he corrected. "It's safer to avoid surnames. Wait here. I'll ask inside." He strode into the tavern.

The back of my neck burned. I touched my tag, the skin tender.

"What is it?" Bronte asked.

"Do you see anything on my skin?" I lifted my hair.

"Nothing except your tag."

"Is it red? Blistered?"

"No. Why?"

"It hurts."

Bronte's mouth turned downward. "Hurts how?"

"It's nothing."

"Althea . . ."

"It isn't important." I added an overly bright smile so she would leave it alone.

A pair of hoplites stumbled out of the tavern, unsteady on their feet. The taller of the two spotted us and weaved in our direction.

"Never seen velos like these," he said, his gaze roaming up and down us. "Such pretty things must be covering up something special."

"We should have a peek at what's under there," said the shorter man.

"Our velos stay on," Bronte answered firmly.

The taller hoplite jerked his head to the side. "Don't be rude. We think you're pretty."

Shorty maneuvered behind me and reached for my velo's ties, but I stepped sideways before he got ahold of them. Bronte dodged the taller man. They were so close I could smell the sour ale on their breaths. Bronte and I turned back to back. Shorty reached for her.

"Don't touch my sister," I growled.

To my surprise—and the surprise of both men—Shorty halted.

Theo had exited the alehouse and was strolling over. "Everything all right?"

"Just having a good time," Shorty answered.

"The women don't look like they're having a good time." Theo extended his arm and slid his hand into mine. I froze, my jaw locked down tight.

The taller man took a step back. "Are they yours?"

Theo squeezed my hand. "We're together."

"Our apologies, Officer," Shorty said. "We didn't know they belonged to you."

My jaw clenched so hard my eyes ached. I didn't belong to Theo Angelos or any man, and I never would.

Theo tipped his head at them. "You both have a divine day."

The tall one paused and looked back. "Aren't you Colonel Angelos?"

Theo's fingers briefly tensed around mine. "I am."

The men's faces burst into grins. The tall one grabbed Angelos by the shoulder and shook him in a brotherly way, part affectionate, part excited.

"You were the youngest soldier in history to join the guard," he said. "You made battalion leader by the time you were, what, sixteen?"

"Fifteen," Shorty said.

Theo inhaled deeply, his nostrils flaring.

"You trained my brother," Shorty went on. "He's at an outpost in the Aegean Sea now. They called you the Bear because you never lose a fight. He said when Theo Angelos declares he will do something, he will do it, no matter what. Didn't I hear you're up for general? That would make you the youngest soldier in Thessaly to achieve that rank."

"So I've been told." Theo couldn't have sounded more lukewarm.

"No wonder he has two wives," the taller one said.

The hoplites chuckled heartedly. They didn't seem to notice that we didn't join in.

"Divine day," Theo repeated, a clear dismissal.

They ambled off, chatting animatedly about "the great colonel Angelos."

I yanked my hand from Theo's. "Those men think we're your wives."

"A necessary story, to divert them."

"I had the situation handled."

"Hmm," he said.

Fire burned in my vision, blurring everything red. I wasn't certain which I wanted more—never to see Theo Angelos again, or to see my mother one more time.

Bronte slid her arm through mine, our elbows locked. "Shall we go?"

"I traded the horses to a server in exchange for his silence." Theo pointed toward the docks. "He said the harbormaster is this way."

I glared at him, willing him to say or do something that would break my thin hold on my temper. He averted his gaze and waited.

"Lead the way, Colonel," Bronte said, her singsong voice too cheerful for my taste.

We left the horses tethered in front of the tavern and crossed to the docks. Our footsteps rang hollow on the wooden planks as we passed boat after boat of fishermen unloading their daily catches and tying off their lines for the evening. At the far end of the main dock, hedged in by water on three sides, a dilapidated hut hung halfway over the sea. Its clay roof had been patched so many times I couldn't discern its original color. A sign outside read: **Go Away**.

Theo knocked. "Hello?"

Waves lapped against the dock.

I stepped in front of him and pushed the door open. Fishing gear and buckets cluttered the cramped interior, and light streamed in from holes in the roof and the cracked shutters.

"He isn't here," I said.

"What now?" Bronte asked.

"We wait for him to return." I took off my velo to let my skin breathe and caught a glimpse of my reflection in a dirty pail. Several bruises discolored my cheek where I had been struck, and I had a black eye.

Theo stayed outside. "We'll wait at your boat. Which one is it, Althea?"

"I don't know."

He blinked at me. "You don't know which boat is yours?"

"I bought it from a merchant friend. He said the harbormaster would direct us to it."

Theo grunted disapprovingly. I must have been dazed from Decimus's blows to have brought him along.

I tugged Bronte aside. "Are you certain about having him as our guide?" I asked.

"I don't know why, but I like him. Maybe it was the way he handled the hoplites or the harbormaster, but I feel he's genuine."

"Genuinely a pest."

Bronte peered upward as if seeking some sort of guidance—or patience—from the heavens. "I think we should give him a chance, but you tell me. You're the one who met with the oracles."

They *had* mentioned a guide. Was it too much to ask that they send a less irritating one?

An old man strolled down the dock hefting a bucketful of oysters. He edged past us to the harbormaster's hut and went in without a word. I exchanged a cursory glance with Bronte, then pushed open the door after him.

"Hello?" I said. "We're looking for the harbormaster."

The stout man had more gray hair on his face than on his head. He kicked over a pail to sit on, then removed from his boot a hunting knife that was so massive, it was a wonder he could walk with it. He shucked a shell with the giant blade and sucked down the oyster.

"What do you want?" he asked with his mouth full.

"Proteus sent us," I replied. "He sold me his boat."

The harbormaster shucked another oyster. "He sold *you* his boat? You're a woman."

I was also not wearing a velo as an obedient maiden should. I jutted out my chin. "I'm well aware of my gender, sir. I paid good silver for Proteus's boat."

"Proteus said the new owner was coming, but . . . you? I could get into trouble giving a boat to a woman."

"Then give it to Theo," I said. "He's our . . . brother. He knows how to sail."

The harbormaster cast him a courtesy glance and then pointed his knife at me. "You just said Proteus sold *you* the boat."

"He sold it to our family," I amended.

Theo and Bronte both hesitated, then they nodded. I much preferred people thinking we were siblings with Theo rather than his spouses.

The harbormaster gave a skeptical huff as he pried open another oyster with his ridiculously large knife. "Oceanus's child," he gasped. He plucked out a pearl as big as his fingertip. "I've shucked hundreds of oysters this season, and this is the first pearl I've found."

"We brought you good fortune, hmm?" Bronte posed.

He chuckled and replied, with an edge of sarcasm, "Fate must have brought you here."

I locked gazes with Theo, then promptly looked away.

The harbormaster picked up a sack by the door and ambled outside. "Come. Your vessel is this way."

We followed him to a quieter area of the docks where the boats were smaller and tied more closely together. He stopped before a weathered wood-planked sailboat. Its raggedy cotton sail hung limply in the windless sky. Seagull droppings speckled the deck and upper hull.

"I scrubbed the barnacles off the hull while it was dry-docked ten days ago," he said. "The sail was patched last month, and all the lines were inspected yesterday . . . No, perhaps the day before. I cannot remember."

The boat was a lackluster prize for the silver we had paid. Proteus was a fair man, but this caused me to question him.

"Is it suitable for open water?" Bronte asked, stating the exact thought I hadn't gotten around to expressing. Crete was two days' voyage across open water. We needed a reliable vessel that could handle the might of the sea.

The harbormaster patted her arm. "Your brother will take care of you."

He drew Theo aside to discuss the boat's history. I caught snatches of their conversation, but every time I crept closer to eavesdrop, the harbormaster turned his back to me. He passed Theo the sack he had brought from his hut, then strolled away.

Theo threw the sack on board and began untying the line.

"Well?" I asked.

"He said we should have calm waters. The Oceanids won't risk violating the treaty between Oceanus and the Almighty by misbehaving this close to the First House Festival."

"The harbormaster couldn't tell me that? I should be included in conversations about my boat."

"*Our* boat," Bronte corrected.

I gave a slight nod and went on. "What's in the sack?"

"Supplies," Theo answered. "Proteus sent food and water for our journey. Low tide is coming. We need to leave, or we'll be stuck in the harbor until morning." He stepped onto the boat as it began drifting away from the dock.

I grabbed the slack line to stop the boat from floating away. "Can you navigate at night?"

"Yes." He stared at the cloudless sky, the twilight deepening to a dramatic expanse of navy. "All I need are the stars."

Bronte chewed her lower lip. "Think of Cleora," she murmured to me.

Truth was, I tried not to imagine how Cleora was faring. After what Decimus said about her first encounter with Cronus, such ponderings were unbearable.

We stepped onto the boat together and found a place to sit out of the wind. Theo took up the oars and rowed us out of the harbor. Once we reached open water, he untied the lines to release the sail. The cloth snapped as wind flooded it, and the boat glided south.

Nightfall crept across the Aegean Sea. Its reflection fused with the starlit sky into a single velvet tapestry. Bronte rested her head against my shoulder and drifted off. I sensed Theo's attention on me and gazed ahead, searching for the blade-thin line where the heavens hugged the ocean to the horizon with its comforting weight.

After a whole night and most of the day on the water, I was certain the ocean was for imbeciles. Bronte had vomited at least once every hour since we entered open water yesterday evening. I held her hair back from her face as she dry-heaved overboard. I hadn't retched, but I had come close more than once. Pride alone kept me from humiliating myself in front of our captain.

Theo manned the sail, poised, at home with the crystal-blue sky and sunshine-drenched waves. Only he had eaten since we'd left. I didn't dare have anything other than water, and Bronte refused even that. At this rate, the provisions Proteus sent with us would easily last until we arrived at Crete the next day.

Daylight had chased away the chill that accompanied the red-washed morning. Bronte lay on the hard deck curled into a ball, sleeping fitfully. I stood vigil beside her, my back against the rail, my face to the wind.

Bronte moaned in her sleep. "Cleora."

This was the longest the three of us had been apart, and I longed for our reunion like a missing limb. I rubbed Bronte's back until she drifted into a deeper slumber. Most of the time, she hummed herself to sleep, but she didn't have the strength for even that.

I pried myself up off the deck and teetered over to Theo. I was less queasy in the center of the boat where the rocking wasn't as noticeable.

Theo had rolled his sleeves up to his elbows, revealing the dark hair on his forearms. "How do you feel?" he asked.

"Well enough."

We cruised past another island with blinding-white limestone cliffs, lush craggy inlets, pallid grasses clinging to razor-sharp hillsides, and a turquoise bay lined with alabaster sandy beaches. Crete lay across the widest stretch of the Aegean Sea, farther south than I ever imagined I would venture. Our small but sturdy vessel rolled over a large wave. I gripped the line, my insides roiling.

"When will we arrive?" I asked.

"By dawn tomorrow, as long as the winds and sea remain calm."

"This is calm?"

One corner of Theo's mouth slid up. "It is for those who have experienced the sea when Oceanus is raging."

Oceanus was renowned for his moodiness. I had heard it said that he had as many faces as the sea had shades of jade and indigo. His temper had claimed the lives of countless sailors and fishermen.

"I've been meaning to tell you," Theo started. "Your mother, Stavra, was—"

"Was what?" I hadn't thought he would have the gall to mention her to me.

"She was an admirable woman. She stood for what she believed in."

"Yes, I know," I said coolly. "You must be worried about your own mother. Do you think Decimus will—?"

"He wouldn't dare harm her."

I hoped he was right. "How did Decimus know you had turned on Cronus?"

"How well do you hide your hatred for the Almighty?" Theo retorted.

"I wasn't working in the palace."

The corners of his eyes tensed. "I've expressed how I feel about Cronus."

"Which is . . . ?"

"The same way you feel, I imagine."

I doubted that. The severity of my loathing ran deep. "Then you don't believe in the Titans."

"I didn't say that."

"You believe in the Protogenoi?"

"You continue to call out my beliefs and allegiances as if you know them," he answered. "Do you do that to everyone?"

"Do you answer everyone's questions with another question?"

His eyes narrowed on the horizon. "Get down."

My gaze darted out to sea. A massive trireme approached us, fast, its gleaming hull flying over the waves.

"Who is that?" I asked, thinking the worst. A slave ship? Drifters come to rob us?

"Rhea's royal vessel."

The trireme was about forty yards long and six yards wide, with three rows of oars, manned by one rower per oar. Two sails puffed in the wind, a large one off the mainmast and a smaller one off the bowsprit. The main propulsion came from the approximately 140 men rowing. The massive vessel dominated our tiny boat, casting us into its shadow.

Theo kneeled and bent his head to the deck, and I sank to my knees.

Titans were known for their elusiveness—they *were* the sun, stars, air, and sea, blending into the world with a seamlessness that was both omnipotent and tangible. Rhea purportedly possessed extraordinary elegance and allure, a consort fit for the Almighty. I craned my neck for a glimpse of her.

"How does that ship carry her?" I asked. "Titans are immense."

Theo turned to me. "Have you ever seen a Titan?"

"No."

The shadow of the trireme raced over us. On the middeck, the piper sat above the sailors and led the rowers' flawless rhythm, the horn of an ibex slung across his chest. I searched for the Titaness in her turret crown, with her legendary guard of tawny lionesses. Rhea was the only Titan I took a genuine interest in, because of her resistance in the face of Cronus's many infidelities. It was common knowledge that theirs was not a love match. They were siblings. All of the Titans espoused each other. Monsters wed monsters, and together they bred monstrous children.

Before long, the ship trailed off into the fading daylight.

"Where do you think she's going?" I asked.

"Back to the Aeon Palace for the First House Festival, I would wager."

A flare of anger hit me. Rhea would likely see Cleora before I did.

"Why doesn't Rhea do anything about her husband?" I asked. "He took away their children. I don't understand why she doesn't stand up to him."

"We don't know that she hasn't," Theo said, somewhat vacantly. "Rhea is as much his subject as we are."

Feeling nauseated again, I returned to my sister's side and lay down close to the rail, in case I needed to retch.

Fate willing, none of us would be under Cronus's rule for much longer.

My nausea woke me from a fitful sleep in the middle of the night. Wiping my clammy forehead, I sat up and leaned over the rail while my empty belly churned. Bronte slept soundly, curled up on her side behind me. I was glad her sickness had abated enough for her to rest, but I was also envious.

Waves slapped against the hull of the boat, and cold, briny spray speckled my face and lips. Currently a mirror of the countless diamond stars, the restless sea spanned from one horizon to the opposite, limitless in its splendor. I had started to drift off again when a cool wind ruffled my hair and brushed past my ear, laced with a man's raspy voice.

Daughter.

A chill prickled across my scalp. Theo sat stern-faced at the sail and paid me no mind.

Daughter . . .

The tag on the back of my neck burned. A black patch on the surface of the sea drew my gaze. The dark waves reflected the stars everywhere except that patch, where a huge shadow slid nearer, just under the surface.

I'm waiting for you, daughter. Release me.

"Papa?" I whispered. My father died when I was too young to remember him. I wouldn't recognize his voice, but who else would call me "daughter"? And my father's spirit would be in Hades, where most mortal souls went after death. My mother insisted that her husband had earned the honor of going to Elysium, where deceased heroes spent the afterlife. If that was true, then she was there too.

The shadow slithered alongside us. Lofty appendages bloomed from it, extending like black-winged night across the water. Everywhere it spread, the starlit sea lost its luster. The wings approached the boat, and a single hooklike claw uncoiled from a wing tip and scratched the hull with an earsplitting screech.

I scrambled back from the rail. My tag burned so hotly that tears pricked my eyes. I pressed my hand over it. My skin there was icy.

"Althea?" Theo asked. "Is everything all right?"

"Did you see . . . ?" I trailed off at his puzzled expression.

The winged figure had vanished.

I crawled back to the rail and ran my hand along the smooth wooden hull until my finger found it—a long, deep scratch.

More unsettled, I moved to the center of the deck and lay between Bronte and Theo while he continued manning the sail. The thing in the water was unlike anything I had ever seen. It had devoured the starlight reflecting off the sea. A Star Eater.

Theo yawned, then splashed his face with seawater. I rested my head in the crook of my arm and wished for a sound sleep, but my mind reeled with what I had seen, and my nausea was unrelenting.

Sometime later that night, still awake, I heard a rich, solemn voice begin to sing.

"Already half my days spread out behind me.
Look, girl, gray hairs sprinkle my head,
Announcing that age and wisdom draw close.
But still, I care only about laughing,
Drinking, and the pleasures of the night.
And yet, in my unsatisfied heart, a fire burns."

Theo hummed a poignant melody that I had never heard before, and then began to sing it again, the mood of the tune shifting from morose to hopeful.

"Oh, Fate, write me an end.
Say, 'This woman, this one here,
She is your soul's reflection. She—
Yes, she—is the end of your madness.'"

As the last note drifted out to sea, I noticed my nausea was gone. I felt almost as good as if I was back on dry land. I pushed up onto my elbows to see Theo better in the dark. "I didn't know you could sing."

"Why would you?"

It struck me how standoffish I had been to this man who had sailed for hours on end without a reprieve. I could be friendlier, at least until morning. "I dance, but Bronte has a talent for singing, like you. What was that tune?"

"It's an old fishermen's ballad." Theo's voice hushed. "My wife and I used to sing it together."

"You're married?"

"Widowed. Charmain, my wife, worked in the tavern her family still owns. She would sing in the evenings for patrons. Sometimes I would join her."

"Did you marry for love?" I didn't care either way, but I found myself curious.

"Soldiers marry when their battalion leader appoints them a wife. I was fortunate Charmain was given to me. She and I were childhood friends. Very few have the privilege of marrying for love."

Decimus's oath rose in my thoughts. He thought he had cursed me never to fall in love with anyone but him, but no outside power could claim ownership of my heart. My heart was the only heart I would have, forever. I wasn't interested in giving it away.

"How did your wife die?" I asked.

Theo licked his lips, collecting his thoughts. "Charmain was born with shallow lungs. She fell ill a year after we wed, and never recovered. Despite how it pained her to breathe, she sang all the way to the end."

"Brave."

"Audacious. Charmain was stubborn about what and who she loved. You remind me of her."

I squinted at him. "Do you intend that as a compliment?"

"Undoubtedly. Your heart lies with your greatest passion."

My pulse picked up speed. "I'm a stranger to you."

"For now."

His serious amber gaze struck me speechless. Its intensity warmed me straight through. Our surroundings fell away, and I was bathing in his light, dazzled.

I blinked, and Theo glanced off into the darkness.

The night rushed in around me, bringing with it a new sense of solitude and confusion. I wanted to see that look of his again. I wanted to understand it.

"What other songs did you and Charmain sing together?" I asked, then yawned.

Theo's voice, soft but with an undercurrent of an emotion I couldn't discern, carried on the wind. "You should rest. Dawn will wake the world soon."

I rested my head on my arm. "Good night, then."

"Good night, Althea."

He began to sing again, more melodiously than any flute. My heart slowed, and my drowsy attention drifted to the infinite vault of stars . . . to looking for the return of the Star Eater . . . to the man across the deck . . . his unguarded expression when he looked at me, as if I were the woman who would end his madness.

8

Splashing drew my gaze away from Theo. I had spent too many of the past twelve hours pretending not to stare at him, hoping for another glimpse of his softer side like I saw last night.

He pointed out to sea. "Althea, Bronte, look!"

Bronte still slept soundly, her face sticky with sweat. I shaded my eyes with my hand and sat up.

A pod of dolphins swam alongside us, their silvery bodies dancing on the waves. Seafarers believed dolphins were a good omen from Oceanus.

Theo changed our course slightly, and the dolphins followed. This continued for about an hour until he pointed at a slice of land on the horizon.

"Crete," he said.

The dolphins split off from us, turning east. We stayed the course south. Had Oceanus blessed our journey? The god of the sea was the only brother of Cronus's who hadn't helped him dethrone their father. Did Oceanus know about our mission?

We approached the leeward side of the island, and I gently jostled Bronte awake. "We're here."

She crawled to the side of the boat and pressed her cheek against the rail.

"Do you need to retch again?" I asked.

"No," she said hesitantly. "Yes. Perhaps in a moment . . ." She poked her head over the rail, then laid it back down. "Wake me when we make landfall."

I joined Theo on the middeck. It was into the afternoon, later than he had predicted we would arrive, but I didn't point this out. He was so exhausted that a stiff wind could have blown him overboard.

Theo drew the sail, and the two of us rowed toward shore. The navy waters paled to crystalline aqua as we approached the beach, revealing the colorful sea life darting about under us in the shallows. A school of small bright-orange-and-red-striped fish scattered from the end of my oar as I dipped it in the water, and seabirds searched for clams in the tide pools, but no people were visible anywhere on land or sea.

The bottom of our boat ran aground. I shook Bronte, rousing her. We stepped into the surf and sloshed together over the sharp, slippery rocks. My knees wobbled a little from disuse, but the feeling of having my soles on solid ground was a relief.

Bronte sat on the beach and picked up fistfuls of pebbles. The color was already returning to her pale face. "I have never been more grateful to have my feet on dry land," she said loudly in a singsong voice.

Up the sloped shoreline, seagrasses sprouted from the reddish stony ground, then shrubberies blended into a forest of leafy trees. A cascade of mountains towered across the skyline, the highest peak still white with winter snowfall.

Theo wrestled the boat out of the water and past the tide line. His soaked shirt clung to his trim stomach and waistline, and his face and upper chest, where his neckline split, glistened with sweat and salt water in the late-day sun. I caught Bronte eyeing him.

"What?" she asked. "Don't pretend you don't notice."

How could I not? He was right in front of us.

"He reminds me of someone," Bronte said, more to herself than to me. "I cannot think who . . ."

Theo trudged over to us. "We should make camp before nightfall."

Bronte scanned the thick woodland. "Is Crete inhabited by natives?"

"A tribe is thought to reside deep in the interior of the island." Theo examined the tree line with a critical eye, then started off.

"Shouldn't we stay close to the boat?" I asked.

"The woods are safer than the beach," he said. "Sea dragons inhabit these waters."

Sea dragons were known for both sliding out of the surf on their bellies and leaping out of deeper waters to ambush their prey. They didn't hunt the waters as far north as Thessaly, but tales of them snatching people off beaches fed many children's fears.

I hastened after Theo into the brush, Bronte trudging behind us. He paused every so often to listen to the insects, the birds, and the other stranger noises of the woods. The longer he listened, the closer I listened, and the less certain I was about why he was on alert.

Bronte paused to pick a handful of black currants from a bush. I spotted red berries next to them and reached for one. She snatched my hand in midair, halting me.

"Those are poisonous," she said.

"Those berries?" I asked.

"Those berries will make you sick to your stomach. That snake will kill you."

She let go and pointed. A bright-green snake was coiled, camouflaged, around the branch I'd almost harvested from.

"One bite from that viper, and you wouldn't live through the day," Bronte said.

I stepped away from the bushes. Bronte wasn't afraid of snakes, but she was cautious as she collected the edible currants. Then we hurried to catch up to Theo.

Bronte passed me half the black currants. I popped a few into my mouth and chewed, bursting their sweet tartness. Theo turned them down, so Bronte kept the rest for herself.

The woodland dimmed little by little, and then abruptly, as though the sun had been covered with a curtain, night fell around us. Long, eerie shadows deepened, and I had to squint not to trip over roots or collide with low-hanging branches.

Theo stopped in a rocky clearing, lit by the ghostly moon and encircled by dense oak trees. "Here," he said, dropping the pack.

He tasked Bronte with building a firepit while we gathered wood. Her side had mostly healed, yet she moved carefully, favoring it.

Nightfall laid down a blanket of cold that pushed into my tired bones. Bronte set to work lighting the fire, and her fifth attempt bore a spark that she coaxed with patient breaths. We soon settled around the flames, huddling close. Theo drew a crude map of Crete in the dirt and indicated the mountain range that ran down the island like a spine.

"Ida Mountain," he said of the highest peak. "The oracles said the Boy God dwells there."

"What else did the oracles tell you?" I asked. And why hadn't they told me where on the isle to find the Boy God?

"They said he was the youngest of Cronus's legitimate children."

The oracles hadn't told me that detail either. Their predictions felt less special when divided between the two of us. Theo might have been an experienced military officer whom they might confide in with more detail, but he didn't seem worthy of that privilege. His service to Cronus should have counted against him.

"That's it?" Bronte pressed. "They told you nothing more?"

"Nothing of consequence," he replied.

I suspected he was lying. The oracles told me personal things that I was unwilling to share with him too.

Bronte threw a branch into the fire, sending sparks into the night. "Does anyone else think it's odd that the God of Gods doesn't know he has a living son?"

"Gods are fallible," Theo said, shrugging.

Cronus's ignorance gave me hope. If something that momentous could be hidden from the Titans, we might actually have a chance at helping to overthrow Cronus. But Bronte's suspicion was understandable. Cronus was the mightiest Titan in all the world. How could a Boy God even have remained hidden from him, let alone rise to defeat him?

"Theo, what do you know about Cronus?" I said.

A slight vibration coursed through the air, lifting the hairs on the back of my arms and quieting the birds and insects in the woods.

"The Almighty is obsessed with protecting his throne," Theo answered in a hushed voice. "He has reigned for nearly four hundred years, though his army and armada were formed just seventy-five years ago. He has a deep-seated fear of his Titan siblings or their offspring overthrowing him, and it has worsened. He used to travel to see his brothers at the four pillars of the earth. Now he spends most days in his great hall at the top of the highest tower, hidden under a misty gloom, watching and waiting for his enemies to rise against him."

"What enemies?" I questioned. "Oceanus?"

"Cronus is suspicious of everyone, but I imagine he is more concerned about his mother gaining allies. Since the fall of her husband, Gaea has been livid at Cronus for neglecting to release her other children from Tartarus, the Cyclopes and the Hecatoncheires, which he had agreed to do when she handed him the adamant sickle. This may be speculation, but I believe Cronus is on guard for her retribution."

This portion of Cronus's history was always omitted from the plays about his illustrious ascension, although it might have been the most crucial part. Without Gaea giving her son the adamant sickle—in exchange for the release of her children, whom Uranus had imprisoned—Cronus could not have prevailed over her husband. Now Cronus assumed that others would betray him, just as he had betrayed his parents. No, we never saw *that* on the stage.

"The Cyclopes and Hecatoncheires don't belong in our world," Bronte said. "They're monsters."

"Not to their mother," Theo replied. "To Gaea, all creations are beautiful."

"How did Rhea hide the Boy God from her husband?" Bronte asked.

"I don't know," Theo admitted, yawning widely. "I worked as a palace guard while Rhea was with child. She handed over the swaddled infant to the Almighty, and he swallowed the babe whole, just as he had his previous five children."

"Did you see it happen?" Bronte asked.

"No, but my mother did. I swear on the sun, moon, and stars, she aged ten years that day. The only other time I saw her that distraught was when the God of Gods welcomed Stavra to the palace."

Iciness washed over me. I wanted to hear more, but after listening to Decimus recount how Cronus received Cleora, I didn't need my mother's introduction to the palace in my head too.

"What did the Almighty do?" Bronte asked, her question punctuated by the crackling campfire.

"It wasn't what he did, it's what Stavra did." Theo sounded amazed, even proud. "She threatened him."

"What?" I replied, my astonishment tumbling out. "What did she say?"

Theo tried to cover another yawn and shook his head, as though disappointed in his own fatigue. "My mother wouldn't tell me. She only said that when Stavra finished whispering in the Almighty's ear, she had never seen him angrier—or more fearful. I thought you might know what Stavra said."

Bronte and I exchanged glances, searching both each other's faces and our memories for an explanation. She shook her head.

"I don't know either," I said.

"Could anyone else have heard her?" Bronte asked.

"I asked every slave and soldier in the throne room," Theo replied. "No one else heard what Stavra said, only that her tone was threatening.

To this day, my mother refuses to tell me." He unloosed another cavernous yawn.

"I'll stand guard," I offered.

Theo murmured his thanks, lay down on his bedroll, and fell asleep.

Bronte lay down beside me. I twisted my ring, and the string glowed softly, as radiant as the moon. High above, the Titaness Selene spied on us with her all-seeing pearl eye. Unlike Helios, the sun god, the moon was ever-present in the heavens, dwarfed by the daylight yet never fully retreating from her throne. Selene's rule in the heavens was fixed and safe. Did Cronus look upon the moon and despise her security?

Bronte and Theo breathed in quiet rhythms. I was too anxious to sleep. Tomorrow I would meet the Boy God, the second-generation Titan fated to dethrone Cronus.

Stars, I wished I knew what my mother would have thought of all of this.

Thinking of her, I took my velo out of the satchel. Mama warned me I would grow to despise having to wear my modesty mask, and I had. I detested what it stood for, but part of me also loved it as much as my arm cuff. I loved that it had been my mother's.

A column of gloom fell over the clearing, a shift so slight that Nyx, the Protogenos goddess of the night, might have flown above and cast her deathless shadow over us. I thought I saw a woman's face in the forest's umbra, but it disappeared in a blink. The memory of the Erinyes' ghoulish faces and long claws sent a shiver through my mind.

Stop it, I told myself. I had crossed a sea today. My efforts to honor my oaths had to count for something. I shuffled closer to the fire, nearer to its light. A crunching noise like a footstep sounded behind me, but before I could look around, a hand clamped down over my mouth.

9

A man bore down on me, one hand over my mouth and the other on my shoulder. I froze until I realized it was Theo. He crouched beside me, so close the darker flecks of amber in his eyes shone in the firelight. He lifted a finger to his lips, motioning for me to stay quiet, then let go.

"We have company," he whispered.

Bronte slept soundly as he rose and drew his sword.

A masked woman stepped out of the woods. In addition to the shield and sword she carried, a braided sheep's-wool sling hung at her waist. Her golden velo resembled my own, with fiery wings flaring out from her eyes. Below the mask, her full lips and slim, pointed chin were visible. She wore leathers and animal furs, knee-high sandals, and a shell necklace with an insignia of a dove in flight with a rose in its mouth—the crest of Aphrodite.

Behind her, emerging from the brush, came at least two dozen armed female warriors sporting identical half-winged masks and necklaces bearing Aphrodite's crest.

"Weapons down!" shouted the one in the lead.

Bronte startled awake and hauled herself to her feet.

"Disarm yourselves!" the leader yelled.

Theo lowered his sword to the ground and raised his hands. "I'm Colonel Theo Angelos of the First House guard. We didn't mean to cause you alarm. We're looking for a resident of the isle."

"You're trespassing," the leader snapped. "No men are permitted on Crete." She whistled, and her comrades rushed in around us.

Theo's expression remained calm as they yanked his arms behind his back and tied his wrists together. They patted him down and took his knife. Next, they bound my sister's hands, and then mine. A warrior went through our only bag.

She held up my velo. "Euboea, look."

The one barking orders plucked my mask out of her comrade's grasp. Seeing it beside theirs, I had no doubt they were identical.

"Where did you get this?" Euboea asked.

"It belonged to our mother," I replied. "I'm Althea Lambros. My sister there is Bronte."

Euboea shook the mask in my face. "Who was your mother?"

"Stavra Lambros."

Several warriors whispered to each other.

Euboea stepped closer, her eyes narrowing. "Where is Stavra?"

"Dead," I answered without inflection. "Cronus took her seven years ago. She died giving birth to his half-Titan babe."

The warriors continued their whispering.

"Your man said you're looking for someone," Euboea said.

"He's not my man." And if men weren't allowed on Crete, where was the Boy God?

"We were directed here by oracles," Theo replied.

"Oracles?" Euboea laughed—a dry, coarse sound—and sauntered over to him.

He stiffened as she lifted her sword. "Our apologies for trespassing," he said. "We mean no harm."

She held her blade to his throat. "Men mean harm."

Theo held perfectly still. Even with his hands bound, he was bigger and stronger and could easily defend himself—he took down four soldiers without becoming short of breath—but he meant it when he said he would do them no harm. His damned honor was going to get him killed.

"Euboea," I said sharply, drawing her attention. "Colonel Angelos is a celebrated soldier in the Almighty's army. His absence would be noticed." Her blade dropped marginally from Theo's throat, just enough to reveal her unease. "You don't want to incur Cronus's wrath."

"The God of Gods has no authority here," she said, lowering her sword from Theo's bobbing gullet. Then to her comrades, she said, "Bring them."

"But the man—" one warrior said.

"If he so much as sneezes on anyone, slit his throat."

A guard hit me squarely in the back, knocking me to my knees, then she struck Bronte to the ground. Theo started to kneel, unprompted, but they smacked him anyway. Theo flinching in pain was the last thing I saw before they covered my head with a sack.

The warriors led us across rocky ground. Disoriented under the sack, I stumbled along, concentrating on putting one foot in front of the other. The earth beneath me changed to softer soil, then grass brushed against my bare ankles.

Pounding music came from ahead. The drums were punctuated by metal clanging, like spears banging against shields. We followed the drumming, getting closer and closer until it was all around us.

Rough hands yanked me to a stop. Not a heartbeat later, the clanging halted.

In the abrupt silence, my breaths boomed in my head. The sack tugged across my lips, drying out my mouth. Sweat rolled down the sides of my face, sticking my hair to my clammy skin and adding more moisture to the already-musty sack. My hands were bound so tightly that my wrist bones pushed against each other. I tried to wriggle them, but that only hurt worse.

Someone yanked the sack off my head. My eyes adjusted to the light of a massive bonfire. Bronte and Theo stood beside me, their hair a mess. Theo had additional bindings around his ankles, and they had gagged him with a leather muzzle, the type hunters used on their hounds.

At least a hundred armed warriors encircled us, all women, all of them wearing velos in the same design as mine. They stared at Theo with hard eyes while he gazed straight ahead at the center of the camp. There, in front of the fire, stood two woodland nymphs.

They wore no masks, and their exquisite beauty was clear in the firelight. Blue sparkles like perfect raindrops decorated their eyelids, cheeks, and foreheads. One was redheaded and the other pale blonde, and their long, wavy hair was adorned with iridescent butterflies and alive with glimmering wings. Elegant robes of evergreen silk flowed around their willowy figures. Garlands of dewy white roses hung from their necks and wreathed their heads in delicate crowns.

The blonde wore a belt equipped with several hunting knives of various sizes. Colorful tattoos, red and pink roses, ran down her arms and legs. The other nymph was unmarked and unarmed. I couldn't tell their ages. A nymph's life span was somewhere between a mortal's and the gods'. They could have been my age or two hundred years older.

Euboea addressed the nymphs quietly, then stepped back.

"My name is Adrasteia," the redheaded nymph said. She pointed at the blonde. "This is my younger sister, Ida. The tribe you've disturbed is the cult of the goddess Aphrodite. Euboea tells me you're daughters of Stavra Lambros."

"Two of them," Bronte replied. "Cronus has our older sister."

"I'm sorry to hear that, and about your mother's passing."

"How did you two know each other?" I asked.

"Stavra and I were colleagues," Adrasteia replied vaguely. "As a favor to her, your party may stay the remainder of the night. But at dawn, you must leave."

"Will you keep the colonel muzzled?" I asked.

"Words can be more damaging than a sword," Ida said, more to her sister than to me.

"A man hasn't set foot on Crete in decades," Adrasteia explained. "We honor Stavra's memory in trusting you to oversee your liege man."

"You can remove the muzzle," I said. "Theo is a well-respected soldier. He won't act out of turn."

"His reputation among men means nothing here."

Bronte popped an eyebrow. "I don't know if you've noticed or not, but my sister and I aren't men."

"We can vouch for him," I added. I don't know why the muzzle bothered me so much, but I didn't like that Theo had been silenced simply because of his gender.

Adrasteia gave a flippant flourish of her hand. "The muzzle can come off, but he stays bound."

Ida glared as a guard removed Theo's muzzle. "Why have you come?"

"We're looking for someone." Theo rubbed at his mouth and jaw. "A boy."

"Did you not hear us?" she retorted. "We've no men here."

"We're not looking for a man," Theo replied. "We're looking for a god."

The silence in camp tightened, the tribe's attention on Theo sharp.

"What is this you speak of?" Adrasteia asked, her voice carrying across the clearing.

"We know Rhea hid her sixth child from her husband," Theo explained. "I couldn't believe it at first, but I served as Rhea's guard, and what the oracles said fits what I know of their marriage at that time."

A few of the warriors gaped at him. I doubted they had ever heard a man talk so much.

"I've heard enough," Ida said. Between the knives at her waist and the tattoos on her arms, she was intimidating. "Let me muzzle him again."

Adrasteia raised a silencing hand to her sister. "Let's hear what he has to say."

"Yes, let's," I said coolly.

Theo hardly glanced at me, though he must have felt my agitation. He could have told me he had been Rhea's guard earlier, maybe sometime before swords were aimed at us? Or perhaps that was the point. Maybe he never would have told me unless our lives were threatened.

"My first official posting in the Aeon Palace was in Rhea's service," Theo continued. "After the Almighty swallowed their fifth child, she sequestered herself in her quarters for several nights and refused his summons. On the seventh night, Cronus ordered us to bring her to him. We escorted her to his chambers and waited outside the door." Theo's gaze and voice both fell flat. "Rhea emerged sometime later. My mother, one of her ladies-in-waiting, met her at the door to her chambers and helped her inside. Rhea hid herself away for two moons, then went to Cronus to tell him she was with child, and she was going south for the duration of her pregnancy. He let her go, but only because she swore to return with the newborn babe. When she left, I was reassigned. Seven moons later, Rhea returned to hand over her infant son to Cronus. But what if she didn't? What if she gave him a different child?"

"All conjecture," Ida declared, her derision increasingly forceful.

Bronte matched Ida's scorn with her own. "That was a lot of detail for a guess."

Ida narrowed her eyes at her. "Send them away now, Adrasteia. Don't wait until morning."

Adrasteia scrutinized us intently, but without Ida's venom. "Perhaps you're right, sister," she said. "I wish you well, travelers, but we cannot help you. Guards? See them out."

The guards pulled the sacks back out.

"Rhea sent us!" I said, ducking as one of them tried to cover my head again.

"Wait!" Adrasteia floated over to me, her strides so graceful I couldn't help but wonder if she was a dancer. "Why did Rhea send you? You best not lie, mortal. I have lived more years than you have seen sunrises. I will know."

I held the nymph's glittering stare. "Rhea has an urgent message for her son."

"Give me the message."

"She instructed us to tell only him."

"Then you will leave having failed," Ida snapped. "No one demands an audience with His Excellency."

That was it. That was the confirmation we were waiting for.

The Boy God was real, and he was here.

I steadied my voice. "We've spent two days crossing the sea. We've no time to waste. We must see him as soon as possible."

Ida rested her hands on the hilts of two knives at her waist. "You bluff. You have no message."

"All right," I said calmly. "We'll tell Rhea you refused to cooperate, and you can explain that to her guards when they come to deliver the message instead."

The thought of more men coming to the isle sent murmurs through the crowd of warriors, just as I had hoped. Adrasteia took note of the tribe's alarm and whispered to her sister. Ida whispered back with increasing vehemence. Their argument escalated until Ida threw up her hands and stomped off.

"I will send a messenger to His Excellency," Adrasteia said. She nodded at Euboea, and the warrior sent a messenger off into the woods.

"Should he accept our request, you will please unbind us," Bronte said. "I can't feel half my fingers."

"Should he deny your request, you will leave the island and never return."

Adrasteia walked to where Ida stood at the outskirts of the group, and the two began whispering heatedly again. Bronte, Theo, and I huddled together. In the firelight, past the wall of warrior women around us, I could see the outlines of big square tents. This was more a camp than an established village, as if they were prepared to pack up and leave at any moment. As though they anticipated that their time here wouldn't last.

Theo scratched his face where the muzzle had left lines in his cheek. A piece of grass had stuck in his scruff, and I brushed it away without thinking. Theo cast me an odd look.

"You had something . . ." I half explained, looking away.

"What if the Boy God refuses to see us?" Bronte asked.

"He won't," Theo replied.

"How do you know?"

"He won't refuse his mother."

Theo might have been projecting his devotion for his own mother, but then he knew more of the story of Rhea and her son. I only knew that she had saved him.

Adrasteia floated back over to us, my mother's velo in hand. I recognized it as mine because the ties on the back were wool, and the warriors used leather ties. "You've kept Stavra's mask in good condition," she said.

"Why does the tribe wear velos when there are no men on the island?" Bronte asked.

Adrasteia scanned the masked women. "They don't trust outsiders," she said. "People from their previous lives might be looking for them."

"Why?" I asked.

She gave me a concentrated stare. "Didn't your mother—?"

"Adrasteia!" the messenger yelled, running into the firelight. "His Excellency will see them right away!"

Bronte cast a smug look at Ida, who was still lingering at the fringes of camp. The fair-headed nymph deepened her scowl and brought her hands back to two knives at her hips.

"Release the girls," Adrasteia said. The guards untied Bronte and me, but they left Theo chained. "I will lead you to His Excellency. Your man stays here."

Euboea strode over, the muzzle dangling from her finger. "I'll watch him."

Theo gave no reaction, though disappointment stained his expression.

"We'll be back," I promised.

Adrasteia and three warriors led us deep into the woods past soaring elms and tamarisks. A bridge spanned a creek with willows, clover, and galingale lining its banks. The messenger hadn't been gone long, so I anticipated a short walk. After trekking up a steep, rocky path with no end in sight, my bad ankle began to hurt, and it occurred to me that they must have some other means of communicating. Searching the trees, I spotted a line running through pulleys high above. Pegs were attached to the rope for holding messages. A person need only pull one end of the line to send a letter in the other direction.

Bronte panted beside me as we both tried to keep up with the nymph. Adrasteia wasn't out of breath, and though her skin was dewy, she could hardly be accused of perspiring. I got the impression she made this journey often.

Giggling sounded ahead, then I saw lights bobbing through the trees. Adrasteia led us to the opening of a cave. More laughter came from within. Adrasteia went inside while her guard stayed with us. Her voice echoed out.

"Your Excellency, the visitors have arrived."

A male voice replied, not as young as I had imagined. "I changed my mind. Tell them to come back tomorrow."

"Your Excellency, they came from Thessaly to bring you a message from Rhea."

"They? They who?"

"Two young women. Sisters."

His voice took on a note of intrigue. "Why didn't you say so? Send them in."

Adrasteia waved us forward.

I swallowed my next breath. This was my first face-to-face encounter with a Titan. Second generation but a Titan, nonetheless.

Bronte poked me in the side. "You first."

"Why me? You're older."

"This was your idea." She dropped her voice to a whisper. "Nervous?"

"No. You?"

"A little." She poked me again, half-heartedly. "Do you really think he can help us get Cleora back?"

I couldn't say for certain, but there was one thing I did know. "We have to try."

Bronte ran her tongue across her upper teeth, then gave a nod.

Facing the cave, I strode forward to meet the god of my fate.

10

At the cave entrance, I was hit with an otherworldly scent—an aroma of the gods. I recognized the fragrance from my childhood and immediately thought of my mother. She would come home from the palace smelling of nectar and ambrosia. When ingested, both were poisonous to mortals.

Except for the undecorated entryway, the cave was not rustic. Inside it resembled an extravagant tent. Torches cast radiance over the red and purple silks draping from the ceiling to the jewel-toned rugs. Plush floor cushions were occupied by masked maidens in loose chitons with long bronze legs and arms, and full busts. They congregated at the center of the room to fawn over a young man with frizzy black hair. His thin face accentuated a sharp, square jawline and scrawny, shirtless chest. He sat with one leg slung over the side of an overstuffed floor cushion, his arms above his head. A baggy wrap hung low on his hips, covering his legs to the knees, and his left foot was missing a sandal. A maiden massaged his shoulders while two more fed him bits of fruits and nuts from bounteous bowls and platters. He sipped amber nectar from a chalice, and on a separate platter that none of the young women touched was ambrosia, which looked like gooey honeycomb.

This was the Boy God? The gods were undying and ever young, but he lacked the size and presence of a Titan in every way. He was older than what I would consider a "boy" yet not quite a man. I wagered he was a few years younger than me, perhaps fifteen.

He lowered his arms and grinned. "It's been a while since my mother has sent me sisters. You're prettier than my last pair." He waved off the maidens and gestured us forward. "Though you're dirtier than I expected, with a bath and scented oils, you'll make a splendid gift."

"We aren't a gift," I said.

"Oh, right. You're 'messengers.'" He winked conspiratorially, the size of his grin doubling. "Go on, then. What's your message?"

"We're—"

"Come here and deliver it."

I shuffled forward.

"Closer . . . closer . . . there." He put his hands around my waist and tugged me into his lap. "All right. Deliver your message."

I sat with my back straight, every muscle on edge. "I think you have us confused with someone else."

"Unlikely. My mother sends me maidens all the time. She believes I should gain experience in all areas of life." He buried his face in my hair and rubbed the small of my back.

Bronte threw her gaze to the heavens. "He really is the Almighty's son."

"Pardon?" he said, lifting his head. "I haven't meant to neglect you. I have plenty of room in my lap for you both."

"I'd rather sit on a bur bush," Bronte snapped.

He laughed. "My mother knows I enjoy a challenge."

"We're not here to challenge you," I replied.

"No? What a pity." He took my hand in his. "What's this?"

I tried to pull away, but he held my left hand fast and touched my string ring.

"It's nothing," I said.

"That is *not* nothing." He showed me his own left hand. There, tied on his middle finger, just like mine, was a ring made of string, identical to my own.

"Where did you get that?" I asked.

"I don't recall. I've had it for as long as I can remember." He threaded our fingers together, our rings touching.

A light burst from them, brief but bright, and a wave of dizziness hit me. Rings of residual light floated across my vision, and a faint voice whispered, *Moira*.

I jerked my hand from his. The boy scrutinized me closer, as though he, too, had heard the voice.

"What's your name?" he asked solemnly, his gaze combing my face.

"Althea Lambros. That's my sister Bronte."

He sniffed my hair and pushed it away from my neck. "Everyone calls me 'Your Excellency,' but you may call me Zeus."

"Are you a son of the Almighty, Zeus?"

"Rhea sent you to ask who fathered me?" He gripped my wrist, his gaze sharpening. "Why have you come?"

"Oracles sent us," I replied. "They said a son of the God of Gods was hidden on this island and that we should find you."

Zeus's eyebrows shot up. "What else did the oracle tell you?"

"There were three of them, actually. Sisters."

"More sisters," he said dryly. "Were they 'messengers' from my mother too?"

"Messengers of fate. They told me the surviving son of the Almighty would overthrow him and assume the throne."

"Did they, now?" Zeus laughed again louder, his retinue of pretty-faced gigglers joining in. He popped a piece of ambrosia into his mouth, then stood, propelling me to my feet. The Boy God towered over me. His height was his only attribute that met my expectation. "You've wasted your time, and mine. I'm not who the oracles said I am. Do you have a message from my mother, or shall my guards escort you out?"

"I . . ." I glanced at Bronte for help.

She stuttered out a reply. "Well, we, she—"

Zeus drooped with disappointment. "It's a shame you aren't who you said you were. Take them away."

"Wait!" I said, dodging the guards. "Cronus has our sister."

A sudden seriousness fell over Zeus and his entourage of maidens, hushing them to stillness. It may have been my imagination, but it seemed that even the torches flickered.

"You speak the name of the God of Gods too openly, mortal," Zeus warned.

I raised my chin, unafraid of uttering a name or of this supposed Boy God. "Cronus has taken our sister captive. She is just one of countless women he has terrorized. He reigns without responsibility. Someone must hold him accountable."

Zeus started to reply, and his adolescent voice cracked. He cleared his throat. "I'm not responsible for my father's actions."

"What about your own?" Bronte demanded. "Is this how you wish to live? Hidden from the world, gorging yourself on food, pandered to by maidens, and guarded by warriors who deserve better than to watch over you?"

He stretched out on the floor cushion and put his arms behind his head again. One corner of his mouth twisted in a smirk. "Glorious, isn't it?"

Bronte kicked his foot, knocking off his other sandal.

Zeus sat straight up. "Pardon you!"

She bore down on him and shook her finger in his face, scolding him as she would a misbehaving child. "The secrecy of your existence is a privilege you don't deserve."

I drew Bronte back from him as Adrasteia rushed forward.

"My apologies, Your Excellency," said the nymph. "I'll take them away now."

"I'll gladly go," Bronte growled, marching to the threshold. "I cannot stand the sight of him."

"You just met me," Zeus said, feigning offense.

I shook my head at him, my own frustration rising. "Rhea saved you and hid you away so you wouldn't become your father, but you're just like him." Too tired to contend with him any longer, I let out a disheartened sigh. "The oracles were right. You *are* a Boy God."

Zeus sank back and rested a hand over his chest as though I had kicked him too. I joined my sister at the cave's entrance, and we followed the guards out.

"I am not my father!" a squeaky voice cried.

I glanced back to see Zeus just outside his cave, his hands balled into fists. "I am Zeus! You shall not forget my name!"

"I will remember you as the biggest disappointment in history," I called back. "Your name will sink away in the sands of time."

Adrasteia grabbed me by the arm and dragged me into the woods. "You and your sister should show the gods more respect."

"We respect those who are worthy," Bronte retorted.

"Respect isn't inherited," I added.

Adrasteia loosened her grip on me. "Stavra spoke in such a way. She did herself no favors."

"Our mother understood more than most people," I said.

"Yes, but she always revered the gods."

I had no argument for that.

Our party continued downhill in silence, Bronte stomping her feet and swaying her arms widely. I trapped my own temper in my throat, swallowing a frustrated scream that I would have rather expelled into the darkness closing in around us.

After returning to camp, with a few hours of night left, the tribe had led us to a tent and ordered us to stay there overnight. Bronte bundled herself into a bedroll and slept, but Theo and I discussed our predicament into the early hours of the morning.

"Tell me again what he said," Theo whispered.

"He won't stand up to his father," I said. "He simply refused."

"You said his name is Zeus?" Theo thought hard. "I've never heard of him. Rhea hid his existence well."

"He isn't eager to change that. He's terrified of his father." I rubbed my tired eyes and tried not to think about the intimacy of sitting so close to this man at such an hour. It was hardly romantic with my sister asleep beside us and two guards posted outside. Still, the closeness of Theo's warm body was enticing.

"You didn't tell Zeus about my mother?" he asked, lying on his back.

"I saw no point after he showed no sympathy for my sister's capture. He's a sheltered, spoiled coward."

"He's lost his way."

"That would imply he was ever on the correct path." I could not understand why fate would choose someone so unworthy to usurp Cronus, and to rule in his stead.

"You're thinking," Theo remarked.

I hugged my knees to my chest. "I'm always thinking."

"We shouldn't discount Zeus so quickly. He may need time to consider your offer. A Titan cannot be contained by a cave forever."

"Or we might have wasted our time coming here," I muttered.

Theo scratched his scruffy chin. "Do you always dismiss people so readily?"

"The gods aren't people."

"Perhaps that's where you're most mistaken," Theo said, his voice gentle. "They're just as mortal as you and me."

"Except they're immortal."

"If Zeus was mortal, would you overlook his weaknesses?"

"I don't know." I rubbed my eyes again and fought off a yawn. "It doesn't really matter what I think. The tribe is sending us away in a few hours, and Zeus won't hear from us again."

Bronte rolled over with a dreamy murmur. I tugged her wool blanket up to her chin and rearranged the bottom to cover her feet. The star mark on her heel made me ache for Cleora. Mother used to say it took a minimum of three stars to form a constellation. Take one away, and the connection between them was lost. Missing Cleora felt like that, like losing part of what made me whole. Part of what made me *me*.

"It may be worth a try to request an audience with Zeus again," Theo remarked. "For your sister's sake."

"For my sister's sake or for your mother's?"

His whisper coarsened. "I won't stop until she's free."

"Why didn't you offer to buy her from Decimus?"

"The same reason you didn't offer to buy Cleora from the Almighty: What price would you put on a soul?"

His breaths grew faint as he drifted off. I wished I had brought back better news, but Zeus wasn't the Titan we needed. Just as Cronus had despised his lustful father, dethroned him, and then went on to emulate Uranus in every way, so would Zeus fail to emancipate us from the oppressive appetites of another Titan ruler.

Noises outside startled me. Footsteps leaving. Our guards? I could no longer see their shadows outside the tent.

I slowly reached for my spear.

A moment later, someone slipped inside the tent. A masked warrior crept between Theo and me. She raised her sword over him, preparing to stab down. I swept my spear out and blocked her strike.

"You," she growled.

"Leave him be, Euboea," I said, identifying her voice. "He's just a man."

"That's more than enough reason to kill him."

Normally, I might agree, but Theo was more tolerable than most. "Adrasteia put him under my care. You want him, you'll have to challenge me first."

"Don't pretend to be noble," Euboea snapped. "Your mother never would have threatened our tribe by bringing a soldier into camp. You're nothing like her."

"All you need to know about me is that I will spear you straight through the heart if you cut so much as one hair off Theo's head."

Euboea withdrew her sword. "You're not worth the time it would take me to clean your entrails off my blade." She stormed out, throwing the flap closed behind her.

I lowered my spear, my heart thudding so hard it echoed in the soles of my feet. I pushed my hair out of my face and caught Theo staring.

"How long have you been awake?" I asked.

"Long enough."

"Were you going to let her chop your head off?"

"I thought *you* might."

"The sun will rise soon," I said, turning over. "You've wasted your chance to sleep."

"It was worth it to hear you threaten her."

"I'm glad your near demise amuses you."

"I count myself fortunate that I'm not your enemy, Althea," he said, chuckling to himself. His compliment bore too much resemblance to mockery.

"Next time, I'll let her skewer you," I grumbled.

He laughed, and his whole body shook. I tossed my pillow at him, striking him directly in the head. He took it in his arms, cradling it to his chest, then rolled over to sleep. I rested my head in the crook of my arm, too annoyed to ask for my pillow back.

Theo began to hum to himself, that same lullaby I had heard him sing on the boat. Again, his melodic voice stilled my restless mind. But as sleep finally began to come over me, the night tucked itself away; dawn began to claim her daily ascension to glory, and the noises of the camp rose with her.

Adrasteia yanked open the tent flap. Theo sat up quickly, his eyes alert like he had never fallen asleep.

"We've prepared a meal for you before you go," said the nymph.

"Would you please petition Zeus to see us again?" Theo asked.

"His request to send you away is final," Adrasteia replied. "The chieftains of the tribe agree, you cannot stay. Come. Eat breakfast."

Bronte sat up blearily, her tawny hair a mess around her sleep-scrunched face. "Did someone mention breakfast?"

The three of us got up and lumbered out. We weren't in a rush to leave, and we wouldn't turn down food. We hadn't eaten a proper meal in a while.

Dew glistened in the grass under a blue sky awash with vaporous clouds. The camp consisted of little more than tent peaks and a few pathways vanishing into the trees. The only wooden structure was a small school with an outside play area. The rest were tents set together in groups. Women everywhere, all wearing velos, had started their usual routines. Huntresses prepared bows and arrows, tanners prepped animal skins, beekeepers collected honey from the hives, and an ironsmith hammered away. A pair of shepherds waved goodbye to Adrasteia and left to tend to their flock.

Euboea waited with Adrasteia.

"Back so soon?" I asked Euboea.

Her cheeks pinkened.

Adrasteia raised a slim brow. "Euboea will take you to breakfast, then I'll escort you to your boat."

Euboea stepped forward to bind Theo's wrists in front of him. She wrapped more cords around his feet, leaving enough slack for him to shuffle walk, but just barely.

"This way," she said.

We followed her across the grassy clearing to the mess hall, which operated under a tent filled with benches and tables. Our table was set at the edge of the area. A porridge of wild rice and short grains was slopped onto plates and served to us by two girls. The odd food smelled of honey and almonds. Other members of the camp lined up to collect their meals. Nearby, a table full of younger girls took turns staring at Theo and whispering. Traditionally, back home, men dined separately from women and children, who ate after the men had had their fill. The lack of males, even among the children, baffled me.

"Where are the boys?" I asked, then added jokingly, "Or did every mother only give birth to girls?"

A flash of pain flew across Euboea's face. "I had a boy once."

"Where is he?" Bronte asked.

"He's with his father." Euboea tilted up her chin, masking her hurt. "When I came to Crete, I gave him up."

"What about the other mothers with male children?" I asked.

"They left them behind too. When a pregnant woman gave birth to a boy here, Ida made arrangements to place the infant in a home elsewhere. That hasn't happened in quite some time. As you know, no men live here, and no woman with child has joined us in almost three years."

Bronte set down her spoon. "The mothers cannot keep their babies?"

"Those babies will grow into boys, then into men, and men don't belong on Crete." Euboea sent a glare at Theo, then waved at our plates. "Eat. Or I will take you to your boat hungry."

Though the porridge smelled good, my stomach was too unsettled to eat much.

Theo tried to lift his spoon to his mouth, but the bindings around his hands made it too challenging, and his grip kept slipping. He didn't sigh or grunt or offer any noise of complaint. He simply tried, again and again, without success.

"Here," I said, "let me."

"I can do it."

"I recall you doing me a kindness by retying my mask for me. Let me repay you."

Taking his spoon, I dipped it in the porridge and fed him a bite. His beard framed his lips, showing off their pink softness. I tried not to think about them as I scooped him food in manageable bites. The women watched us closely. I doubt I could have convinced a single one of them that Theo wasn't my man, but I wasn't about to let him starve, no matter what impression this gave them.

Bronte cleared her plate, then finished mine. After I served Theo his last bite, she noticed a bit of food on his beard and wiped it off.

"Neither of you deserves to be Stavra Lambros's daughter," Euboea muttered.

Bronte played with her necklace and whispered in my ear, loud enough for Euboea to overhear, "Don't let her bother you. She's a sour sow."

Euboea pushed to her feet. "Time to go. This sow has better things to do than watch you."

As I followed her out of the mess hall, I noticed a familiar burn mark on the back of her neck.

"You were tagged?" I asked.

She cast a glare over her shoulder. "We all bear scars from our past lives, some visible, some not."

She led us out of camp and past a large enclosed tent erected around twin brick smokestacks. A woman came out the door, and I glimpsed inside. Within the greenhouse were rows and rows of low-growing, little red flowers.

"Poppies?" I asked.

"The tribe must have a taste for opium," Theo replied.

Adrasteia and several armed guards met us at a wide pathway.

"Zeus asked me to give you this." She offered me a ring made of string, red and braided, the workmanship simple. "He wanted you to have something to remember him by."

"Oh, I won't soon forget him," I replied, each word dripping with derision. "Tell him thank you, but I don't want it."

"Don't look down upon him," Adrasteia implored. "Zeus has never known another life. Ida and I have been Rhea's loyal servants since our apprenticeship ended with Mnemosyne, goddess of memory, when she became a councilor to the Almighty. We watched as child after child of Rhea's was taken away, as she grew brokenhearted, a shell of the goddess to whom we first gave our allegiance. When Rhea told us her plan to come to Crete and birth her sixth child in secret, we accompanied her and hid the sound of Zeus's wails by banging our swords against our shields. We acquired another newborn boy from a slave trader, and Rhea took that child to her husband, leaving Zeus with us to raise and protect. We've done our best to teach him about the world, but he's still learning."

I flattened my lips. "He has the luxury of setting himself apart."

"His life is not without sacrifice. Ida and I have tried to be mothers to him, but we're not his blood. Rhea cannot risk visiting him more than once every few years, so she sends him maidens to keep him company. They satiate his need for affection, but he longs for his kin."

"Mmm," Bronte replied, unimpressed. "He cannot hide forever."

"Perhaps, but it's my duty to protect him for as long as possible." Adrasteia gestured down the path. "The beach is this way."

I was so turned around from entering camp blindfolded the night before that I was astonished to discover we were a short walk to our boat. The guards heaved it down to the water, then undid Theo's bindings and returned his weapons. He got into the boat first to stabilize it.

"Farewell, Althea and Bronte," Adrasteia said. "It was good to meet Stavra's daughters. I wish it had been under different circumstances."

"You said you two were colleagues," Bronte stated. "What did you mean?"

Adrasteia stood in the sea as the waves crashed around her. "Ida and I used to live alone on this island until Stavra began bringing women that she had helped to escape from their homes. In exchange for swearing an oath that they would never leave here, we let them stay."

"Our mother helped all these women?" I asked.

"All of the original members of the tribe," Adrasteia replied. "Stavra and Tassos moved the refugees together."

Bronte and I shared a look of astonishment. "You knew our father?" I asked.

"Tassos was your mother's most vital ally. His death was a great loss for us all." Adrasteia's wispy lashes lowered to her cheeks. "Because of them, you were permitted to stay here as long as you have. Please repay us by never telling a single soul about the tribe or Zeus."

"I swear," I said sincerely.

"I swear," Bronte agreed.

Theo rested his hand on his sword, a common sign of good faith among soldiers. "You have my silence as well."

Adrasteia smiled her gratitude. "May Gaea guide you to your next destination, wherever that may be."

Bronte and I climbed into the boat with Theo, and the guard pushed us off. Theo took up the oars, and then hesitated.

"What's our destination?" he asked.

"Home, I suppose," Bronte murmured.

I wasn't ready to leave the island yet, or to spend another few days nauseated at sea, or to return to Thessaly, but I doubted I could convince the tribe to let us stay.

Bronte laid her hand over mine. "We'll find another way to Cleora," she said.

I had already come up with another way. It's what I should have done all along—trade my freedom for hers—but I couldn't tell Bronte, or she would try to dissuade me.

Theo rowed us out to sea, then threw open the sail and tripled our speed. The isle shrank away, and our short time there began to feel like a dream. The farther we sailed, the more Bronte and I slumped into each other, listening together to the tumbling, clamorous sea.

"I don't understand," she said, her voice rife with disappointment. "The oracles told us to find Zeus, and Prometheus says, 'We are never defeated unless we give up.' Why did the oracles send us here, only for the Boy God to send us away?"

Tears welled up behind my eyes, blurring my view of the glittering waves. I wished I knew.

11

At the height of noon, we sailed through a grouping of alabaster islands. Rocks jutted out of the shallower water, the stone splinters resembling shards of broken bones. Only smaller watercraft could navigate these channels without running aground. Theo stayed vigilant at the sail. With little foliage and rocky beaches, the isles appeared uninhabited and untamed.

"Where are we?" I asked.

"The fastest current north to Thessaly takes us farther west, toward the coastline, through Oceanid Passage," Theo replied. "Not many boats venture through these waters. They aren't for deep-sea-going vessels."

A rock scraped along the hull below the surface. Theo quickly lowered the sail and handed oars to Bronte and me.

"We need to row," he said. "Navigation will be easier."

He stationed himself at the stern, and each of us took a side. We rowed while he steered through the treacherous rocks. Beached ships testified to how swiftly things could go wrong.

Just when I thought we had navigated through the worst, the current strengthened, propelling us along, reducing our need to row. Theo remained calm, his orders short and direct. Bronte and I heeded his calls without question. My sister's color had paled, sweat beaded along her upper lip, and her nausea had returned, but she didn't quit rowing.

In fact, she sang at the top of her lungs, an old tune about Gaea and Uranus meeting for the first time. The lyrics were muddled by the splashing, but her voice carried like a battle cry.

The hull scraped an outcropping of rocks, screeching so loud I winced. Finally, the waters deepened and the current eased. Bronte sang her last note, and I relaxed my death grip on the oar.

"That was . . . exhilarating," she huffed.

"Can we use the sail now?" I asked.

Theo studied the path ahead, a narrow channel between two island cliffsides. "Not yet."

The current picked up again, swifter than before. Theo directed the rudder at the helm and fought to keep the boat from drifting into the limestone cliffs. Big waves kicked water over the rails, soaking our clothes. I blinked salt water out of my eyes. We were too close to the cliff on my side, and I felt sure that we were headed for a collision.

We flew up to the wall on the crest of a wave. I stuck my oar out and pushed off as hard as I could. Bronte joined with her oar, and together we drove the boat away and back toward the middle of the passage.

The gap between the isles expanded, and the current loosened its grip on us until finally we flowed into quieter waters.

With the passage behind us, we released the sail again and set aside the oars. Bronte and I sat back to dry in the sun. The boat slid past more rugged islands, their cliffs high and steep. Birds nested in their overhangs, hovering around them like bees to a lilac bush.

Bronte pointed up. "What is that?"

A domed structure with grand columns sat atop the next isle's cliff line. From the look of the antiquated architecture, it had been there a long time. Domed roofs hadn't been built in Thessaly in decades.

"What are you looking at?" Theo asked.

"There's a structure up there," I said, pointing. My string ring began to glow, but as I lowered my hand, it stopped.

Peculiar.

Theo looked up. "Where is it?" he asked.

"There," I said, pointing again. Once more, my string ring began to glow while my hand was raised. My pulse began beating in double time. I thought my ring was trying to tell me where to go next. "We should go ashore."

"Why?" Bronte asked.

"I have a feeling." Since Bronte's seasickness had returned, she didn't need much persuasion. "Find somewhere to go ashore," I called to Theo. I anticipated some resistance, but he changed course.

The current flowed in our favor. Moments later, we sailed up to the rocky shoreline. My ring glowed brighter. I tucked it into the folds of my still-damp chiton while we navigated the coast in search of a quiet cove or inlet.

"There." Bronte gestured at a rocky outcropping. "Are those stairs?"

Indeed, a crude set of stone stairs led from the sea to the beach. Nothing but the structure above suggested that this isle might be inhabited.

Theo steered the boat alongside the stairway and jumped off onto the top step with the line. He dropped the bow stones and tied up, then helped Bronte and me disembark. The moment I set foot on shore, my ring quit glowing.

Now what?

A steep pathway of switchbacks rose all the way up the vertical cliff. I was exhausted from little sleep and really didn't want to climb. Every movement felt arduous.

"Shall we?" Bronte asked. Apparently, she had recovered from her nausea.

I had led them here—or more accurately, the ring had led us all here, I assumed—so I couldn't very well turn back. "You first," I sighed.

Bronte started up the trail, and I followed. Theo took the rear.

The ascent was painstaking. Bronte stayed away from the edge, practically hugging the wall. Theo plodded along in his usual steadfast and stalwart manner. He was as fast as a lion on the attack, but otherwise, the man had one pace.

I took the lead up the final switchbacks to the grassy plateau. The stone structure—a temple—was set on a slight incline away from the cliff edge. Detailed arrangements of roses and doves decorated the entablature. The open façade comprised nine tapered columns, and the other three sides were walled.

My ring glowed again as I mounted the seven steps to the towering columns, but I hid my hand in my cloak to avoid questions from the others.

"Hello?" I called into the dim temple. "Hello, is anyone here?"

A gust of wind stirred the silence.

"It's deserted," Bronte said, going inside.

"Careful," Theo warned.

The tile floor had buckled in places, and the ornate stonework along the cornice had crumbled off and fallen around. In the middle of the tile floor, half covered in dust and crushed stone, the crest of Aphrodite was inlaid.

"This must be Cythera," I said in a hushed voice, "the isle Aphrodite sailed past on seafoam before making landfall on Cyprus. This is one of her temples."

When Cronus castrated Uranus, his drops of blood spattered the earth and sea. From those drops, the Erinyes were born from the earth, and from the sea rose Aphrodite, come ashore as a fully formed female and, some believed, the first woman ever.

Theo picked up a toy I would have played with as a girl, a doll with a simple clay face on a cotton body stuffed with straw. It was in relatively good condition, but who had left it?

Bronte tripped over a tile and fell forward. She caught herself with her hands and stood to brush herself off.

"I told you to be careful," Theo said.

"I *was* careful. My foot caught on that broken tile. Look. It's hollow beneath." She pulled aside the pieces, opening up the hole and exposing a wooden box within.

We hefted the box out of the floor. The exterior was plain, nondescript wood of low quality. I lifted the lid to uncover a folded piece of parchment inside. Bronte took it out and opened it—a map. A path had been drawn from Othrys to several islands, ending far south at Crete. A tiny pair of wings marked each stop along the way.

"For traders and merchants?" Bronte said.

Theo read the map over her shoulder. "The course is too remote. I think it's something else." He followed the curved line with his finger. "It stops at every temple of Aphrodite between Thessaly and Crete."

"What do the wings mean?" Bronte asked.

Something about the map tugged at my memory. I took it from my sister to examine it closer. At the bottom, in the right-hand corner, a name was written beside the key. My breath caught. "Bronte, is that Papa's signature?"

She examined the mark for herself. "It is. But why?"

Theo wandered the dais with a look of concentration.

I waited as long as I could before asking, "What are you thinking, Theo?"

He pivoted toward me. "Starfall."

"Pardon?"

"A few years back, reports came in of women going missing. The Almighty asked Decimus to investigate." The back of my neck burned at the mention of Decimus's name, but I stopped myself from scratching it. Theo went on. "I was assigned to his company. We discovered no one was capturing the women, they were running away—and they had help. An underground group was moving them out of Thessaly to an undisclosed location. We tracked their movements to the sea but never caught them." He ran his finger down the route, from place to place, all the way to Crete. "This route would have been ideal for smuggling. And look here." He pointed out a small star, like a comet, near our father's name. "The emblem of the Starfall operation."

"Adrasteia did say Mama and Papa moved refugees," Bronte said.

Theo held the doll in both hands. "Their operation smuggled dozens of women out of Thessaly, some with children. Cronus was convinced that a Titan was conspiring against him. His brothers accused him of paranoia, but the operation was successful for so long, it might have been true."

"Was a Titan helping our parents?" Bronte asked.

Theo considered the route on the map again. "I'm not sure they needed a Titan's help. This route bypasses naval forts along the coastline and takes advantage of the swiftest currents. It's risky, but under the best conditions, it would be nearly impossible to follow or chase down a vessel on this path. Still, I wouldn't discount it."

My parents' sacrifices left me speechless. The risks they'd taken, and the struggles they'd gone through to help others, were immeasurable. I wondered exactly how many women and children were free because of them. And I was intrigued by the possibility that they had teamed up with a Titan.

Theo passed me the toy doll. "Their work became known as Operation Starfall because trying to find the escapees and their supporters was like trailing a shooting star."

"Did Cronus discover that our mother was leading the operation?" Bronte asked. "Maybe that's why he took her?"

"As far as I know, he didn't figure that out. We had been searching for a man. The Almighty would never admit that a mortal was outsmarting him, particularly not a woman." Theo scratched his beard. "Stavra's plan was brilliant, really. She correctly assumed that Cronus and his liege men would never think the head conspirator was a woman."

Brilliant, perhaps, but ultimately lethal.

I walked out of the temple and crossed the plateau to the seaside cliff. Scanning the view, I imagined my parents leading women and children up the winding, steep incline to hide them in the temple. How brave those women were to run from their homes, knowing that the consequences of getting caught would be dire. Why had my mother chosen Aphrodite's temples for shelter? Aphrodite's place among the gods had always seemed frivolous, but perhaps I had dismissed the goddess of love too quickly. After all, love takes many shapes in a woman's heart.

Theo came to stand behind me. He said not a word, but his presence felt immense. I sensed his sympathy before the words left his lips.

"I'm sorry about your parents."

"You're not the reason they're gone." He wasn't responsible for the death of my baby sister either, yet I still hadn't entirely decided whether he was culpable for not stopping it.

"That may be so," he said, "but I may still express my condolences. I don't know what sort of man I would have become without my mother to raise me."

I glanced slantwise at him. "Well, it's a good thing I don't have to worry about what sort of man I will become."

He chuckled, but it had an undertone of exasperation. "Is everything a debate to you? Even a compliment?"

"Especially a compliment. Men compliment women because they want something from them, or to flatter themselves. Oh, look how kind I am! Oh, see how generous I am with my praise! I don't want your praise. What you think of me doesn't matter in the—"

Into the sky, a scream went up.

Both our gazes flew back to the temple.

"Bronte." I took off in a run.

Theo sprinted after me across the plateau. He nearly surpassed me, but I arrived at the temple just ahead of him.

Bronte sat crouched in the far corner, her face buried in her knees. I kneeled and rubbed her back. Her whole body trembled.

"What happened?" I asked.

"They, they, they—the Erinyes."

Theo drew his sword and swept it in a circle. His sword would do him no good. No mortal weapon could outmatch the Erinyes' vicious, brass-studded scourges, and no prayers, tears, or begging could move them.

In the middle of the temple floor, sunny-yellow narcissus sprouted from the cracks. Sacred to the Erinyes, trails of narcissus were found near the souls they hunted. Sometimes their victims also saw white turtledoves, their most revered animal.

"Where were they?" I asked, my voice raspy.

Bronte gestured to the back of the temple where the walls cast foreboding shadows into the corners.

"Did they speak to you?" Theo asked.

Bronte shook out her trembling hands and pulled away from my touch. "They surrounded me. I couldn't see the light of day, then one of them trailed her scourge down my cheek and said, 'The oath breaker will suffer.'"

Theo sheathed his sword and strode out of the temple, his shoulders rising and falling with each labored breath.

"Who were they talking about, Althea?" Bronte asked.

"It must be Theo."

She squinted at me. "You swore an oath too. How can you be certain they aren't after you?"

I couldn't be, which was why my hands had gone icy and I couldn't catch a full breath. Before we left Thessaly, Bronte had seen the Erinyes at the Mother Temple. Neither Theo nor I had been there at the time. Had they been waiting for him or me?

The map had fallen to the floor. I picked it up and, for the first time, noticed the words written on the back.

By the hand of faith, destiny is found.

Written under it in big letters was one word: *moira*.

Clotho said fate worked in mysterious ways. I turned the map over and considered the route from Thessaly to Crete again. Why take the refugees to Crete? Had my mother learned about Rhea's betrayal? Had she known about Zeus?

My ring began to glow again.

Perhaps our mother didn't die because she smuggled women out of Thessaly. Maybe she died to protect Rhea's secret. To protect Zeus.

My ring brightened. I shoved my hand into my pocket to smother the light. Could the ring hear my thoughts? I nearly ran outside, took it off, and pitched it over the cliff, but a soft voice rang in my ears: *Trust the Boy God.*

I could not say why my mother had chosen Crete as a refuge for women, and whether that choice had ultimately led to her death, or even whether Operation Starfall had assistance from a Titan. But I did know that, for Cleora's sake, and for the sake of fulfilling my oath, I needed to return to Crete and try once more to gain Zeus's partnership.

I helped Bronte to her feet. On the way out, the eerily bright-yellow narcissus blooms seemed to turn toward us. Bronte stopped at the base of the temple, both hands on her necklace. I left her to collect her thoughts and went ahead to join Theo, who was waiting for us at the cliff's edge.

"We're returning to Crete," I said. "I understand if you don't want to—"

"I have a plan."

"So do I."

Without so much as a glance in my direction, he said, "We'll follow yours."

The nighttime noise of cicadas and frogs in the woodland hid the sounds of Bronte, Theo, and me crouching in the brush. Returning to Crete had taken us the remainder of the day. As it turned out, Theo and I had similar plans—sail back to the island, make landfall on the south side, sneak inland to the tribe's camp, and while the north wind slept, distract their guard so we could climb Ida Mountain.

Our plans were the same in every way except for one.

"Absolutely not," Theo said.

"We won't have time to sneak past unless you cause a distraction." I elbowed Bronte in the side. "Aren't I right?"

"I don't know if it matters what he's wearing." She monitored the torchlit camp from our hiding place. "They'll probably spear him dead regardless."

Theo's eyebrow ticked.

"We need to stun the guards," I said. "What's more shocking to a group of women who hardly ever see men?"

"A nude one," Bronte agreed, slapping Theo on the back companionably. "Try not to get speared."

"I'll do my best," Theo muttered.

He slid out of his clothes, leaving his bottom undergarments on, then stepped out of the brush. In the firelight, the bronze skin across his chiseled shoulders appeared too perfect to be real. The patch of hair covering his solid chest looked soft to the touch, like his beard.

I shook the thought out of my head. It had been too long since I'd lain with a man.

Theo dropped his undergarments.

"Well, well, well," Bronte drawled. "He's built well for an older man."

"Old" was not what came to mind. "Statuesque." "Chiseled." "Magnificent." Any of those. All of those.

"He really does remind me of someone," Bronte said. "Why can't I think of it?"

"Do you think he knows?" I posed.

"Knows what?"

"How handsome he is?"

Theo glanced over his shoulder at us and smiled as though he had heard us.

Bronte sighed. "He knows."

Theo stepped farther out into the field. His buttocks hardened and softened as he walked.

"Althea, we need to go." Bronte picked up my spear and sneaked into the woods.

I crept around the perimeter of the camp. Theo approached the bonfire, his chest out and chin high.

"You there," shouted a guard.

Euboea.

I groaned. Of all the warriors we could have encountered tonight, fate chose her.

"Stop," she called, drawing her sword.

Theo halted.

She approached him slowly, her blade forward. Her gaze wandered down the length of him. "Where are your clothes? Your weapons?"

"Our boat ran aground," he began, just as we'd planned. "I swam back to land. My clothes were torn away by the rocks and my weapons were lost."

Euboea kept glancing down the front of him. She looked up to the moon and then back to him. Just as I hoped, she saw his nakedness as vulnerability. She held her sword out but did not strike. I sneaked past them to the main footpath. With one last glance at Theo's naked back, I took off up the dark gravel path.

I ran with one eye on the treetops. The rope for the message trolley was already moving. Bronte had attached our letter to the line, and it would reach the top before me. I ran faster. The message flew ahead of me, out of sight, but I could hear the line moving through the pulleys and used that creaking noise as my guide. When I was almost to the top, the noise stopped.

The mountain seemed to never end. My legs and lungs burned, and my bad ankle throbbed, but I pushed myself to the end of the path. The message was still on the line outside the cave. Just as we'd hoped, Zeus's guard came out to retrieve it. I crept up behind her, hooked my arm around her neck, and covered her mouth with my opposite hand.

"Shh," I said, muffling her protests.

She flailed, wore herself out, and ran out of air. I laid her unconscious body on the ground and strode to the cave.

"Sibylla!" Zeus called from inside. "I'm cold without you."

I pulled Theo's knife from the sheath at my waist and padded in.

Scant light danced from a candle on the floor near a pile of satin pillows. No more guards were anywhere to be seen, nor was Zeus. Then suddenly, he was behind me, kissing my neck.

"Mm," he said, his hand slipping down my hip. "You're not Sibylla."

I'd thought I might need to seduce him to gain his attention, but I should have known that he would attempt it first. In one motion, I grabbed his hand from my waist, spun around so I was behind him, twisted his arm, and pressed the blade of the knife to his throat. He wore breeches and nothing else. Even his feet were bare.

"You've a real eye for women, Your Excellency."

"Oh, it's you. Again. Didn't I send you away?"

"I have trouble obeying imbeciles." I pushed the blade closer to his skin. "Move."

He shuffled out of the cave with me. "I hope we aren't going far. My feet hurt."

"You should try wearing clothes."

"What did you do with Sibylla?"

"She'll wake up in a little while."

He winced as he stepped on a pine cone. "Where are you taking me? You *are* aware that we're on an island and you've nowhere to hide?"

"You're the one who likes to hide." I yanked on the arm I had twisted behind his back and shoved him forward. "How big an escape boat do you think your life is worth to the tribe?"

"You're overestimating my value."

"Or you're underestimating it."

"Are you kidnapping me?" He laughed. "I thought you were ambitious before, but now? You ask me to dethrone the God of Gods, all right, I can see the merit in that. But kidnapping me on your own?"

"She isn't alone." Bronte stepped out of the trees, aiming my spear at him.

He preened a little. "Good evening, fair sister. Look at the two of you. Are either of you wed? But, of course, you aren't. Any man would be a fool to trust you."

"That may be the first sensible thing he's ever said," I remarked.

"You couldn't have grabbed him a robe?" Bronte asked, making a face.

"I don't think he owns different clothes."

"Oh, really," Zeus scoffed. "What do you two sleep in?"

Bronte held up the muzzle she had swiped from camp. "Can we gag him now? Please?"

"That's a delightful toy," Zeus remarked. "Would you like to know how I use it on my maidens?"

"No," Bronte and I replied in unison.

"Oh, I see. Your exoticism only applies to ambushing people in their homes at night."

"Stop your harping," I said.

"Is this kidnapping another plea to make me ruler of the world? I've no interest in leaving this place, let alone to conquer the First House. Why would I? I have everything I need right here."

"My sister told you to shut up," Bronte replied. We each grabbed one of his arms and started into the woods.

"Althea!"

I stopped. "Did you hear that?"

"Althea!"

"That's Theo," Bronte said.

"Who's Theo?" Zeus asked.

The three of us had agreed to meet him at the boat. Something must have gone awry.

Theo ran up the trail and into view, still naked. A blush fired across my cheeks.

"The guards are coming," he panted. "Euboea woke them. I held her off as long as I could."

"Not long enough," Bronte said.

"How long did you think she would be distracted by my nakedness?" he retorted.

I was still distracted, but I didn't say so.

Shouts sounded nearby, and torches bobbed in the trees.

"We still have our prisoner," I said. "Let's return to the cave."

Bronte and I dragged Zeus inside. Theo took his sword back and watched for the incoming guards.

"Could you ask him to put something on?" Zeus asked.

Bronte rolled her eyes. "The irony of that request . . ."

I threw Theo a robe, which he yanked on. It fit so snuggly across his chest and shoulders that he might as well have still been naked.

I *had* to stop thinking about him naked.

"Zeus, is there another way out of here?" I asked.

"No."

"He's lying," Theo said. "He has no reason to help us."

Zeus laughed, once. "Who *is* this man? And why isn't he dressed?"

"He's covered now," I pointed out.

"Hardly an improvement," Zeus countered.

Theo lowered his voice. "I see what you mean, Althea. You took no liberties when you described him."

"What . . . what did she say about me?" Zeus asked, his face falling.

Voices and the clatter of armor approached from outside. Theo backed away from the cave's entrance, ready with his sword. The noises grew louder, and then Adrasteia called to us inside.

"We have the entrance surrounded! There's no other way out."

"The Boy God was telling the truth," Bronte muttered.

Zeus's sky-blue eyes flashed. "I am many things, but I am not a liar."

Just our luck. He had one noble trait, and it worked to our detriment.

We were trapped.

12

Don't panic.

I thought I might have said this aloud, but a moment later, Theo said the same thing, as though it was a new idea.

"Don't panic. Zeus is a valuable hostage. We can use him to negotiate."

But our hostage was the Titan we returned here to negotiate *with*.

"Colonel Angelos!" Euboea called. "Come out, and no harm will come to you or your party."

"When someone promises to do no harm, they probably intend to do just the opposite," Bronte grumbled. She pushed a stack of parchments off a floor cushion and plopped down.

"Careful!" Zeus kneeled and picked up the scattered parchments.

Bronte picked one up. "Who's Metis?"

"That's private." He snatched it from her grasp.

Bronte scanned the other parchments still on the floor. "She must be of importance. Most of these letters appear to be from her."

"I don't see how that's any of your concern." Zeus gathered the letters and set the pile out of her reach.

One of them slid from his grasp and fell at my feet. I noticed Rhea's royal seal, a lion's head, and her elegant signature at the bottom. I retrieved it before he could and started to read.

My dearest Zeus. You will bring about monumental change. Reorganize the sky, my beloved stormking—

"Give that back!" Zeus cried.

"Your mother believes in you," I said, holding the letter away from him. "She risked everything to protect you. She didn't do that so you could laze about all day eating and fornicating."

"To be fair, he would probably be doing that at the palace," Bronte chimed in dryly.

Zeus locked his jaw and spoke through clamped teeth. "My staying in hiding doesn't only protect me. It protects Adrasteia, Ida, and the tribe. If my father discovered that they and my mother secreted me away . . . I dare not imagine what he would do."

I respected his caution and his desire to protect his friends and family, but not at the expense of mine. "Cronus raped our mother. She died giving birth to his child." My voice trembled. I cleared my throat, hardening myself. I would not gain Zeus's respect by dissolving into hysterics, as men were wont to think all women did. "Now he has our sister Cleora. We cannot abandon her."

"I'm sorry," he said, "but there's nothing I can do."

"You'd rather be alone?" I asked. "As long as Cronus rules, you will be without your mother and the rest of your family."

Zeus threw up his hands. "Even if I wanted to stand up to my father, I could never overpower him. He watches the whole of the world from his great hall. Using my strengths as a Titan could draw his eye, so I've never even tried."

His Titan strengths were inborn. All Titans could run faster, jump higher, lift more weight, and hit harder than any man on earth. I couldn't fathom not utilizing such advantages.

"No mastery comes without practice," Theo said. "You must train, like any good soldier."

My mind lit up with an idea. "Theo, *you* should train him."

"Me?" he asked skeptically. "No."

Bronte munched on a nectarine. "That isn't a bad idea."

"Yes, it is," Zeus argued.

"Listen to the boy," Theo replied. "He's not nearly as impressive as the rest of his kin. Maybe he's right to stay in hiding."

"Do you think I've wanted to hide in this cave for fifteen years?" Zeus rejoined. "If Cronus finds out I'm here, he will send mercenaries to punish anyone who has ever helped me, then he will capture me and cast me into Tartarus. I live in constant fear that he will come for me."

"You just described every day of every woman's life in Thessaly," I said.

"We're wasting our breath." Bronte picked up the box of letters, flipped the lid open, and took out a fistful of the parchments. "Zeus isn't going to listen to reason, but this might convince him." She tossed a letter into the fire.

"No!" Zeus sank to his knees and tried to fish out pieces, but the parchment disintegrated in the flames.

Bronte held another letter over the fire.

I put up my hand. "Wait."

"I'm not ignorant of my father's capacity for cruelty," Zeus said, teary-eyed. "It's because I know who he is that I hesitate." He hung his head, his shoulders bowed. "Cronus cannot fall."

I felt an overwhelming desire to help Zeus up. The oracles had shown me future Zeus on his throne. I couldn't imagine how this boy would ever become that great ruler, but I wouldn't stand in the way of his destiny.

I offered him my hand. "You're Zeus, son of the God of Gods, and the next in line to rule. You don't kneel to anyone."

My ring began to glow.

Half a second later, his ring began to glow too.

Zeus reached for me, and as his palm slid into mine, warmth coursed up my arm, and the vision of him reigning from his great hall returned, so vivid I could hear the clouds sliding past the tower. Zeus *would* become a true god worthy of respect. Far inside him, past his fear, this was his mission.

He rose to his feet, paling. "Who are you?" he asked slowly.

"You know my name."

He blinked several times. He looked at me differently now, as though he had suddenly shared my vision of what was to come.

Euboea called from outside. "Your Excellency? Are you all right?"

Zeus withdrew his hand from mine. Though the slight glow of our rings faded, the warmth lingered, humming through my veins.

"Call them off, Zeus," Theo said.

"You're not doing this alone," Bronte added. "We'll be with you."

Zeus glanced from her to me and grinned. "You know how much I favor the company of sisters."

"Oh, Gaea help us," Bronte groaned.

Zeus chuckled. "Colonel Angelos, can you train me without getting yourselves and everyone on the isle slaughtered?"

"That would be to my benefit," Theo replied.

Zeus smoothed back his frizzy hair. "Euboea, stand down!"

She called out cautiously. "Your Excellency, are you certain?"

"I am."

Silence.

"Oh, for stars' sake, Euboea!" Zeus said. "It's the middle of the night. Send away the guard. Our guests will return to camp soon. Provide them with anything they need. They're staying."

"Including the colonel, sir?"

"Him as well, and he may retain his weapons."

After another long pause, Euboea spoke. "Yes, Your Excellency. Good night."

The clatter of armor faded away.

Zeus flopped into the bed of cushions. "Could anyone else use a drink?"

"I could," Bronte mumbled, putting his letters back in the box.

Theo picked up Zeus's chalice, sniffed the contents, and immediately dumped it into the firepit. "No nectar while you're training. Your senses and faculties cannot be dulled by spirits."

Zeus rolled over onto his stomach and dramatically stuck his head between two pillows.

I dug through a trunk and threw some clothes at him. "Dress appropriately for training tomorrow."

"Tomorrow?" Zeus replied. "Must we start so soon?"

"We have a lot to do," Theo answered, already sounding weary about the work ahead. "Be ready. We start at dawn."

13

We had won no one over with our attempted kidnapping. In the morning, I left Bronte asleep in our tent, and as I crossed camp, every masked woman I passed paused to glare at me. I couldn't leave fast enough.

I followed a well-worn path to the beach, gulping in the cleansing sea breezes, and padded across the wet sand to a pair of figures in the distance. Theo stood on a boulder that was half buried in the shoreline. Zeus picked up a massive rock and hurled it into the surf. A high tide pummeled the shore with roaring, rolling waves of gray under a moody sky.

Zeus bent his knees and hefted another boulder. He spun in a circle and cast it easily into the sea, where it sent up a tremendous splash. As far as I could tell, the Boy God's strength was typical for a Titan, though still impressive.

Theo folded his arms across his chest. "You're still working too hard. Release the rock before you make the full rotation and let the impetus of your spin finish the throw."

Zeus's knees shook as he picked up the next boulder. He spotted me in midrotation and stumbled, crashing backward, the boulder landing on his chest. Theo and I both ran to him.

"How many times must I tell you to watch your feet?" Theo said.

Zeus pushed the boulder off and wiped at his sand-speckled brow. "I got distracted."

"You're not concentrating." Theo used his ultra-calm voice, which was much scarier than yelling. "You're a Titan. Your strength is intrinsic, but you must not shy away from it."

"I'm only a second-generation Titan."

"Keep thinking like that, and you *will* be second rate."

Zeus sat up and brushed off his sandy hands. "I'm not my father."

"Your father wouldn't trip over his own feet."

The Boy God stood, too fast on his gangly legs, and nearly fell over again. "Agh! I cannot do this."

"You fail only by giving up," Theo barked. "Quitting isn't an option. Too many lives depend on you."

"Then you save them." Zeus took off down the beach.

"Zeus!" I called.

"Let him go," Theo replied. "He's due for a break anyway."

"You should go easier on him."

"Cronus won't hold back. Zeus must think of himself as greater than his father, or this will never work. I've no patience for wasting our time."

"Maybe I can help by training with him," I said.

"No," Theo answered immediately. "I need time alone with him. You'll be a distraction."

"Zeus wasn't expecting me earlier. That wasn't his fault."

"It was absolutely his fault. Rhea sends him maidens for his entertainment and pleasure. He has no self-control."

I had never seen Theo blush, but this seemed the proper moment for it. My own face felt on fire. "You won't let me train with him because I'm a woman?"

"That's not what I said."

"You might as well have."

Theo offered no apology. I wondered who he was worried about me distracting—Zeus or him? Or did he simply think I couldn't train like a proper soldier?

I walked to a boulder, squatted, and wrapped my arms around it like I had seen Zeus do. I heaved, but the rock didn't budge.

Theo flapped a hand at me. "Stop. You'll strain your back."

"I can do it."

"Don't be ridiculous. That's too heavy."

Theo didn't want me training because I was a woman. The matron didn't like me using my spear and shield because I was a woman. I had to dress like a hoplite to go anywhere without permission, and when I did go, I had to mask myself.

Because I was a woman.

I pushed into my legs and hefted the rock. Careful of my footing, I spun in a circle and hurled it out to sea. The boulder didn't go as far as Zeus's, but it went farther than I thought it would.

Theo gaped. "Althea . . . you—" In a heartbeat, his expression changed. "We need to leave the beach. Find cover in the trees."

"Why?"

"Slave ship. Go now."

I spotted the vessel on the horizon as Theo urged me to run. We retreated to the tree line and crouched in the underbrush. The back of my neck burned as the trireme sailed closer, propelled by hundreds of rowers.

"Will they come ashore?" I asked.

"I don't know. I've never heard of slave traders coming this far south."

"Could they have found out about the tribe?"

"They're trolling for something. They're moving too slowly just to be passing by."

I rubbed the back of my neck. I didn't want to think about what the flashes of pain meant, but I had put off wondering why my tag suddenly hurt. Blood oaths tied two souls together, the benefactor and the victim. Both were beyond even a god's power to break. Did my neck burn when Decimus thought of me? When he spoke my name? What did it mean?

"I don't think they saw us." Theo helped me stand. "You threw that boulder farther than I thought you would."

"I was angry."

"You have a temper."

I brushed sand off his shoulder. "I've never denied it."

Our closeness stirred up mixed feelings. I had two impulses: to touch his soft, scruffy face again, and to shove him for not letting me train with Zeus.

The latter won.

I pushed him in the chest and took off. "Race you back to camp!"

"We're not finished for the day."

"Then you forfeit!"

I sprinted down the path. When I no longer heard the waves, I began to feel that my feet weren't touching the ground. Sometimes when I ran, I imagined I had wings and could soar, but this felt different. This was in my chest, a feeling like fire. Like the firelight had glowed across Theo's naked back . . .

All right, so this was lust, plain and simple. It happened from time to time. Occasionally, when some of the more attractive village boys had watered their sheep at the pond near the temple, I found myself daydreaming of their broad shoulders and big hands. After we had a good romp in the woods, I never had the urge to see them again.

That's what I needed from Theo. Once I felt his weight on top of me, I would be satisfied. Then I wouldn't have to think about him in that way ever again.

Over the next four days, Theo and Zeus trained, sleeping only a few hours a night. Bronte and I tiptoed around the tribe and tried to stay cool in the unseasonably warm spring weather. The tribe would not remove their velos in our company. Having worn a mask in the sticky summer months back home, when every breath felt heavy and wet, I pitied them.

We tried to keep busy. The younger girls, born on the island from mothers who were with child when they fled their homes, would gather outside the schoolhouse and listen to Bronte sing and act. She captivated her audience, and the girls liked her so much they asked her to help them put on a play. Bronte would also forage in the woods for currants, mushrooms, herbs, berries, and nuts. The tribe's cooks happily accepted her offerings. And once they discovered that she was a skilled shot with a bow and arrow, the huntresses took her out with them. She brought back her first deer within an hour, then spent another hour in a friendly debate with members of the tribe about philosophy.

I kept to myself. As hard as it was, I stayed away from Theo and Zeus, training with my spear and shield in the woods alone, and taking long walks up the mountain to the cooler air. I discovered a stunning beach with pink sand and a cozy cove with aquamarine water where I could swim with colorful fish. Though the isle provided endless opportunities to explore, I was still restless. Bronte and I ate meals at our own table, avoiding the nightly bonfire where everyone congregated to socialize. Sleep came in fitful bursts.

Adrasteia visited camp daily to check on us, but she never stayed long. She and Ida lived elsewhere. I hadn't discovered where, though they couldn't have been far. Euboea was in charge of tending to our needs. We rarely saw her, except in the evenings when she returned with the day's catch of fish.

On the fifth day of Zeus's training, I planned to practice with my shield and spear, only to find them missing. Bronte's new bow and arrow, given to her by the tribe, were there in our tent, but my gear was gone. I went to ask Bronte at the schoolhouse, where she was organizing the play with some girls. Across the field, a crowd had assembled, all of the women cheering and shouting.

"Have you seen my spear and shield?" I asked one of them.

"Euboea and another girl borrowed them. They said you knew."

The women had gathered around a marked circle. Euboea and a second woman were in the center, locked in hand-to-hand combat. Euboea threw her opponent to the ground and landed on her. The cheering erupted. Euboea let the woman up, then paraded around with her arms over her head victoriously.

My shield and sword were off to the side, propped against a bench. I slipped through the crowd and pulled up short. A girl sat by my gear, and she stood when she saw me.

It was Sibylla, the guard I'd ambushed outside Zeus's cave the other night.

"Do you remember me?" she asked.

"I do."

"Do you remember giving me this?"

She pulled back the scarf around her neck. Her throat was bruised where my arm had pushed down on her windpipe. My mouth soured with regret. I didn't recall holding her that tightly.

"I spent the past few days with no voice," Sibylla said, still sounding scratchy. She began stripping.

"I'm sorry," I said. "Sometimes I don't know my own strength."

"Keep your apology," she spit. She continued to remove her clothes, down to her undergarments, a band across her breasts and loose trousers. Her body was sculpted and lithe, like a wildcat's. "Meet me in the ring."

"Excuse me?"

"You want your gear back? Wrestle me for it." Sibylla walked to the center of the ring. "Or is Stavra Lambros's daughter a coward?"

My mother's name sent a veil of quiet over the crowd. Their respect for her was probably why they hadn't cast us into the sea. I couldn't fail to live up to her memory.

After undressing to my undergarments, I stepped into the ring. A wrestler's goal was to throw her opponent to the ground from a standing position. A point was awarded when an opponent's back or shoulders touched the ground. Three points won.

Euboea came forward. "No time limit. Holds are restricted to the upper body." She lifted a salpinx to her lips—a straight, narrow bronze tube with a bell—and blew into the bone mouthpiece. A piercing noise shot across the field. The crowd shifted closer, right up to the edge of the ring.

Sibylla's arms encircled my upper body. The next thing I knew, I was on my back, staring up at the morning sky.

"One!" Euboea yelled. She stood over me and hefted me to my feet while my opponent chuckled. "You awake now?"

I shrugged out of her hold and faced Sibylla. I wasn't much of a wrestler, but I had been in enough tiffs with my sisters to dodge throws.

Sibylla grabbed for me again. I twisted around her, keeping out of her range. She anticipated my next evasion, caught me by the middle, tripped me, and threw me to the ground.

"Two!" she shouted, glowering. "Euboea was right. You're nothing like your mother."

I leaped up and grabbed her, pulling her to the edge of the ring. The crowd shoved us back toward the center of the ring. I held Sibylla and threw her to the ground.

"One," I said.

After I let her up, she launched at me again. We locked arms, pushing shoulder against shoulder, legs low, knees bent. She gave ground and plowed into the crowd. I kept pushing, and we broke through the spectators and toppled to the soil on our sides. She shoved at me, pushing my back closer to the dirt.

I wedged my knee beneath us and thrust. She flew back, almost landing on her back. I leaped at her, brought my arm across her bruised neck, and shoved.

"Two!"

Euboea waved us back to the ring. I started to return, but Sibylla was on me. She threw me down, yet I spun before my back hit the dirt. I crouched at her and charged. My head plowed into her middle and drove her backward, farther from the ring. The rest of the audience followed. Bronte and the girls at the schoolhouse came out to watch.

It didn't matter.

I was done with their games and their glares and their judgments.

Grabbing Sibylla about the waist, I pushed. I shoved and shoved all the way to the mess hall. Her back struck a table, and I threw her down and kneeled on top of her. She cast me off, and we tumbled to the ground. Then she was on me, her lips at my ear.

"I'm going to enjoy your spear and shield."

I pushed up with all my strength, rolled her beneath me, and held her shoulder blades to the ground.

"Three," I breathed.

Another piercing sound carried across the field. Euboea came over with the salpinx in hand and raised it above her head.

"Althea Lambros: the victor!"

I rotated onto my knees, chest heaving. Bronte ran over from the schoolhouse and helped me up. Sibylla was still recovering her breath. I had landed on her hard and knocked the wind out of her. The crowd didn't cheer much as Bronte drew me away.

I called over my shoulder. "I expect my spear and shield delivered to my tent!"

Sibylla glared back.

Bronte led me faster. "What were you thinking?"

"Did you see me?"

"Everyone in camp saw you."

"Good."

"Good?" Bronte shook her head. "These women are our allies, Althea."

"Tell that to Sibylla."

We entered the tent, and Bronte poured water from the pitcher into the washbasin. "You strangled Sibylla until she was unconscious. She had good reason to challenge you for her honor."

"Honor? That was an ambush."

"Then you're even."

I threw up my hands. "Why are you taking her side?"

"I'm not. I'm reminding you that we need their hospitality. Throwing one of their guards across camp isn't going to earn their respect, and we certainly don't want their fear. We know what it's like to live in fear. It breeds contempt."

I sat on the edge of my bedroll. "I had to win."

"But you didn't have to brag about it."

My lips spread wide, showing my teeth. "Did you see that last throw?"

"Althea," Bronte groaned.

"Sorry. Last time."

She went to the doorway. "I need to return to the schoolhouse. You should keep to yourself for the rest of the day, and maybe tomorrow as well."

"I'm not hiding like a coward."

"You're safer here. I'll worry less knowing you're not getting into more fights. Now I have a play to put on. I cannot be interrupted by more distractions."

"Fine," I grumbled.

She slipped out of the tent.

My arms and legs were caked in mud and dirt. I scrubbed them until the clean water was too muddy to be of use, then changed my clothes. A few bruises had already darkened on my sides. I was going to be sore all over, but at least everyone knew that I was, in fact, Stavra Lambros's daughter.

That was worth any pain.

14

That evening, nightfall scattered the irritating itch of the daytime heat, but I still felt mucky from the wrestling match. I did as promised and stayed in the tent all day, taking supper there with Bronte, who brought us bowls of venison stew.

She chatted as she ate, telling me about the play she and the girls were putting on. They were reenacting the birth of Aphrodite, the tribe's favorite tale to recount. "It isn't very long, just one act, but they're so excited, especially for the final song. They have no idea how fortunate they are. They wouldn't be allowed onstage anywhere else."

"When does it start?" I asked. "I want to arrive early to get a good seat."

Bronte stirred her stew without meeting my gaze. "Things have been tense since this morning. You disgraced Sibylla not just once but twice. Her friends are rightly unhappy. Some of them have children in the play. You should probably keep to yourself, at least until tomorrow."

"You don't want me there?"

"Of course, I'd like my sisters there."

Sisters.

"Cleora would be proud of you," I said gently.

"She would, hmm?" Bronte asked. "Or would she wonder why I'm teaching little girls to act and sing, instead of helping her break free?"

"Dethroning Cronus is only one way the world needs to change. We also need to teach girls who they are, and offer them new options for who they can become."

Bronte set on her head a leafy crown that the schoolgirls had made her. "That's me, changing the world, one children's play at a time."

It stung that she didn't want me to attend that night, but I put on a smile and walked her to the door. "If I wasn't grimy, I would hug you."

"You smell too." She kissed my cheek warmly and left.

I finished my supper, then sniffed myself. She was right. I collected my bathing things and set out.

The small pond just outside the main camp in the woods was deserted. Silvery moonlight sparkled across its surface, undisturbed. Slipping out of my clothes, I stepped into the cool water and waded in up to my waist. I scrubbed my hair and scalp with soap that Adrasteia had given us when we arrived. I had more bruises on my body from the wrestling match, but some of them were already fading.

I finished lathering and waded farther in to rinse off. The light on the surface of the pond around me dimmed. I looked up through the treetops at the sky. Strange. Not a single cloud, and the moon was now accompanied by a masterpiece of stars.

A cold current slithered around me. The dark spot on the water widened, eating up the starlight, and shifted closer. I made out the shape of a man's shadow hovering below the surface, like the one I had seen on the boat. The Star Eater.

Daughter . . .

His raspy voice vibrated through the water, pushing in around me. I froze, my head and hair dripping. Something cold and slimy slid across my upper thigh. I jumped and covered my bare chest.

"Who are you?"

We are the heavens. The sun is our throne, the moon our footstool, the stars our retinue. We are the true alpha and omega, the first and the last.

His tone held an undercurrent of rage.

Because he spoke with the royal "we," I couldn't tell if he referred just to himself or to someone else as well. Whoever he was, he was not my father, and he was not overstating his influence over the heavens. His mere presence shrouded starlight and paled even the moon.

I started to carefully wade back toward shore. The Star Eater caught my leg and pulled. I went underwater so fast I had no time to take a breath.

Darkness blanketed me. No moonlight penetrated the water. I tried to kick free, but the Star Eater grasped my other leg too. His cold snaked up my body, pinning my arms to my sides and anchoring me under. My lungs throbbed. The pond felt bottomless. My skin burned with bitter cold.

Daughter, you must set us free. The voice boomed all around me and rang in my ears. *Open your wings and rise.*

My back burned as though two fiery hands had been pressed against my shoulder blades. I arched in pain, and my arms and legs broke free. I kicked hard, hoping I was headed toward the surface. My hollow lungs felt close to collapsing.

Bursting into the air, I swam hard to the embankment and dragged myself out of the water. I choked, gasping, and rested my cheek against the pebbled ground. The bathing pool once again shone with the heavens' light. The Star Eater had gone.

My shoulder blades still burned. I looked over my shoulder and saw handprints high on my back, seared into my skin. As I watched, they faded away.

A shadow fell over me. I lurched to my knees, looked up, and saw Euboea there with a bath sheet in her arms. She wasn't wearing her velo. Her face bore scars in a crisscross pattern across her cheeks and forehead, but they didn't have the red, puckered look of burn scars. They were too fine, like knife cuts.

"You're not Stavra Lambros's daughter," Euboea said.

"You keep saying that. I know my mother was a great woman. You can express that without putting me down."

"No," Euboea said thoughtfully. "Stavra was a good woman. You . . . you will be great."

I pushed my wet hair from my face. "But you hate me."

"I'm not willfully ignorant. You impressed me during the wrestling match."

"No one else seemed impressed."

"They *are* willfully ignorant. Anyone with eyes could tell the shape of your soul is powerful. Your body barely contains it. It practically shimmers off you."

I had no response. Her praise was generous and unexpected, and I wouldn't humiliate her by rejecting it. "Thank you."

"That wasn't a compliment," she insisted. "You're terrifying."

"Oh."

She set a bath sheet down beside me. "Consider this a gift from my father. He would want me to repay your parents for what they did."

"Your father?"

"Proteus. He's a fish merchant in the city."

"Yes," I said, surprised. "I know Proteus."

Her eyes grew wide. "How . . . how is he?"

"He's well. His fish shop is the best in the agora."

"Good," Euboea said, albeit sadly. "I haven't seen him in a long time. Years ago, I was married to a man who threw a jealous fit if I spoke to another man. It didn't matter if I was haggling with a merchant over our supper ingredients. My husband would wait until I was home and strike me until I couldn't walk. My father reached out to Stavra and Tassos for help. I was one of the first women they smuggled here to Crete."

"Do you know why my parents started moving refugees?"

Euboea picked up a handful of pebbles and began tossing them into the pond, one at a time. "Your mother's older sister, Hebe, was married to my husband's brother. My husband was awful, but his brother was worse. Stavra tried to help Hebe get out with the first group of women, but Hebe was too afraid. My father lent Stavra and Tassos one of his fishing boats, and I was to operate the sail. We had to leave, or we would miss our opportunity, so we embarked, and your mother and father promised Hebe they would return. Three days later, while we were at sea, Hebe was found dead with her tongue cut from her mouth. Her husband was questioned, but he denied ever touching her."

My tongue suddenly felt sticky. "I never knew my mother had a sister."

"Stavra didn't talk about her after that, but Hebe was the reason she began running refugees." Euboea threw the last stone into the water and watched the ripples spread. "The velo design that the tribe wears emulates Stavra's mask to honor the sacrifices she made for us."

I hadn't thought it possible, but now I was even prouder of my mask. "My mother never said anything about this place or the tribe or the refugees."

"She wouldn't have. The only women who come now are those fortunate few who hear the rumors about the island. Stavra didn't want to stop helping women escape their homes, even after your father died, but Cronus's guard was getting close to finding us. She wouldn't risk our discovery."

"She said my father died in an accident?" I got the impression that Euboea knew more, but I didn't want to inquire too much.

"Unfortunately, yes," she replied. "From what Stavra told me, she and Tassos were loading a supply boat when the pulley snapped. Your father was swept underwater with the rope, pulled away by the current, and never recovered. His loss changed Stavra. She said that when Tassos drowned, she lost the best part of herself."

I clenched my jaw, my eyes misting. Learning more about my parents was bittersweet. I wanted to hear about them, but at the moment,

I needed to understand something else. "Euboea, who gave you your scars? Was it your parents or your husband?"

"Ida did it, soon after I came here. She performs all of the tribe's ritual purifications."

"Ida?" My head whirled. "Wait, are the other women scarred? But why? They're safe from the outside world here."

"Safe?" Euboea chortled once, humorlessly. "As long as men still think we're their possessions to buy and sell and trade, we will never be safe."

My tag on the back of my neck itched. "But why cut yourselves?"

"Aphrodite is the most exquisite female in the world, the goddess of love. Her perfect beauty draws the eyes of men, who are so blinded by her outward appearance they do not see the goodness in her heart or the worth of her soul. Our tribe knows that our worth doesn't depend upon our looks. Ida suggested we all perform the ritual to emancipate us from our pasts, and to unite us. I'm safer with my scars. Should my husband ever find me, he won't want me anymore."

I didn't have the heart to tell Euboea that the women scarring themselves electively in Thessaly had only increased their popularity among men.

Euboea opened the bath sheet and laid it over my shoulders. She looked up at the moon. "It's spooky, isn't it? To think that Selene sees everything, and that she's indifferent to it all?"

I wasn't certain about the indifference, but Euboea's remark brought to mind a question I had been circling around. "Do you think my mother and father had help moving refugees, from anyone else, perhaps a Titan?"

Euboea spoke quietly, as though to avoid the goddess of the moon overhearing her. "Your parents never mentioned a godly accomplice, though I doubt they would have told anyone if they had one. That sort of betrayal against Cronus could start a war."

Gooseflesh scattered up my arms. I told myself it was the night air on my wet skin, but a war between the Titans would devastate the world, and we mortals would be stuck in the middle.

"Bathing alone at night isn't safe," Euboea said, straightening. "No one would be here to help you if something went wrong. Take someone with you next time."

"I will. And, Euboea? Thank you."

She pursed her lips. "Why thank me? You pulled yourself out of the water. I probably would have let you drown."

"Probably?"

"I guess we'll never know." She turned to go, then paused. "How did you do it?"

"Do what?"

"Stay underwater that long?"

My shoulders still ached, a visceral memory of the burning hands on my back. "I must have caught my foot on something at the bottom of the pond."

"Yes, but how did you hold your breath for so long?"

"How long was I under?"

"I thought you might have left the pond somehow, without me noticing. Then I saw air bubbles and realized you were still down there. Four, perhaps five, minutes."

Five minutes? She must have been exaggerating. "I suppose I got lucky."

Euboea eyed me suspiciously, let out a ponderous "harrumph," and left me at the edge of the wine-dark water.

15

A message from Zeus was delivered to my tent as dawn in her rosy robe awoke the world. A girl handed me the message and ran off. I was so distracted by what Zeus might want that I didn't notice until after she left that she hadn't been wearing a velo.

"What does it say?" Bronte asked, brushing her hair.

I skimmed the brief message on parchment. "His Excellency has summoned me."

"Hmm." She sent me a wicked smile and went on in a singsong voice. "Zeus fancies you."

"What?"

"You said he kissed your neck."

"He must have kissed a hundred girls' necks."

Bronte yawned. She had been up late, cleaning up after the play, which was praised by all who attended. "What happened between the two of you in the cave the night of the kidnapping? For a moment, you gazed at each other so intently, it looked as though I was seeing a pair of battle-ready soldiers, as though you two could rival the heavens. Prometheus would say, 'Where is there a mightier pair than they?'"

I wasn't certain how to explain the vision the oracles showed me, so I decided it was best not to put it into words, and settled upon a simpler answer. "Zeus decided to trust me."

Bronte gave a skeptical "hmm," and then the two of us stepped outside.

The camp bustled with women busily hanging strings of flowers between tents and from trees while others built up the woodpile in the massive communal firepit.

"What's all this for?" I asked.

"Tonight the tribe will honor Aphrodite with the spring hecatomb," Bronte said. "It's all the girls have talked about since we arrived."

Across the way, two shepherds led six black ewes and six snow-white rams—tonight's animal sacrifice to the goddess of love—into a temporary pen at the center of camp. Sometimes as many as one hundred cattle or sheep were slaughtered for a hecatomb.

"Do you notice anything different?" I remarked.

None of the women were wearing velos. Last night before we fell asleep, I told Bronte everything Euboea had told me, both about our mother and about the tribe's practice of cutting themselves.

"Why are you smiling?" Bronte asked, her tone reproachful. "All their faces are scarred."

"The first day we arrived, Adrasteia said the tribe wouldn't remove their masks because they didn't trust us."

"So they trust us now?"

"At least one of us." I bumped Bronte with my shoulder, then took off for the path up the mountain.

"It has to be me!" she called at my retreating back.

She was probably right, but I stuck my tongue out at her anyway.

The morning air refreshed my skin and lungs as I ran up the trail. Last night, I had been plagued with nightmares about fiery hands groping my body. I had no explanation for what I'd seen or felt in the pond, and until I did, I wouldn't tell anyone about it.

Upon reaching the top, I called ahead into the cave. "Hello?"

No one answered.

I stepped inside and drew up short. The walls had been stripped of most of their luxurious silk drapes. What remained of them bore slashes, as though a pride of lions had come through and shredded them.

My gaze fell to Zeus sprawled out on his belly on the floor, unconscious. "Stars above," I cried, and ran to him.

Kneeling, I turned him over, and he grinned.

"Divine day, Althea."

"What are you doing?" I demanded.

"Playing dead."

"Why?"

"It's a common offensive ploy."

"You scared me."

He sat up. "The colonel doesn't care for that maneuver either."

"I imagine not." I pushed to my feet and looked around again. "What happened here?"

"Theo and I practiced swordplay yesterday," Zeus said, rising. "I kept retreating out of his range on the beach, so he moved us here to the cave. It made for a bit of damage."

With the draperies gone, I could see the painted pairs of wings on the stone walls. They resembled the ones we'd put on my mother's gravestone. Wings had many meanings, but to my mother, they'd represented the basic shape of each person's soul, and its ability to soar beyond this life and into the hereafter.

"Where did these come from?" I asked.

"My mother had them put up, the night I was born, I think. Perhaps just before. She labored a long time to deliver me. Ida painted them at her behest."

I counted the wings—five pairs in total. "What do they represent?"

"There is one set of wings for each child Cronus swallowed. The Almighty has no qualms about murdering his own children." Zeus shoved at his messy hair and laughed lightly to dispel his darker mood. "May I offer you something to drink and eat?"

"Yes, thank you. I ran here without stopping for breakfast." I strolled over to the platters of fruit and sampled berries while he poured us drinks from two different pitchers. He handed me a chalice of wine. "Don't confuse your drink with mine. Your death would be difficult to explain to Colonel Angelos."

I asked after the contents of his chalice. "Nectar?"

"You won't tattle on me, will you?"

"Not a chance. I'm no sycophant." I sipped my wine and held back a cough. It was strong. I doubted it had been watered down at all. "How is training?"

Zeus swallowed half the contents of his chalice before answering. "Abysmal. Colonel Angelos is a bear."

"That's what the other soldiers nicknamed him."

Zeus nearly spit up his next sip of nectar. "He's relentless! The only reason I'm not training with him right now is that I said I was nauseated, so he let me sleep in."

"I thought you said you never lie."

"At times, when the fib is benign and it behooves me, I will stretch the truth. Last night, after running for hours, I vomited all over his sandals."

I snorted. "Sorry, I shouldn't laugh."

"Go ahead. It's humorous, isn't it? I'm the only child Rhea managed to save from her dastardly husband, and I'm the worst Titan ever born."

"Self-pity doesn't suit you."

"Oh, but it's so tempting." Zeus stretched out on his mound of pillows and considered me over the rim of his chalice. "I heard you and Bronte won over the tribe. They're a difficult group to appease."

"They're just tired of wearing their velos. We're hardly good company."

He tipped his head to the side. "Do you always do that?"

"Do what?"

"Minimize your accomplishments? Remind people of your faults?"

"Help me remember who just said he's the worst Titan ever born?"

Zeus raised his glass. "You're not wrong."

"You're the one who said it."

"Yes, and I never lie. My performance of late has been less than noteworthy. Every genuine effort I make toward progress ends in failure." Zeus sank his head back and stared up at the ceiling. "What if I cannot do it?" His voice came out so small, I nearly missed his question.

"Do what?"

"Make my mother proud."

My shoulders lowered, releasing some of the tension. "Your mother is already proud of you. You're her son, and the heir to your father's throne."

"Those are hardly things I earned."

"So earn them. Become the god she believes you are."

His gaze fastened on me. "Was your mother proud of you?"

The question hit me from the back, burning almost as much as those invisible hands in the pond. "I—I think so."

"Would she be now?"

His concentration rattled me. I paced away to give myself a reprieve from his stare. "Did you summon me here to discuss my mother? Everyone else has things to say about her."

"I never met Stavra, though I've been told she was indomitable," Zeus said, "until Cronus finally caught up with her."

"That's been the fate of many women."

"I ask because I've always wanted a family." Zeus's attention swung to the wings on the wall, symbols of his lost siblings. "I would prefer a world where my father doesn't wish me dead, but evidently, that's asking too much. Even knowing he would end me without batting an eye, I don't hate him. He has a vast family, and most of them support him, but he only thinks of himself, his own needs and desires, how to retain his precious throne. I pity him."

I swung back toward Zeus. "Your compassion must be why fate chose you."

"Does fate choose us?"

"Sometimes I think so."

"Why? What comfort comes with turning over control to a cosmic power?"

I stared down at my chalice. "I hope there's a reason for the pain, for the tragedies and the loss. Believing in fate means trusting that everything will turn out as it should."

Zeus straightened, and his face lit up. He jumped to his feet, pulled the chalice from my hand, and set it aside. "He's here."

"Who's here?"

"Come along. You'll see," Zeus said, dragging me out of the cave.

We stood outside, the Boy God vibrating with excitement. I had never seen him so happy, not even with his horde of giggly maidens, yet the trees were quiet, and nobody came up the pathway.

"What's going on . . . ?"

He tilted my chin up. "There."

At first, all I could see was the sun, and I had to shield my eyes. Zeus nudged me to look again. A sunbeam took shape in the sky, turning into a golden chariot drawn by four white-winged steeds with long blond manes and matching gold barding. The driver landed the chariot in the clearing outside the cave. I had to blink several times before he came into focus. I didn't need anyone to tell me this young man was a Titan.

Everything about him was eye catching. His floor-length dark-burgundy robes with the high collar that framed his face, a simple yet practical style often worn by the desert nomads from the east to protect them from sunlight. His majestic crown was like the shining aureole of the sun. On his left earlobe, he wore a half-sun cuff that spanned the whole length of his ear and spiked out like rays. His hair was cut short on one side and long and shaggy on the other, the color a golden red I had only ever seen in the kitchen fire that Cleora had lovingly tended to in the temple. He was clean-shaven, and gold lined his eyes, tapering out to appear catlike. His eyes themselves were molten, almost luminescent, contrasting with his rich brown skin and intensifying the stunning perfection of his splendor. Even his red lips shone glossy, as though he had just sipped morning dew from a rose.

The driver stepped down, and a tremor shook the crags and forest under his immortal feet.

"Helios!" Zeus said, jumping on him.

"Cousin," the visitor replied. "You've grown since I last saw you."

"You come too seldomly. I see you fly over every day."

"Work, work, work. I should visit you in the evenings, but by then, I've flown halfway around the world, and I'm exhausted." He hugged Zeus again. "I brought you something. Metis has been pestering me day and night. I cannot return without a letter for her, so you best write your response quickly."

Zeus snatched the letter from Helios and went into the cave.

The Titan god of the sun laid eyes on me. "Good day."

I couldn't find my tongue. Somehow, it had fallen out of my open mouth.

"It's a pleasure to meet you." Helios took my hand in his and raised it to his lips. A warm zap went through my skin, an exquisitely euphoric feeling. "Would you like to meet my horses? They're friendly."

Helios was quite simply dazzling. Even when I blinked, I saw his light behind my eyelids. "Ah, all right."

"They were bred in the east, in my homeland. My father keeps his most prized stallion in his stables at his home in Coral Mansion. That stallion stud has fathered every horse that has ever flown this chariot."

I nodded dumbly. The Titan Helios was here, telling me—*me*—about his father, the first-generation Titan Hyperion, the god of light.

The Fourth House, the pillar of the east, was known for two things: horses and cultivators. Many of its people migrated all over the world to plant and harvest crops. They could supposedly grow any plant or tree in any climate or soil. A superstitious lot, the eastern nomads were permitted to pray to Gaea because of their kinship to the earth. They were the only exception Cronus made regarding the worship of his parents, besides the vestals, who were allowed to worship Gaea because he didn't want to incur any more of his mother's wrath.

I petted the coat of one of Helios's steeds. Unlike other horses, they didn't have hair but short, birdlike feathers that were downy soft. One of them raked the ground with his front hoof and snorted.

"He likes you, Althea," Helios said.

"How do you know my name?"

"I see and hear all, which is a blessing of being the god of the sun. Or curse, depending on your point of view." He grinned, showing his radiant teeth. "My cousins say I'm a pragmatist, but don't worry. I can keep a secret."

I wasn't certain what secret he meant, but then it occurred to me that he was reassuring me that he wouldn't betray Zeus. I wondered how many other gods knew of his location, and what sort of threat that presented to our plan.

Zeus returned with another parchment. He blew across the wet ink to dry it and then rolled up the letter and passed it to his cousin.

"What did Metis say?" Helios asked.

Zeus shrugged nonchalantly. "She asked me to pick a special flower from Ida's garden and keep it with me at all times."

"And when you look at it, you're to think of her." Helios grinned. "Shall I describe your betrothed's loveliness for you once again?"

The Boy God blushed. "I've heard about it enough, thank you."

I turned toward him, shocked. "You're betrothed?"

"To his cousin, an Oceanid," Helios answered, wagging his eyebrows.

Oceanids, daughters of Oceanus, were notoriously clever and charming beauties. Many a sailor had been beguiled by the tricksters, who delighted in harassing mortal men. "Zeus, have you ever met Metis?" I asked.

"When? I never leave the island."

"One day, this probationary period will end," Helios said, "and I will take you around the world with me." He mounted his chariot. "Now I must be going. The sun won't set itself. It was an honor to meet you, Althea Lambros. Put aside your concerns, and rest well. Your sister Cleora is safe."

I gripped the side of the chariot. "You've seen my sister?"

"I am the god of the sun," Helios replied. "I see everything."

"Except what occurs at night," Zeus said. "Only Selene sees that."

"Yes, well, we cannot all be my sister," Helios replied wryly, picking up the reins.

"Can you tell me more?" I asked. "How is Cleora?"

Helios closed his eyes. When he reopened them, rings of fire glowed around his pupils. "Your sister misses you." My throat swelled shut. Helios blinked again, and the rings of fire disappeared. "Cleora is stronger than she seems."

I knew then that he had truly seen her. People often mistook Cleora's cautiousness and patience for weakness, but in many ways, she was more resilient than Bronte and me.

"Goodbye, cousin," Zeus said, slinging his arm around my shoulder. "Fly safe."

The god of the sun cracked his whip over his steeds' backs, and his team raced upward, leaving a trail of stardust in their wake. We watched as the chariot shrank into the sunshine until they became one.

Zeus dropped his arm from my shoulder. "I'm hungry."

How could he think of food after that? I followed him into the cave in a daze. I could hardly process what I had seen or heard. Zeus sat on some pillows and munched on almonds while rereading Metis's latest letter.

"I didn't know you were betrothed," I said.

"All Titans have arranged marriages." A smile stretched across his lips and grew wider and wider. "Are you annoyed that I pulled you into my lap, even though I'm betrothed?"

"No." At least, I didn't think so. "I didn't realize any Titan besides your mother knew you were here."

"No one can hide from my cousins Helios, Selene, and Eos. They favor my mother over my father and have no investment in their parents' alliances. They can be trusted."

"And Metis?"

"Metis is a prophetess, a goddess of wisdom. I cannot hide anything from her either. She sent me a letter last year . . . or the year before, I cannot recall. In it, she told me someday soon two sisters would travel from Thessaly to see me, and she advised that I was to hear what they had to say."

I twisted my ring, my thoughts turning back to what the oracles told me about fate and destiny and inescapable knowledge. "What else has she predicted?"

Zeus rose and took my hand. "That I would love many women in my life but only one would be my equal."

The rings on our hands began to glow.

My pulse banged around inside my head. "As your betrothed, Metis must have been talking about herself."

"Yes, that's what I thought too."

Someone behind us cleared their throat.

Theo stood in the entrance to the cave, his face expressionless. "Pardon the interruption," he said, his voice cool. "It's time for Zeus to begin training."

Zeus slowly let go of my hand, skimming the back of it with his thumb. As soon as we were no longer touching, our rings went dark.

"Fascinating," he murmured.

Theo's lips tensed. "We'll be continuing our swordsmanship lessons today."

"I don't think my cave can withstand another lesson," Zeus said, gesturing at the tattered draperies.

"We'll train in the forest." Theo stepped back. "I'll wait for you to get ready."

I took that as my hint to leave and followed him outside. "How is his training going?" I asked.

"It's proceeding well," Theo said.

"That's not the way Zeus tells it."

"He resists me at every turn, but I expected that." One corner of Theo's mouth turned up drolly. "He's mastered playing dead."

"Yes, he practiced that trick on me this morning." I felt the urge to explain the touch he saw between Zeus and me, but I didn't see the sense in drawing more attention to it. After all, Zeus and I were merely friends.

"I saw the slave ship again," Theo said.

"When?"

"Yesterday afternoon, along the northern coast. They're definitely patrolling. Stay off the beaches, just to be safe."

Zeus sauntered outside and gave a great yawn. Theo tossed a second sword at him, and he barely caught it in time.

"Let's go," Theo said.

I wished them farewell and watched as they walked off into the woods, Zeus dragging his feet. Their mixed reports about the training had raised my curiosity. I decided to trail them, far enough back that they wouldn't see me. Their route led us into a part of the woods that I had not yet explored.

Ahead, tucked away in the trees, a cottage appeared. A garden of brightly colored flowers grew around the front door. Most of them I had seen before—hyacinths and violets and yellow crocus and wild roses.

But there was a sapphire-blue violet with red-edged petals that I didn't recognize. The rainbow of colors was alluring. I didn't want to fall too far behind Zeus and Theo, but I was interested in whether this was the home of the woodland nymphs. I peeked through the window into a tidy room that was full of plants and had butterflies pinned to the walls.

A soft cooing sounded above me. I looked up to see a white turtle-dove on the edge of the rooftop. More cooing came from behind me. Perched on the branches of the trees closest to the house were more turtledoves, a whole flock of them.

My scalp prickled. Every last bird was watching me.

The turtledove on the roof dived at my head. I batted it away, but more flew at me, flapping their wings and pecking at my hair. I dashed into the forest with my hands over my head, swatting at them, but more and more chased me. Then, through the fog of white feathers, I spotted three women clothed in dark furs and animal skins soaring toward me through the trees on wings of blackest night, a red glow in their eyes.

I screamed and ran faster, turtledoves still surrounding me and limiting my sight. Suddenly, my foot hit air. I pinwheeled my arms and corrected my balance. I was at the top of a ravine. The bottom was a long way down.

The turtledoves pecked at my head and arms and shoulders. I turned, and the Erinyes flew at me. They rushed me so fast, I fell back and dropped over the edge. Staring up at the sky, I saw them halt above and watch as I plummeted.

Immediately there were arms around me, and then I slammed into the ground.

I waited for the pain, but only my head hurt, and just a little.

"Agh," a voice moaned in my ear. It was Zeus, beneath me. "You're heavier than you look," he groaned.

"How did you know I needed help?"

"I followed the sound of your scream." Zeus sat up, cradling me against him. "Are you all right?"

"I think so." Sitting up, I felt a sore spot at the back of my head, and my finger came away damp with blood. "Ow."

"Stars, I thought I covered all of you." He pushed my hair aside to see the wound. "It's not bad. Just a small cut."

"How did you get to me so fast?"

He thumbed at himself. "God."

Adrasteia and Theo came running. She went to Zeus. Theo came to me.

"Is anything broken?" he asked.

"I don't think so."

He lifted me to my feet, and my ankles wobbled. I grabbed him for support and winced. Theo reached around me and saw the blood in my hair.

"You're hurt," he said.

"Zeus took the brunt of my fall."

"What happened?" he asked. "We heard you scream and came running. I've never seen Zeus move that fast."

I lowered my voice so only Theo could hear me. "Did you see them?"

"Who?"

"The Erinyes. They sent a flock of turtledoves after me and then chased me through the woods. That's how I fell."

Theo's eyes went wide in alarm. "Did they say anything?"

"No."

Zeus's voice rose above ours, interrupting us. "Quit fussing, Adrasteia. It's Althea you should be worried about."

"I'm fine," I said. The adrenaline from my fall was wearing off, and my head hurt more now, but I didn't want to worry them.

Adrasteia plucked a white feather out of my hair. "You gave us quite the scare. Be careful in these woods. There are lots of ravines and steep areas with loose rocks."

"I wasn't . . ." I stopped myself, deciding not to explain. *Let her think I went on a hike and got careless.*

"I'll walk you back to camp," Theo said, more a demand than an offer.

Adrasteia placed a hand on his shoulder. "I'll take her, Colonel. You and Zeus can return to your training."

My gaze fell to her hand on him, and my jaw tightened. "I can walk back on my own."

Theo scowled. "You shouldn't be alone."

I didn't appreciate him treating me like Adrasteia was, like I was a hysterical woman who just saw a few birds and went carelessly falling into a ravine.

"Camp isn't far," Zeus said. "I'll take her to the main trail, and she can go the rest of the way by herself."

I accepted that compromise, and we set out together. Zeus blathered on about his sword practice and what it felt like to finally knock Theo to the ground while I vigilantly searched the trees. No turtledoves in sight.

I glanced behind us. Theo and Adrasteia followed at a distance. She walked awfully close to him, laughing and touching his arm.

We reached the cottage, and Zeus stopped to pick a flower from the nymphs' garden. He chose the one I didn't recognize, a violet with red-trimmed petals, and shoved it into his pocket.

"For your betrothed?" I inquired.

He shrugged. "Metis asked me to find it and carry it with me, so I will."

Theo and Adrasteia had almost caught up. She touched his arm again, her laughter ringing out. What was he saying that was so damn funny?

"What do you think?" Zeus asked.

"I think she's too familiar with him."

Zeus put on a silly grin. "You fancy Theo."

I knocked my shoulder into his, and he pretended to tip back on his heels and nearly fall over. I took a step to go, then paused. "Zeus? We don't have much time. You know that, don't you?"

His expression sobered. "I know."

I left just as Theo and Adrasteia arrived. The trail was well worn, and when the cottage was far behind me, a single bit of light on the forest floor ahead caught my attention. I wandered up to it and stopped.

There, in the middle of the trail, was a single sunny narcissus.

My gaze darted around for any other sign of the Erinyes. Nothing. I could have crushed the flower under my heel in frustration, but I didn't want to risk vexing them. The Erinyes wanted me to know that they were close, and they were watching.

16

After returning to camp with a bad headache, I lay down in my tent to rest. I must have drifted off, because the next thing I knew, drumming woke me, and it was dark.

Bronte threw open the tent flap. "Oh, good, you're awake." She held a wine chalice in one hand, and her eyes were glassy, as though it weren't her first cup. "You missed the slaughter of the hecatomb, but the revelry is just starting. Theo was looking for you. He said you fell and hit your head?"

I rubbed my eyes. The back of my head felt tender, but the pain was manageable. "I'm all right."

"Are you certain? I cannot recall the last time you slept in the middle of the day."

"I just needed a little quiet. I'll be right out."

"I hoped you'd say that." Bronte drank from her cup and grinned. "Oh! I remembered who Theo reminds me of."

"Who?"

"Prometheus! Suits him, doesn't it? After all, he is a bearish-looking man." Bronte threw back the rest of her wine, downing it in one gulp. "I need another drink. Meet you outside?"

"Get me one too?"

"Already planned to." She sashayed out, humming to herself.

I changed my clothes and left to join the festivities. The bonfire burned so brightly that I could see clear across camp. The flames licked the sky, flirting with the tree branches. Everyone wore white chitons, their hair down and brushed to a shine, their bodies perfumed in shiny oil. Bronte ran over and shoved a full wine chalice into my hands.

"To the moon," she said. "May she ever shine."

We clinked glasses and drank. The wine was watered down quite a bit, and its fruitiness verged on too sweet, but it quickly quieted my throbbing head.

Lyre, cymbal, and drum players performed while women danced around the bonfire. Bronte pranced about, her arms waving and hips swaying in time with the music. I had never seen her more carefree, or more drunk.

"Want to dance?" she asked.

"Desperately."

I couldn't remember the last time I'd danced, let alone with other people. Moving to the music was a release I didn't know I needed until I felt myself soaring.

Bronte and I swayed and spun, laughing and drinking. She sang along wordlessly with the music, her eyes shining a little too brightly for someone who had consumed only wine.

"Did you have any opium?" I asked.

"Just the wine. Mine is gone again, and so is yours. I'll refill our cups."

She spun away on her toes with our cups raised over her head.

Euboea found me dancing alone and dragged me into the thicket of people. Bodies rocked all around us, spinning and shimmying and twirling. Throughout the clearing, half-naked women danced, laughed, talked, and made silly faces, played games, drank, and smoked opium. I couldn't picture anything like this taking place in Thessaly. The women there would never be allowed to be this carefree.

The drums slowed to a sensual beat. My hips and my bottom swung and shook. The crush of the bodies was carnal and intoxicating as people writhed, their figures glowing in the light of the fire stirred by the beat of the drums. At eleven, when I came into womanhood and started my monthly bleeding, my mother had told me I would learn that the pleasures of the night belonged to women. The gods gave us the most glorious form in all existence, not to be admired by men but for the simple appreciation of living.

Women pressed together, legs linked with legs, hands on waists and backs. Euboea moved in next to me, gripping my hips. We swayed in tandem, her knee slowly sliding farther and farther up between my thighs. The heady music was provocative, and I lost myself in the rhythm, giving in to the sounds and smells and touches of the night. Every sense was heightened by the firelight and the continuous press of flesh around me.

I don't know for how long I danced, but when Euboea's lips brushed my ear in the barest of kisses, we were both sweaty, faces pink and bodies glistening with sweat. I was tempted to stay, but the wine was wearing off and my headache had returned.

"I'm dizzy," I said. "I need to sit."

Euboea let me go, her fingers outstretched, beckoning me to return. Another woman took my place, and the two of them slid against each other under a sky of shifting stars. I left the fire and the music to rest on a nearby bench.

Theo wandered toward me. "Bronte asked me to bring you this." He handed me a cup of wine. "I helped her to your tent. She had a lot to drink."

"Thanks for looking after her." I drank down half my cup, seeking relief from my aching head, and now my aching ankle. I had been on my feet for too long.

"Be careful. They lace their wine with opium juice."

That explained Bronte's giddiness, and my dizziness.

Theo sat next to me. The velvety night swathed us intimately.

"How is your head?" he asked.

"The wine helps. Where's Zeus?"

"He wanted to come, but I told him to rest up for his training tomorrow. I'm concerned his heart still isn't in it. The idea of the throne is abstract." Theo stared at me intently. "Today was the bravest I've seen him. He heard you scream and tore off into the woods without a thought."

"I was fortunate he got there in time."

Theo fell quiet.

"Zeus is betrothed," I said. "The connection between us is only friendly." At least, it was for me.

Theo stretched his legs and crossed his ankles. We sat in silence for a while, then his gentle voice reached out to me again. "Why will you never marry?"

Normally, I wouldn't discuss something so personal with anyone but my sisters, but I had just enough wine in me. "I'll shrink myself for no one. The chance of finding one's equal is rare."

"But not impossible."

"Maybe an equal doesn't exist for everyone."

Theo's eyes softened like liquid honey. "Mine does."

Heat built beneath my cheeks. I sipped more wine, the warmth of the spirits flowing through me. Perhaps it wasn't entirely the wine . . .

The music took up a lively beat again, drawing more dancers into the field. Others left in pairs, escaping into tents together. I longed to find a dark corner to cozy into with Theo, but not yet. I wasn't finished dancing.

"I'm going to go back out there," I said, ignoring my sore ankle. "You should join me."

"I doubt the tribe would appreciate me spoiling their fun."

"They're too drunk and happy to pay you any mind." I took his hand and pulled him to his feet. "Stay close to me."

His lips slid upward. "Gladly."

I lifted onto my toes and twirled. Theo laughed—a short, bright sound—then mimicked my twirl with his own. With his big feet and body, he looked utterly ridiculous. I swayed side to side, and he mirrored that as well, so I began to spin around and around, and he tried the same, a feeble attempt. We broke into laughter.

Some women kept their distance from us, but as we rocked to the beat, they came in close again. Theo's arms went around me, and I hooked mine over his shoulders. Our hands slid over one another, caresses more intimate than any romp in the woods with a village boy. No part of him was off-limits. By the time the drums slowed, I had explored every part of him.

He held me close, our faces sweaty and clothes sticky. I tilted my chin up to kiss him, but then the music stopped. The tribe gathered around the bonfire to toss little things into the flames, sending orange sparks into the night.

"What are they doing?" I asked.

"I don't know."

We moved in closer and saw that dozens of women were throwing roses into the fire, then shutting their eyes and whispering to the heavens. Even little girls were participating.

Adrasteia approached us. "As part of the spring hecatomb," she explained, "we burn a rose as a sacrificial representation of ourselves, Gaea's creations. And we ask Aphrodite to forgive our shortcomings, replacing our sorrow with her love." She passed us each a rose. "Would you like to join in?"

"This will bring me forgiveness?" Theo asked, raising a brow.

"It's a renewal. All souls carry burdens. Let them go, and open yourself up to new beginnings."

I wasn't convinced that such a simple act could have that much influence, but I was still basking in the pleasures of the wine and dancing, and I was willing to participate for the sake of the evening.

"No one need know what you seek forgiveness for, Colonel," Adrasteia said, resting her hand on his shoulder. "That's between you and the goddess."

Theo shifted closer to me, away from Adrasteia. She glanced from him to me, then smiled and left us.

"You first," I said.

Theo stepped toward the fire, his expression set in concentration, and tossed his rose into the flames. He wore his sadness with absolute conviction as he watched the tender bloom alight.

I twirled a rose under my nose. What I needed forgiveness for, I doubted the goddess could give me. I couldn't turn back time and save my mother or my infant sister, and I couldn't go back and switch places with Cleora. The Erinyes had every right to hound me. I vowed to my mother that I would protect my sisters. If I couldn't forgive myself for falling short of that promise, how could I expect anyone else to forgive me?

"Althea?" Theo asked. "Are you all right?"

Tears smeared my vision. "The wine must have gone to my head."

He drew me away from the fire, back to our tents. I slipped inside mine to check on Bronte while he waited outside. My sister slept soundly on top of her blankets. I pulled her sandals off one by one, brushing my finger over the star-shaped freckle on her heel, then laid my blanket over her. I rested the rose beside her and stepped outside again.

"How is she?" Theo asked.

"Comatose."

The closeness we shared while dancing seemed far away already. I thought about reaching out to touch him, to reclaim that intimacy, but the sadness in his eyes stopped me. "What did you ask forgiveness for?"

His shoulders tensed.

"You don't have to tell me."

Theo rolled his head, releasing the tension in his neck, then dropped his chin to his chest. With a downcast gaze, he replied. "I asked for forgiveness for not protecting your baby sister."

My whole body stilled.

"I could have done something. Taken the baby. Hidden her."

"Why didn't you?"

"Because of my mother," he admitted. "Had I run off with the babe, they would have used her against me. Punished her as though she had committed the betrayal."

My heart sped up. "Doesn't she face the same threat now?"

"It was a risk I had to take in order to win her freedom."

All those years ago, on the night my mother died and my half sister was taken, Theo had only followed orders. I understood that now. I couldn't expect him to stand up to Cronus on his own, especially when I was incapable of doing the same.

"I forgive you."

His hand reached toward me across the dark. Our fingertips touched, and the distance between us evaporated. We leaned in, and our lips met.

Theo sucked in a breath so deep that I thought he might inhale the world, then he carefully took my chin in his warm hand, and he kissed me deeper.

My lips pressed against his hungrily, fast and full of pent-up need. His kisses were slower, delicate, measured, with the thoughtfulness of a man who believed he had all the time on earth. His depth of affection was beyond what I had anticipated, and I couldn't help but sink into it.

Theo caressed my back, hips, breasts. Everything moved slower than I had patience for, yet I matched his thoroughness, my touch lingering across his chest and shoulders.

As Theo trailed kisses down my throat, my head lolled back, and my mind spun. This wasn't merely a satiating of carnal desires.

This was meaningful.

This was stupid.

I had oaths to keep, and this was no time for distractions. All the other times I had let a man touch me had been strictly physical. This . . . this was complicated.

I rested my forehead against his. "I should go."

Theo took my chin in his hand again and kissed me, achingly slow, turning my legs to mush. I almost changed my mind and invited myself into his tent, but he stepped back and whispered, "Good night, Althea."

He started to go, then paused and crouched. A single narcissus had bloomed where we had been standing.

Theo stood up again, suddenly on high alert.

"Was that there earlier?" I asked.

"No."

He stomped on the flower and ground it into the grass with his heel.

A frigid grimness sank through me, straight to the marrow in my bones. I wrapped my arms around myself and shivered. We were almost out of time.

Theo continued to scan around us for any sign of the Erinyes. Finally, he said, "Sleep with your weapon close."

After another look around, he went into his tent. I slipped into mine and found my spear in the dark, then lay down next to Bronte. I tucked myself into her body heat, but I could not shake the chill clinging to my insides like hoarfrost.

The Erinyes would never stop hounding me. Forgiveness and new beginnings were a lovely thought, but I would have no peace of mind, no renewal of self, until I fulfilled my oath. The next day, I would do what I should have done in the first place.

I would go to the Almighty.

17

Sunup came too quickly. Bronte was still asleep when I got out of bed. I tried to be quiet while I changed clothes, but I made just enough noise to wake her.

"Oh, my head," she said, moaning.

"Go back to sleep. Your headache will pass." I kissed her forehead and pulled back. "Your skin is hot." I touched her face with the back of my hand. "You're feverish."

"I just need sleep," she said.

"And water," I said, setting the waterskin beside her. "I'll see what I can do about finding a remedy."

She mumbled something that I couldn't understand and drifted back to sleep.

I left the tent and shielded my eyes from the morning sun. Bronte wasn't the only one who'd drunk too much wine last night.

The camp was quiet. I had hoped to catch Euboea before she went out fishing, as she did most mornings, but her gear was still hanging by the mess hall, including the spear she took to defend herself against sea dragons.

Theo stepped out of his tent. I pulled up short at the sight of him. His eyes were red rimmed, and his mussed clothes were the same ones he'd worn yesterday.

"Good, you're awake," he said, adjusting the strap of the sack slung over his shoulder. A gust of wind ruffled his wavy hair. "I'd like you to join Zeus's training session today. I thought about what you said, and you're right. Your attendance would be good for him."

"I was looking for Euboea. Bronte is feverish. I was hoping she might have a remedy."

"Ida would be the one to ask," Theo said. "She gave Zeus a tea for his upset stomach the other day. He said she has a way with remedies."

Bronte did need something for her fever, and I was worried about her, especially since it would be difficult to leave her here if she was unwell, but I also needed to speak to Euboea about sailing me back to Thessaly. Since she was nowhere to be seen, it could wait. "All right, but I need to come back soon to check on Bronte."

"This shouldn't take long."

Theo and I set off into the woods. The air was cooler in the trees, the forest floor damp from dew and the wind calmer. We were quieter than usual. Perhaps he was thinking about last night too. I tried to forget about it, but every time he rubbed his beard or licked his lips, I remembered his kisses. *This will pass,* I told myself. Leaving the isle, and leaving Theo, would cure me of my infatuation.

The trail led us past the nymphs' cottage and flower garden. Their shutters were closed. I thought to stop and ask Ida for something for Bronte's fever, but I would rather Zeus or Adrasteia ask her on my behalf. Ida was more likely to assist them. We continued onward, all the way back to the area of the woods I never wanted to see again. The ravine that I'd fallen into when the Erinyes had chased me was just as steep and precarious as I recalled, though a rope had been installed, strung from one side of the gulch to the other.

"Althea!" Zeus came jogging down another trail from uphill, his face and chest slick with sweat. I wondered how long he had been running. "The colonel said you might join us today."

"He did?" I glanced slantwise at Theo.

"We're training on the high rope today," he said, setting down the sack he had brought. "It's better with multiple participants."

Zeus clapped me on the shoulder. "Don't worry, Althea. There's a net."

Indeed, they had strung a fishing net along the bottom of the ravine, though the drop was still quite far. Theo pulled out a waterskin and a timepiece. He set up a clepsydra—a portable water clock—on top of a flat rock, explaining that it would keep time for approximately six minutes.

"I have a prize for whoever is fastest at crossing to the other side and back," he said.

Zeus's eyes lit up. "What's the prize?"

Theo took a pair of bracers from his pocket. The leather armor, worn around the wrists and forearm, was engraved with lions in a design almost identical to the one on my mother's arm cuff.

"They were part of my first set of battle armor," Theo said. "They haven't fit for years, but I keep them with me for good luck."

"Those bracers are mine," Zeus said, hopping on his toes like a jackrabbit. "I'll go first."

He walked to the edge of the drop-off and stretched his arms overhead.

"He's entirely too jovial about, well, everything," Theo grumbled.

"Wait until you see how annoying he is when he wins," I replied.

Theo extended his hand and brushed his fingertips down my forearm. "Thank you for coming. Zeus does better with an audience."

A dart of guilt struck me dead in the chest. I couldn't tell either of them that I was leaving. They would try to talk me out of it, but I had made up my mind. The best way for me to help Cleora wasn't waiting around for Zeus to grow up. It was trading myself for her like I should have done in the first place.

Zeus started across the rope. He placed one foot in front of the other, his arms out. Theo began the water clock, then took a crossbow out of the sack and aimed it at Zeus.

"What are you doing?" I asked.

"Increasing the level of difficulty."

"What if you hurt him?"

"The bolts are dulled at the end."

"That doesn't mean it won't hurt."

"A little discomfort would do him good." Theo locked the bolt in, sighted his target, and let the bolt fly.

Zeus bent backward to avoid getting hit, then righted his balance.

"Your turn," Theo said, offering me the crossbow.

"Me? I don't think so."

"Zeus will take the opportunity to shoot at you when it's his turn." I accepted the crossbow.

"Tuck it at your side," Theo said. "Now add the bolt and pull back. There, it's locked and ready for release. Squeeze the trigger lightly . . ."

I released the bolt and narrowly missed Zeus.

"You've done that before," Theo said.

"A hoplite left a crossbow in our field once. I played with it for a few days before he came back to retrieve it."

Theo handed me the rest of the bolts. "Have at it. Don't hit him too many times."

I didn't. A couple times, I came close to grazing him, but Zeus was light on his feet.

He reached the other side, grew more confident, and increased his speed on the way back. I couldn't reload quickly enough to keep up, and soon he was back on our side of the ravine.

"Whoop!" he cried, pumping his arms over his head.

"How did he do?" I asked Theo.

He checked the water clock. "He beat my time."

"What was your time?"

Theo pressed his lips together. "Longer. Much longer."

"He's going to be unbearable," I groaned.

Zeus bounded over to us. "I did well. Didn't I do well? Did you see how well I did?"

Theo rubbed at his forehead. I shoved the crossbow at Zeus and rolled up my sleeves.

"You better not lose to a puny mortal," I said. "That would be so embarrassing."

Zeus removed from his pocket the violet that Metis, his betrothed, had asked him to carry on his person. He sniffed the flattened petals in a familiar way that made me think he did this a dozen times a day. "I'm already a winner," he said dreamily.

I envied his confidence.

Stepping forward, I peered over the edge. The net below appeared secure, but since Zeus hadn't fallen in it, I couldn't be certain. I wasn't afraid of heights, but standing near the drop-off left me winded.

"Althea, you don't have to do this," Theo said. "Zeus's time will be difficult to beat. You don't need to put yourself in danger."

The implication rankled. All my irritation at having to depend on Zeus had been building up, and the last thing I wanted to hear from Theo, or anyone else, was that it was impossible for me to beat a Titan.

"I'm going, Theo. Time me, or don't. I'm doing this."

Zeus grinned. "Good luck, puny mortal."

I extended my arms out and set one foot on the rope. It swayed a little. The first few steps were shaky, but farther out, I found my balance. Staring ahead, I tried not to look down or think about how high up I was.

A bolt whirred past my face. I reeled backward, arms windmilling, then redistributed my weight.

"Well done, Althea!" Theo called.

I wished he would be quiet. He hadn't cheered on Zeus, and it was distracting at best, patronizing at worst. Theo didn't say another word until I reached the far side, then he shouted that I had made it halfway. He really needed to shut up.

I set out to return. After my first few wobbly paces, Zeus shot a bolt. He missed, but he followed it with another, and that one hit my leg with bruising force. I gritted my teeth at the immediate throbbing. My concentration wavered, and I glanced down.

My next step missed the rope, and I fell forward. I grabbed the rope around my chest, catching it on my underarms. I didn't want to drop into the net.

"Zeus, go get her," Theo said. "Althea, hold on!"

My position was too precarious for me to pull myself up, but I wasn't finished.

"I can do it!" I let myself hang and moved down the rope, hand over hand, swinging side to side to propel myself. Despite my assertion, Zeus reached me in only a moment. He swung on the rope effortlessly, hanging by one hand, and slipped his free arm around my waist.

"Climb onto my back," he said.

"No." My hands ached. Blisters were rising along my palms. But I didn't grab for him.

"Althea, let go and let Zeus carry you," Theo called.

I ignored him and kept going. Zeus stayed right behind me, almost effortlessly. The unfair ease of his movements fueled me forward.

Theo waited, his arms outstretched toward us. I reached the end, and as I hauled myself up, he grabbed me by the back of my chiton and pulled me to safety. I lay on my back, staring up at patches of blue sky between the treetops.

Zeus landed right behind me. "I'm sorry, Althea."

"Your aim is good," I replied, panting.

Theo inspected my leg. "Are you all right?"

"It's just a bruise."

He didn't seem to hear me. "Zeus, you should have grabbed Althea and brought her back."

"She didn't want me to—"

"Go again," Theo said. "You're still training."

Zeus's eyes hardened. "You forget who you're speaking to, Colonel."

"I know exactly who I'm speaking to," Theo countered. "You think because you're the son of the Almighty, you're not accountable for your actions? Your privilege makes you more accountable, not less. Go again."

Zeus slammed his jaw shut. "I *am* sorry, Althea."

"I know," I said. I didn't understand why Theo was so angry.

Zeus shot Theo another glare, then stepped back on the rope to cross the ravine again.

Theo helped me to my feet. "He's a child," he groused. "Our lives, and the lives of everyone we love, hinge upon an overgrown boy."

"He's still learning."

"He's Cronus's son, Althea. Do you think he inherited nothing from his father? I've never met a more selfish, womanizing, unfaithful braggart than Cronus—but Zeus may exceed him."

"He won't. He has a good heart."

"Does he?" Theo scrubbed a hand over his beard. "He should have brought you back."

"Why? I finished on my own." Then it suddenly dawned on me, the reason that Theo had invited me to join. "I'm here as, what, bait?"

"You're motivation. Zeus acts quickly when others are under duress."

"It's a good thing I continue to need saving," I snapped, trying to shove past him.

Theo cut me off. "Althea, that's not what I meant. Zeus needs a cause, something that motivates him to think about someone other than himself. Look how he responded when you almost fell out there. He rushed to your aid."

"Only, I ruined your plan. I should have let him save me like a good little girl, right?"

"What do you want from me?" Theo demanded. "I'm doing all I can to make something out of that boy. He has everything—*everything*—in the palm of his hand, and he squanders his strength away on pints of nectar and pretty maidens. Zeus might become a hero, but it won't be me who teaches him."

"Theo," I said exasperatedly. "You cannot give up. You *don't* give up."

"I need time to think."

He stalked away.

Theo was disproportionately upset over what was just a bruised leg. Something else must have been bothering him. Maybe the waiting, the wondering, the worrying, not knowing how his mother was faring. Didn't I feel similarly impatient and frustrated? Wasn't I ready to leave?

The moment Theo disappeared into the woods, Zeus rejoined me.

"Althea, I'm sorry—"

"I'm fine. Don't bring it up again."

He shoved his sweaty hair out of his eyes. "Theo doesn't understand what it's like. He doesn't have to stand up to Cronus."

"He's trying to help you."

"He's trying to save his mother," Zeus said seriously. "And you're trying to save your sister. Neither of you cares if my father casts me into Tartarus, as long as your families are safe."

I jolted. "That isn't true."

"Isn't it?" Zeus began to turn away, then stopped. "You may have your qualms about the outside world, but at least you're welcome there. If I leave here, Cronus will discover I'm alive and stop at nothing to destroy me."

Every word of my oaths boomed through my mind. "I know what's at risk. My mother *died*."

"So will we. We might as well stop pretending we have a chance at defeating the God of Gods."

My temper flashed, hot and fast. "Fine. Go back to drinking and fornicating and hiding. My first impression of you was right. You are *just* like your father."

Zeus's face fell, and I immediately regretted my words. I hadn't really meant it.

"Zeus, I'm—"

"You've said enough." He marched off into the woods.

I didn't know who to follow, Zeus or Theo. The answer was neither. I should never have listened to the oracles and come to this place. Believing in fate had wasted time and distracted me from fulfilling my oath. I should have known better than to trust a cosmic power. Faith always failed me.

A tingle coursed down my spine. I turned to see Ida behind me, watching me. The frowning nymph beckoned me with the crook of her finger, then disappeared down the path that led to her cottage. I didn't care to speak with her, but I still needed a remedy for Bronte's fever. Favoring my sore leg, I trudged after her.

18

Ida had left the front door cracked. I approached it, walking on the stepping stones between the beds of colorful flowers, and pushed inside. The interior was meticulously clean, with a shiny floor and well-crafted wooden furniture engraved with detailed leafy vines. The ivy décor continued in the form of real plants. Their pots were everywhere: on the side tables, chairs, shelves, and in the corners of the room. My nose picked up hints of aloe and basil, but I didn't recognize many of the herbs and plants. Bronte would have adored this collection. She could probably have identified them all. I followed the sounds of clinking and clanging to the kitchen at the back.

The blonde nymph placed a kettle over the fire in the wide stone hearth. "I'm preparing a tea for us," she said. "Take a seat."

I sat in a low chair.

"I sense two great burdens on your soul, Althea Lambros." Ida turned her bright-green eyes on me. "The Erinyes hunt you, and you're afflicted by a curse."

"How . . . how can you tell I'm cursed?"

"I saw the blight on your soul the second we met—it's like a black spot." She touched her chest to indicate the same spot on my body. A chill emanated through me. I looked down at myself, but I saw nothing there. "Your soul is resisting the curse, but you cannot hold it at bay forever. Symptoms will soon manifest."

"What symptoms?" I asked, thinking of the burning sensation of my tag.

"Hard to say." Ida set out two cups. "The symptoms will vary depending on the syntax of the curse."

"How do you know so much about curses?"

Her lips spread into a cutting smile. "I've seen much pain in my long life."

"Can the curse be broken?"

"The only way to break it is for the benefactor to revoke it," she said. "In doing so, the curse would claim the benefactor's life as compensation. If he perishes before it's revoked, the curse will drive you mad until eventually you also perish."

My stomach sank. Decimus would never release me from his curse, especially not at the expense of his own life.

Ida poured tea. "Drink it all. It will ease your headache." I stared at the steaming cup. "Drink," she pressed. "I've nothing to gain from poisoning you."

I sipped a little. The astringent taste dried out my mouth but wasn't entirely off-putting. "Do you have anything for fevers? My sister Bronte is unwell."

Ida dropped a small bag of herbs on the table. "This will help." She then set a damp cloth and bandages beside me. "For your hands."

I cleaned my blisters and wrapped the bandages around my palms. "How did you know the Erinyes are pursuing me?" I asked.

"Their prey reek." She sniffed the air and made a face. "Like a rotting wound. The Erinyes will continue to hunt you, either until you fulfill your oath or they catch you."

"They won't catch me," I whispered. When I became a prisoner of Cronus, and Cleora and Bronte were safe, my oath would be honored, and the Erinyes would no longer hunt me.

Ida raised a single pointer finger. "There is another way," she said as though she had read my thoughts. "You could ask them for an atoning task."

"A what?"

"Think of it as a back door."

My breath caught momentarily. *A way out?*

"Be careful, though," Ida warned. "The Erinyes are tricksters. They would just as soon torture you to death as offer you a break. Their mercy is fickle."

An atoning task didn't sound like a solution after all.

Ida picked up her belt of knives and spread them out on the table. "They will come for you very soon. I can help you if you wish." She pulled an old, sharp-looking scythe from its sheath. "We have a ritual on the island. Every girl of age has undergone it."

"You mean the ritual cuttings," I stated.

"With this rite, your fear, sorrow, and pain will hurt you no longer. You will be more focused, more resolute, more capable of fulfilling your oaths." Ida lifted the scythe between us. "What pain would you remove?"

I knew instantly—my memory of the night my mother died.

Ida ran her finger down the curved blade. "This scythe was forged from a shaving of the adamant sickle that Cronus used to castrate Uranus. When Rhea gave it to my sister and me in exchange for guarding her son, I remembered my apprenticeship with Mnemosyne, goddess of memory, before she became a councilor to the Almighty, and I found a greater purpose for this great tool. The scythe's godly power can wash away the bindings of the mortal world. Emancipation means cutting ourselves loose of the bindings that tie us down. Elevation requires separation."

"If the ritual is so great, why haven't you done it?"

"Adamant works differently on nymphs and immortals."

Emily R. King

I thought of how Cronus's sickle castrated Uranus when no other weapon could. "Why faces? Why not cut the women somewhere less visible?"

"Every time they look at themselves, they see a courageous woman who took destiny into her own hands." Ida ran her fingers up and down her arm, over her tattoos of roses. "Each flower represents a woman who has gone through the renewal of self, letting go of her past and growing into her potential. The power of the adamant bestowed these markings on me as the wielder of the blade. The women wear their scars with pride, and I wear these, their hopes."

The night my mother died replayed in my head. I was haunted by every detail, straight down to the musty smell of the birthing room. I couldn't undo my oaths or the curse, but I could unburden myself of my guilt and sorrow. The shameful truth was that if I had not feared Cronus, I would have immediately traded myself for Cleora. My own greatest fear—that I would perish like my mother—had kept me from fulfilling my oath.

Ida walked over to a chair fitted with adjustable bindings for wrists, ankles, chest, and neck. I realized this was how she bound her victims before slicing their faces.

"Uncomplicate your life," she said. "A moment of pain for a lifetime of joy. It's more than most people could ever hope for."

Indeed, many women would agree. Cleora had been willing to burn her face, with no guarantee of forgetting her pain. So were countless others. The thought of unburdening myself was tempting. Too tempting.

Ida approached me with the scythe, a sort of wildness in her eyes. "You see something inside yourself that you want gone," she said. "Free yourself from the bonds that tie you to the past so that you may move forward and fulfill your oaths without fear."

Staring at the blade, I imagined the relief of not carrying all this grief, all this anger. I could face Cronus without fear. But my mother had suffered too much for me to forget all that she had sacrificed. Her example, sealed with her death, pushed me to do better. As imperfect as I was, I wouldn't wish that away.

"I'll take my chances with the Erinyes."

Ida's lip curled. "The Erinyes will not be merciful."

"No, but they will be fair."

As I turned to go, Ida slashed out at me. I caught her wrist and twisted it back, aiming the scythe at her throat. Terror froze her face.

"You may have forced your ideas on others," I hissed, "but not me."

"I set the tribe free," she snarled. "They live without putting a man first. They can do what they want, *become* who they want."

"As long as they stay on the island," I countered. "What of the rest of the women in the world? We cannot continue to harm ourselves in an effort to meet men's expectations. We must stop shrinking ourselves to accommodate them."

"The world doesn't care what happens to women and children. You cannot change men, and you cannot change the gods."

I wrenched the scythe from her grasp. "I can rise despite them, despite what you and they would have me believe about myself. I used to think the world didn't belong to women. We were spectators, disciples, slaves. But this world is ours."

I dropped the scythe on the table and strode out of the house.

My hands shook. Thanks to the tea, my head hurt less, but that merely amplified my aching heart. For all my assertions of bravery, I had never felt more cowardly. Leaving the island wasn't running away. It was righting a wrong. Bronte would be safe with the tribe, and I could send Cleora here to join her. My obligation, my oath, would be satisfied. So why did I feel like I was abandoning Zeus and Theo?

I twisted my ring. I was wary to trust its authority, but I needed reassurance that I could face Cronus on my own. Whatever cosmic force powered my ring, I wanted to know that I had worth beyond the fulfillment of my oath. Beyond fate's use for me.

What makes a soul precious? Is it what we do for the gods, or what we achieve in spite of them?

A few paces beyond the porch, I halted. The front of the cottage looked different. Narcissus had taken over the flower beds, choking the other flowers with so many yellow-starred blooms that I could scarcely count them all.

A hissing came from above. I glanced up at three winged women perched on the roof watching me with burning red eyes. A shiver crossed my scalp.

The Erinyes.

I retreated a step, then two. Another step, and one of them slithered her brass-studded scourge across the roof threateningly.

"You're almost out of time," she hissed.

"I'm going to fulfill my oaths," I said, my head held high. "I figured out a way to see that both Bronte and Cleora are safe."

"Not enough."

Her words drove through me, as swift as a blade. "What else can I do?"

The three harbingers of justice stood and shook out their wiry wings. The same one spoke. "You've three days."

"Three days? Three days until what?"

They stretched their wings—their spans more than twice their height—and dropped off the back of the roof.

I ran around the cottage, searching for them. "Three days until what?" I pleaded.

But they had vanished.

19

Bronte wasn't in our tent. I found her sitting under a tree in the school-yard teaching a song to a group of girls. After meeting with Ida, seeing the young girls' scarred faces was too much. What past had Ida freed them from? None. The girls had paid for the fears of others.

Bronte spotted me and frowned. "Girls, we need to take a break. Why don't you go play? I'll join you in a little while."

The girls groaned in complaint but ran off to the clearing to play *ephedrismos*, a piggyback racing game.

"What happened to you, Althea?" Bronte asked. "You look like death."

"I'm not the one who had a fever this morning," I replied. "Shouldn't you be in bed?"

"Euboea said I had too much opium. She gave me a seaweed tea that helped."

I had forgotten the remedy from Ida in the cottage, so this news was a relief.

"Where did you last see Euboea?" I asked.

"After she gave me the tea, she left to fish. What's wrong?"

"Not here." I tugged Bronte inside the schoolhouse and checked to see that it was empty. "The Erinyes visited me."

My sister bit her lip. "What did they want?"

"They gave me three days to fulfill my oaths."

Bronte rested both hands on a desk and hunched forward, her expression grim. "What are we going to do?"

I appreciated her taking on this dilemma with me, but this was not her problem to solve. I had to return to Thessaly. Traveling there would take two days, leaving me just one day after I arrived to figure out how to convince Cronus to take me instead of Cleora before the Erinyes dragged me down to Tartarus.

Shouts came from outside the schoolhouse. We ran out to see women grabbing shields and spears and darting off into the trees.

"Sea dragon!" one woman cried. She was drenched and covered in sand. I recognized her as one of the women who fished with Euboea.

Bronte and I dashed for our tent to collect our weapons—her bow and arrows, my spear and shield. As we ran toward the sea, some warriors began returning from the beach. They were retreating. With them was Euboea, who was bleeding from a slash on her arm and another on her head. She stumbled forward with blood dripping down her forehead and between her eyes.

Bronte slipped her arm around her waist to steady her. "What happened?"

"A sea dragon attacked the boat," Euboea replied. "Smashed it to pieces. My crew and I swam to shore. It followed us. The colonel held it off so I could get away."

A gut-shaking roar sounded in the distance.

"Is Theo still there?" I asked.

Euboea nodded.

"Take her back to camp," I told Bronte, then I took off for the beach.

I ran out past the tree line and stumbled to a halt. A sea dragon, half beached on the rocky shoreline, bent its long neck downward and nipped at Theo's sword.

The beast was massive, with sleek scales in every shade of the sea; large, pearly teeth; and big round golden eyes. Tapered horns protruded from her head, accented by spiky whiskers that extended away from her bony cheeks like a groomed mane. Tall spines rose from her vertebrae, connected by skin that formed a sail. Her squat, serpentine body—built for maneuvering gracefully in the water—was lodged in the sand. Her short hind legs strained under her weight, and her front claws, with talons for gripping and slashing, had limited reach.

Theo swung at her. The dragon grabbed him with her teeth by the back of his shirt and lifted him off the ground. He dangled as she shook her head. His weapon fell to the sand, and she tossed him, soaring, into the water.

I ran at her with my spear and shield. She batted me aside with her front claws. I flew down the beach and landed in a heap, my weapon and shield beside me. She smashed my shield and my spear under her weight, then arched her head down to peer at me, her eyes luminous. Her snout was longer than my whole body. She peeled back her teeth, her nostrils flaring.

"You smell like a—"

"Ahhhh!" Zeus barreled out of the trees, sword in hand, and slashed at her.

The dragon reared back her head, blood dripping down her cheek.

I scrambled to my feet and retrieved Theo's fallen sword. Zeus stood between the dragon and me. I scanned the shore and sea for Theo, but I didn't see him.

The dragon lowered her head and used it as a battering ram to knock Zeus to the ground. She began to snap at him, then jolted upright.

"You're a Titan," she growled.

Zeus rose to his feet. His sword had fallen out of reach.

She sniffed the air over and over. "Your blood . . . It cannot be."

Zeus eyed his sword.

"It's true," the dragon continued. "My snout does not lie. A child of Cronus lives . . . but not for long."

She peeled back her lips, her pearly teeth shiny with saliva, and lunged. He dodged her, leaping to the side. His sword was almost within range. Zeus ran to it, and the dragon pursued, but she maneuvered too far inland and couldn't wriggle any farther up the beach. Just before Zeus got to his sword, she tossed a wall of sand, showering him and burying his weapon.

I charged forward, cutting at her flank. She reared back, then wrapped her claws around me, trapping me in a vise of talons. Her mouth opened and her teeth came at me.

A crackle and rumble rent the air.

Directly overhead, a storm stewed in an eddy of black thunderheads. Zeus stood in front of the dragon, his chest heaving, his blue eyes sharply focused. Another thunderclap clashed so loudly that I would have ducked and covered my ears on instinct if I were able to move.

Zeus threw his hands above his head, then lowered them. A lightning bolt flew down from the storm cloud and struck the sand in front of us. The dragon released me and reeled backward. I stumbled away while she tried to retreat, but she was well and truly beached.

The sky darkened all the more, immense thunderclouds shrouding the sun. Mighty gusts flew in from the sea, and with them came waves. The rising surf crashed over the dragon and pummeled the shore. The next wave grabbed the sand beneath me and dragged me into the sea.

Theo swam against the high waters and climbed onto the dragon's ridged back. He reached for my open hand as I swept past, caught me, and heaved me up onto her with him. We pulled ourselves up to sit on her massive shoulders, high above the spiny sail.

Zeus raised his hands again. His ring burned brightly. More thunderclaps boomed, then blinding lightning zigzagged down, narrowly missing the dragon.

The beast whipped her serpentine body from side to side, trying to wriggle into the sea. Each movement threatened to toss us off. Theo and I lost our grip and slid down her left flank. I raked my fingernails down her side, searching for a perch. An arrow flew past me and sank into her side. I grabbed it with one hand and hung on.

Theo kept sliding and dropped into the sea, where he fought the currents. On shore, Bronte stood behind Zeus, her bow and arrow in hand. She shot four more arrows into the dragon's flank, creating more perches for me to hold on to. I used them to climb up the beast's back and straddle the nape of her neck.

The dragon bore down on Zeus, catching him in her claws and shoving him to the ground. Bronte let more shafts fly. One of her unerring arrows struck the dragon in the face, near her eye. The dragon snapped, barely missing Bronte, but she bit the bow and broke it to pieces.

I lifted the sword above my head and plunged it into the beast's neck.

She roared and writhed. I held on as she finally squirmed back down the beach and plunged into the waters. My feet flew out behind me with the force of the dive, and the sword slid out of the dragon's back. I kicked to the surface, where I saw her sail breach and begin to circle back.

I swam hard for shore, aiming for where the beach was shallowest, and arrived just before the dragon caught up. She couldn't come any farther without beaching herself again.

With an outraged snarl, she dived into the deep.

I sloshed my way to shore. Theo had emerged from the water. The thunderheads began to clear, unmasking the sun, and the winds died down. Up the beach, Zeus lay face-first in the sand. Theo and I ran to him and turned him over.

Zeus grinned. "Did you see that?"

"How could we have missed it?" I huffed tiredly.

Bronte ran up the beach and caught up to us. "Good work with the sword, Althea."

I sat back, breathless. "Not as impressive as what you did with those arrows."

"I was easily the most impressive," Zeus said.

"How long have you known you could summon thunder and lightning?" Theo asked.

"About as long as you have."

"You did well, trainee." Theo ruffled his hair, tossing sand everywhere. His eyes held something else, though, an emotion beyond pride that I couldn't discern.

Zeus stood on wobbly legs. "I feel strange. I'm so tired. I can hardly keep my eyes open." His words slurred, then his eyes rolled back in his head, and he collapsed.

Theo caught him before he hit the ground.

"Zeus, this is not the time to play dead," I said, exasperated.

Theo shook him, but Zeus couldn't be roused.

"I don't think he's playing dead this time," Theo said.

"What's wrong with him?" Bronte asked.

"I don't know," I replied. "Bring him to our tent."

Theo carried Zeus into camp. When the women and girls saw the Boy God passed out in his arms, they quieted and moved out of their path. Theo laid Zeus on my bed to check him over.

"He appears to be sleeping," Theo said. "What he did must have taken tremendous strength. We'll let him rest."

"The entire tribe is waiting on word," Bronte said. "I'll let everyone know he's all right."

She left the tent.

Theo took my hand. His fingertip rubbed circles across the tender spot at the inside of my wrist. "About earlier."

"I understand what you were trying to do. Zeus needed something to inspire him, to let go of his fear."

"I've no doubt he still fears his father—we all do—but he needed to fear something more, such as losing you." Theo shifted closer, our breaths mingling, and rested his hands on my hips. "Earlier, when you were on the high rope and almost fell . . ."

At that moment, I was more concerned about falling for Theo. The longer we were alone, and the more he touched me, the more I felt that last night's kiss deserved an encore.

Suddenly, without warning, the back of my neck started burning. I felt for my tag. The scarred skin felt normal, yet spots danced across my vision. I swayed forward, and Theo held me closer, supporting my weight.

"What is it, Althea?"

"I feel . . . wrong."

Shouts and calls to arms sounded outside the tent. We went to the opening and looked out. The camp was in disarray. Women were arming themselves and gathering in the main clearing. Bronte caught sight of us and called out. "We're being invaded."

"By whom?" I asked.

"Slave traders."

Theo drew his sword. "Althea, stay in the tent. I suspect they aren't here only for themselves."

"But—"

"*Stay here.*"

I flinched at his tone.

"Protect Zeus," he said more gently. His eyes displayed worry not just for the Boy God but for me too. Theo threw back the tent flap and hurried out.

The chaos of the camp evolved into organized readiness. Warriors took their stations, positioning themselves to defend their homes and families. No one wept. No one dissolved into hysterics. It was as though they knew that this day would come, that it was only a matter of time before the outside world penetrated their quiet lives.

Bronte ran by with a group of girls, hurrying them along. "I'm taking the children to the schoolhouse," she called to me.

The girls held hands in a long line, clinging to one another. For many of them, the only man they had seen besides Zeus was Theo. I would have helped my sister move the children to safety, but I couldn't leave Zeus.

I ducked back into the tent to look for a weapon. My spear and shield had been destroyed, and I lost the sword in the ocean. I had nothing to defend myself with. Not even a kitchen knife.

The tent flap flew open, and Adrasteia stormed in.

"Zeus, I warned you not to—" She pulled up short at the sight of him passed out on my bedroll. "Oh, my dearest boy. Althea, is he injured?"

"Sleeping deeply."

"The thundercloud and lightning he summoned could be seen from clear across the sea. The slave traders followed it right here."

Male voices shouted nearby. The loudest of them all froze my veins.

"Lay down your weapons!" Decimus commanded.

The tag at the back of my neck burned so deeply I winced as Adrasteia and I peered through the small slit between the tent flaps. Decimus stood in the center of the camp, fully armed in sword, helmet, breastplate, and shield. The general's company of uniformed liege men was scattered throughout the clearing and in the trees, so many of them I lost count. Some of them were not soldiers but were instead dressed in loose, short robes and hats with wide brims.

"Who are the men with the soldiers?" I asked.

"Slave traders. The First House's armada isn't permitted to come this far south. It would violate the treaty between Cronus and Oceanus. They would have needed another form of transportation to hide their presence in the southern isles."

It was unsurprising to hear that Decimus would align with a slave trader. But how had they found us? The slave ship was already patrolling these waters before Zeus's spectacular show in the heavens. The southern isles were vast. It could not be a coincidence that they were already nearby.

Across camp, Bronte ushered the last girl inside the schoolhouse and shut the door. Theo was nowhere in sight.

"Goddess help us, we're surrounded," Adrasteia breathed.

Decimus stomped around, his chest puffed out, while his liege men encircled the tribe. The warriors' shields and spears were mighty, but not against these numbers.

Ida entered the clearing. Two liege men aimed their swords at her, threatening her to stay back. Decimus waved for them to stand down. The nymph strolled up to him and a second skinnier man with long, sun-bleached hair and a scraggly beard down to his chest. The three of them exchanged private words, then Ida pointed at the schoolhouse.

Adrasteia and I shrunk back inside.

"My sister," she said, whispering to herself. "What are you doing?"

"Who is the second man with Ida?"

Adrasteia answered in a fainter whisper. "The slave ship captain Rastus. We acquired the newborn that Rhea used to trick Cronus, the one he thought was Zeus, from Rastus. Ida dealt with him a few more times after Stavra began bringing refugees here. As the tribe formed, everyone agreed not to allow boys on the island. We thought if it were a place just for women, no one would ever suspect that Zeus was hidden here. When the pregnant refugees gave birth to baby boys, Ida would deliver them to Rastus, but their last meeting was years ago."

"And General Decimus?"

"I wasn't aware they were acquainted."

We heard screaming, so we peeked out again. Several soldiers had begun to break down the door to the schoolhouse with a battering ram. Decimus waited close by. The mothers attacked, but they didn't even make it into the schoolyard. The liege men dispatched them with double-edged blades, merciless and unflinching in their slaughter.

They broke the door open, and Decimus stormed inside. He came out of the schoolhouse a moment later, dragging Bronte by the hair. More liege men led the girls out and shoved them to their knees in the clearing. Their weeping was agony.

The slave traders rounded up the women and began counting them and the girls as they would heads of cattle. Sometimes auctions of captives like these were held in Othrys. My mother had never let me attend one. She said it would desensitize me to the priceless value of a soul.

Decimus hauled Bronte into the middle of the camp, near Rastus and Ida, and threw her to the ground. Then he grabbed her again, by the back of the head, and raised his sword to her throat.

"Where is Althea?" he bellowed. "Where is Cronus's child?"

Bronte spit in his face. He slammed the hilt of his sword over her head, and she crumpled.

My heart hammered, and my mind swam with fears, heavy and cloudy and so, so cold.

"Althea Lambros!" Decimus bellowed. "I know you're out there!"

This was it, my moment to step forward and fulfill my oath. But how could I trade myself for Bronte when I was supposed to offer myself in exchange for Cleora? I could not do both. Again, I could only save one of my sisters.

"Come out, Althea! Don't make me tear this camp apart to find you!"

Something pulled at me, drawing me toward him, as though my mind had no will of its own. I moved for the opening of the tent, but Adrasteia tugged me back.

"I'll go," she said.

"But my sister—"

"I need to speak to Ida."

Before I could argue further, Adrasteia stepped outside and strode directly over to her sister. Ida stood beside Decimus, her hands on her knives.

"What have you done?" Adrasteia asked her.

"I've done what should have been done years ago when Rhea asked us to give up our lives for the gods."

"You agreed readily at the time. You were so loyal, she even named the mountain she hid her son on after you, sister. Rhea did that to show her appreciation for your sacrifice."

"Where is her support now? I wasted fifteen years investing in a child's future while giving up my own. The God of Gods would have found Zeus eventually. What do you think he would have done when he discovered we betrayed him? I've saved us."

"You've doomed the world." Adrasteia approached her sister, her steps cautious.

"The Almighty will forgive us."

"But how can you forgive yourself?"

Ida looked from the warriors held at sword point to the girls crying softly to my unconscious sister and then back to her own sister. "A war is coming, Adrasteia. We must be on the winning side."

"There is no winning. You will always be just a woman to the Almighty."

Ida drew a knife from her belt—the adamant scythe. "Someone was going to claim the praise for turning Zeus over to Cronus. We deserve that glory."

Adrasteia stepped right up to her sister, unconcerned as the liege men nearby reached for their swords. "Betrayal never breeds glory."

"You promised that if we stayed on the island, someday we would be free," Ida spit back. "Yet we're still the Titans' slaves."

Adrasteia extended a hand to Ida. "Sister, please. Don't you remember? We accepted a posting here so we could stay together."

Ida's jaw softened a little. "Join us, Adrasteia. Let's finally be free."

"What good is it to stay together when one of us has lost her way?" Adrasteia cupped her sister's face. "I want your happiness."

"And I want yours, which is why this will be swift."

Ida slid her scythe into Adrasteia's side.

"No!" Euboea cried.

A guard struck her, and she spun to the ground, gripping her cheek.

Adrasteia wilted, gaping up at her sister. The two nymphs embraced as the evergreen silk of Adrasteia's robe bloomed scarlet. Ida gently lowered her to the ground, where she went limp, her eyes washed blank.

Ida lifted her hand, and there, on the inside of her wrist, appeared another rose.

Women and girls wept. My head spun, my breaths too shallow, my heartbeat sprinting.

Bronte stirred awake and pushed to her knees.

Decimus put the blade to her throat again. "Althea, your sister is next! Don't make me search the tents!"

I panted, cold yet feverish. The part of me that knew I shouldn't heed him was overruled by a louder shriek in my head telling me I must. *I must.* I started to leave the tent, but hands gripped me from behind and pulled me back.

Theo held me against his chest. He had slipped in through the back of the tent while I was preoccupied with the scene out the front. "I won't let you go to him, Althea."

"I have to."

"Decimus won't kill your sister."

"You don't understand. I *have* to go to him."

Theo gave me a perplexed look. "You are Althea Lambros. You don't have to do anything a man tells you to do."

I fought the frantic desire to go to Bronte. Sweat trickled down my back and my joints quivered.

Theo bundled me closer in his arms. "Bronte will be all right."

"How can you be certain?"

"She's a valuable hostage. Decimus could use her against you, or against Cleora, but only if she's alive." Theo lessened his hold on me and rubbed the small of my back. "I'm going to let go now. Stay with me. Do you hear?"

I heard him, but I could not promise that I would do as he asked.

"Althea, are you listening? You're no good to Bronte or Cleora if you're captured. We need to get Zeus to safety. You saw what he's capable of. The oracles were right. He's our only hope."

Theo let me go, and he went to Zeus. Slinging the boy's arm over his shoulder, he lifted the Titan out of bed with a grunt.

"Althea!" Decimus cried. "Come to me now!"

Theo held my gaze. "Let's go. I've readied the boat."

Conflicting desires tore at me. Zeus could never be more valuable to me than Bronte, yet how could I deny his invaluable worth to the rest of the world? For a moment, I considered trading Zeus for Bronte's and my freedom, but Decimus would never agree. He was here for me.

"Althea," Theo whispered. "Trust me."

I did trust him. It was myself I didn't trust. The need to obey Decimus's summons quivered inside me like a starved mutt crouched on the floor waiting for scraps from its master. This was a symptom of the curse. It must be. His hold on me made it impossible to think straight, to know with certainty what was wrong and what was right.

Theo crept out of the back of the tent, leading the way. I forced myself to follow. My string ring began to glow, as did Zeus's. That reassurance, from whatever cosmic force had brought us together, compelled me. Protecting Zeus was the right choice. To consider otherwise would be the end of us all.

A soldier lay sprawled on the ground with a gaping, bloody wound in his chest. We passed the dead man and came upon another. Theo had left a trail of bodies all the way back from the beach.

The boat had been dragged to the water. Theo loaded Zeus in, then I heard shouting behind us.

"Althea!"

Decimus's booming voice halted me. Something slithered around my neck, like a chain tethering me to him. I turned to go back, my tag burning so badly that tears formed in my eyes.

"Althea," Theo said, grasping me by the arms, "stay with me."

But my body had a will of its own. I started to walk away from the boat, away from Zeus, away from Theo.

Strong hands grabbed me and shoved me underwater. I pushed against the force holding me. Then those same hands let me up for air. I gasped, and they drove me under again. I came up a second time, sputtering and coughing but more clearheaded.

Theo clutched me against him, and those hands now stroked the back of my head.

"Althea Lambros," he said firmly, "get in the boat."

I climbed in beside Zeus. My wet clothes clung to my cold, shivering body. Theo pushed the boat into the water, fighting the incoming tide.

A dozen or so liege men ran out of the woods toward us. Theo, still in the water, shoved us farther out until the surf picked up the boat. The rising tide propelled us back toward land. Theo pushed harder, but the sea was unrelenting.

The soldiers caught up, wading into the shallows, and attacked. Theo cut the first soldier down with his sword, then the next, staining the water crimson with blood.

I grabbed oars and rowed against the current. The tag on my neck sent a spike of searing pain deep into my skull. A moment later, Decimus emerged from the trees.

"Traitor," Decimus yelled. "The Almighty asked for your head, Colonel!"

"He'll have to wait until I'm done with it," Theo replied.

Decimus prowled toward him. "You haven't inquired about your mother."

Theo paused attacking the other soldiers, reverting to parrying their blows. "She's still in my service," Decimus went on. "But I would trade her for Althea. Get her for me, and your mother goes free."

I rowed harder, my arms trembling. Should Theo accept, I would not have the strength to fight both him and the curse tying me to Decimus.

"Your word means nothing," Theo said.

"This from a traitor," Decimus snapped. "I suppose I could trade your mother back to the Almighty. He's looking for a new slave to wash his dusty feet."

Theo raised his sword and started toward Decimus. He cut through five liege men, working his way toward the general. Despite my rowing, the boat continued to drift down the beach, the gap between Theo and us widening.

Decimus waded into the water, joining his comrades in their assault. There were so many soldiers approaching that I could hardly make out Theo among them.

Archers lined up on the beach.

In one last attempt at retaliation, Theo threw his sword at the general. Decimus stepped aside, and the blade hit the water.

Theo swam to the boat and hauled himself in. The first volley of arrows sank down around us, most disappearing into the sea, some striking the boat. Theo threw himself over Zeus, and an arrow sank into Theo's shoulder.

I opened the sail and tied it off like I had seen Theo do. Sea winds swept us up, carrying us away from shore. The next volley of arrows came close enough for me to hear them whizzing toward us, but they fell short.

Theo rolled off of Zeus with a groan. I tied off the rigging and then went to him. It was a clean shot; the arrow had pierced straight through his shoulder and out his chest.

"Remove the arrowhead," he said, handing me his knife.

I cut the head off.

"Now pull the stock out from the back with both hands."

Gripping the arrow so hard that my bandaged hands hurt, I yanked. Theo sank forward with another pained groan, clutching his shoulder. The wound was bleeding freely. In seconds, he, too, lost consciousness.

My body broke out in a cold sweat. The urge to go back to shore, to Decimus, writhed within me. Defying it ignited a pain so hot it burned like a bitter chill. I held myself firm and our course true until the isle sank away into the horizon. Exhausted and shivering, I lay down in the sunshine, hoping it would warm me. The day grew brighter and brighter, blindingly so, yet the icy agony worsened until, at last, I succumbed.

20

Sunlight shone through my eyelids, waking me. The most unique-looking woman I had ever seen hovered beside my bed.

"You're awake," she said, her voice silky.

She was so . . . pink. A cascade of rosy curls spilled down her back and over her willowy shoulders in soft tendrils. Her heart-shaped face was graced with satiny, puffy lips; catlike golden eyes; and wide-set cheekbones stained cerise. Her skin seemed to change colors, depending on what angle she tilted her head, shifting from a rose to a golden shimmer that felt hypnotic. Her blush-colored robes draped her slender upper body and thin waist and clung to her full hips before cascading to her heels. Looking at her gave me that same strange, floating sensation one experienced in the peaceful moment between dreaming and wakefulness when neither slumberland nor the physical world felt quite real.

"Who are you?" I asked. "Where are Theo and Zeus?"

"I'm Eos, Zeus's cousin. He's with the colonel and Metis, his betrothed. They've been waiting for you to wake. My brother, Helios, found the three of you drifting out at sea and brought you here to the Midnight Mansion."

The goddess of the dawn fussed over my blankets. So many layers of bedcovers were piled on me that I was toasty warm, everywhere except my lips, which felt as though they had been pressed against ice for hours.

This was Helios's home in the west, his place of rest after dragging the sun across the heavens in his chariot each day. The bedchamber was swathed in rich ivory fabrics and accented by lush potted greenery. A wide archway opened to a spacious balcony that overlooked a fountain courtyard, the azure sea, and swaying palms. The sound of cows nearby drifted in on a tepid breeze, and the late-day sun cast gold light across the marble floors, which reflected it and gave the chamber a coziness.

I pushed off the blankets and set my feet on the floor. A shiver pulsed through me. "Why am I so cold?"

"Your inner chill is a consequence of defying the curse that was put on you," Eos said. "You have a stubborn, restless soul, Althea. Most mortals are helpless against such a curse."

"I don't have time to be helpless."

"Time," Eos said wistfully. "What a convenient incentive. We Titans forget how motivating the hours can be."

I got to my feet. My bones felt brittle, as though they had been left out during the first autumn frost.

A knock sounded at the door, then a boy slave entered.

"Mistress Eos," he said. "Master Helios will return soon. He wishes to see all the guests in the receiving room before supper."

"We'll be there soon," Eos replied, dismissing him. "Are you well enough to attend, Althea?"

The sensation of icicles in my lungs made it hard to breathe, but I wouldn't let her know. "I can come."

Eos gestured at clothes and sandals that had been laid out for me. "I'll leave you to dress." She swept out of the room, leaving a cloud of pinkish glitter in her wake.

I wandered out onto the balcony. The terrace overlooked the verdant oasis, boasting undisturbed views of palm trees and sand in every direction. I wished my sisters were here to share the view with me. My homesickness rose to a simmer, and my eyes brimmed with tears. I returned to the room and changed clothes, my movements numb and hollow.

A rap came at the door. I bid the knocker enter.

Theo stood in the threshold wearing clean clothes as well. His long hair was slicked back and wet, and he smelled strongly of soap. His right arm was in a sling to protect his shoulder where the arrow had struck him.

He noticed my red-rimmed eyes and approached. "Your sisters will be all right, Althea."

The fact that he knew why I was upset brought more tears.

"The soldiers invaded Crete because of me," I whispered. "It's me Decimus wanted."

Theo drew me into his arms. "Eos told me you've been cursed," he said. "Was it Decimus?"

"That's why I had to struggle so hard to resist him. His curse compelled me."

Theo's finger trailed up the back of my neck, tracing my tag. "The next time you feel him calling you to him, remember what you told me: you shrink for no one."

I rested my head against his uninjured shoulder. Outside, dusk dropped a navy haze over the mansion and grounds. Slaves lit torches to brighten the stone pathways and corridors. The bedchamber had no such light, so we stood in the falling darkness, swathed by the accession of eventide.

"You're finally warm," Theo said, his voice husky. "You were freezing before when I visited while you were sleeping."

"My lips are still cold."

His gaze dropped to my mouth, his eyes heavy lidded. I told myself I wouldn't kiss him again, yet when his lips brushed mine, I melted forward, seeking to forget my worries, but the opposite happened; his kiss heightened my sadness. My lower lip quivered, and more tears rose. I didn't deserve this comfort, this escape. Not when my sisters were prisoners.

Theo sensed my fluctuating emotions and bundled me against his strapping chest with the utmost care. I burrowed into him, mindful of his injured shoulder, and let his embrace smooth the sharpest edges of my grief. I wasn't affectionate with anyone other than my sisters, but touching Theo was a balm I hadn't known before, and now it was the only one I wanted.

Someone cleared her throat in the doorway.

"My apologies for interrupting," Eos said. The goddess's eyes danced. She wasn't sorry at all for catching us in an embrace. "The others are waiting."

Theo ran his hands down my arm, reluctant to let me go. "It will be all right, Althea."

It may have been naive, but I believed him.

We followed Eos out of the bedchamber and down torchlit corridors that lay open to the balmy evening through grand columns and archways. Slaves in the gardens waved torches, the smoke scattering the buzzing insects and fogging the air with a slight dreaminess. Cicadas serenaded us, their song growing louder as twilight deepened to night.

We arrived at the dazzling receiving room. Decorated in golds and silvers, the open space boasted a stunning view of the gardens and coastal waters. The walls were painted with floor-to-ceiling murals of the sky in its phases, blending seamlessly from daybreak to midday to sunset to midnight. The artistry was so precise, rendered with such care, that the room felt lodged in the heavens.

Helios and Zeus sipped from chalices and sampled tiny pastries from a platter. They were accompanied by two women who could not have been more different in appearance. One of them had long, straight, ashy hair with luminous silver eyes and ivory skin. Her fitted gown gleamed as if moonshine were caressing her curvy figure. The second woman had skin as dark as Helios's. Her short, raven curls were a soft backdrop for her startlingly blue eyes. Her plain robes hung loosely around her body. Zeus's hand rested on the small of her back, whereas the woman that shone like a moonbeam had no male companion. I speculated that she was Selene, goddess of the moon, and the woman with Zeus was Metis, his betrothed.

A slave offered wine to me and Theo. I passed, but Theo accepted a cup. Zeus left Metis to greet us. He looked the same, physically—still a scrawny boy with unruly curly hair—yet he carried himself differently, with more confidence.

"Althea," he said. "I'm glad to see you're better."

"Same to you," I said.

Metis joined us, threading her fingers through the hair at the nape of Zeus's neck. She smelled divine, of sharp sea salt and sage. "Althea," she said. "I've been looking forward to this visit."

I was curious whether the Oceanid prophetess had foreseen this meeting, but asking felt like prying.

Helios wandered over to us. He wore thick gold liner around his eyes and was hung with more jewelry than when last we met. "Colonel Angelos," he said by way of greeting, "I hear you had some trouble with the First House's liege men."

"We're in your debt for taking us in," Theo replied.

"We're pleased to have you. I hope you enjoy the wine. It's from my storehouse. Many say my private collection is the finest in the world. Pardon my lack of introductions. You've both met Eos. Let me introduce you to our sister, Selene, and our cousin Metis."

Metis was still preoccupied with running her fingers through Zeus's hair, but Selene gave us her full, luminous attention. Her watchful stare, intensely direct, felt familiar, almost comforting.

"Selene doesn't speak much," Helios said. "She communicates by projecting her thoughts."

Selene smiled shyly at Theo and me. A voice as soft as a nighttime whisper filled my mind. *Pleasure to meet you.*

"Can she hear our thoughts too?" Theo asked.

"No," Eos replied. "You must answer her aloud."

"It's nice to meet you too," I said.

Helios clapped Zeus on the back. "What a delight it is to have us cousins together. At last, a family reunion. Had you arrived a day sooner, you would have met Aphrodite as well. She was just visiting."

I was suddenly stunned with a deeper realization of where I was. These were second-generation Titans, kin to the God of Gods.

"Aren't you all allies with Cronus?" I asked.

Helios's golden gaze flashed in an unexpected show of temper. "Not everyone agrees with how our uncle rules. Yes, it's been a time of peace and happiness for men, but his building up of an army and armada has ruffled some family members. Many of his nieces and nephews are unhappy with his decision not to elect a successor. Should tragedy befall him . . . well, it would be outright war among the Titans for who would take his place. We would like more stability. A named successor would ease many minds."

"Isn't Zeus the successor?" Theo asked.

"Unofficially. Until today, most Titans were unaware that he was alive. But the thunder and lightning he summoned were visible from all four pillars of the earth. I was flying my chariot high above at the time. It was difficult to miss."

Zeus paled, then finished his drink and signaled for a slave to serve him more.

"Such a strength is not possessed by any other Titan," Metis said quietly. "The entire family had gathered in Othrys for the procession that commences the First House Festival. Cronus questioned everyone and deduced that he had been betrayed."

"He canceled the rest of the festivities and sent everyone home," Eos added. "We are all under strict orders to turn Zeus in. The House of the individual who does so will receive special recognition. Every summer equinox, its name will be hailed alongside the Almighty's."

For a god who lived forever and already had riches beyond the imagination, such recognition and worship were more valuable than treasure.

"What about Rhea?" Theo asked. "Will he punish her?"

"Our aunt fled to the southern isles," Helios said, his tone wrought with worry. "Metis sent a warning to Rhea a few hours ago. She left the palace well before Zeus lit up the sky."

Selene turned her big, moonlit eyes on Helios.

"Yes, sister," he replied. "I know you haven't much more time." To the rest of us, he explained. "Selene cannot stay long. These are her busiest hours. Let us sit for our evening meal."

On cue, a slave appeared in the doorway. We followed her outside to the terrace, where a grand table had been set beneath the stars and quarter moon. I didn't understand how Selene was both here and there. With all these Titans around, I was tempted to ask, but then we were directed to our seats.

Theo sat to my left; to my right, Metis and Zeus. Helios, Selene, and Eos were across the table. Seeing the magnificent trio together, side by side, dazed me. It was like viewing the dawn, day, and night skies all at once.

"I've envisioned this moment many times," Metis said as the slaves set plates of wild boar and a colorful array of peculiar fruits in front of us. "Each of you is of great importance to the future of the world. My betrothed, of course, has his calling, as does his fierce guardian, Althea. Even the colonel plays a part." She turned her solemn gaze on Theo. "Your father was invited for this conversation, but he declined."

Theo stiffened.

Why would his father receive an invitation?

"Wait," Zeus said, his mouth full of meat. "Who is Theo's father?"

Metis glanced from Zeus to Theo. "You didn't tell him?" she asked.

Theo reached for his cup of wine. "It isn't something I discuss often."

"Yes, but now you're in the company of Titans," Metis said. "Your secret is safe with us."

"Why is your father's identity a secret?" I asked.

Theo avoided my stare. "Very few know I'm his son."

The three gods across from us listened disinterestedly while they dined. Apparently, everyone knew Theo's parentage except Zeus and me.

"Well?" I pressed. "Who is your father?"

"Pardon me," Metis replied, as though it hadn't occurred to her to finish telling us. "Theo's father is our cousin Prometheus."

I nearly choked on my spit as my gaze on Theo turned incredulous. "You're a—a—a *half Titan*?"

"Well, that explains why you're as tough as a bear," Zeus said, shoving another too-large piece of meat into his mouth.

Theo drank the rest of his wine and lifted his cup for more. A slave immediately refilled it. Theo was red around the neck and clearly uncomfortable, but I was not finished.

"Does Cronus know you're Prometheus's son?" I asked.

"Not that I'm aware of," Theo answered. "As far as I know, Prometheus doesn't even know. My mother never told him."

Metis reached across me to rest a hand on Theo's arm. "Your father would be proud of your accomplishments, Colonel Angelos."

"Angelos?" I said. "Your mother's surname?"

Still avoiding my gaze, Theo nodded.

Zeus's head snapped up, and a bright grin spread across his boyish face. "This makes us second cousins. Now I can call you Cousin Theo."

"Or not," Theo said.

I had never met another half Titan besides my baby sister. My mind jumped back to the memory of Theo dispatching four men without losing his breath. Was his strength half that of a Titan's or twice that of a regular man's? Could he drink nectar and eat ambrosia? I had a hundred more questions, but Helios set his elbows on the table, clasped his hands over his plate of food, and addressed the group.

"Prometheus's attendance would have been appreciated for his gift of forethought, but in many ways, his predictions would have been redundant. We here—my siblings and cousin Metis—believe the long-time prophecy that Cronus's time on the throne will come to an end. We volunteer to help facilitate this change, as much as we can, given that we have sworn oaths to uphold the God of Gods' throne and cannot break our vows without suffering great consequences."

"What prophecy?" I asked.

Metis pointed at my ring. "That string came from the oracles," she said. "They told you a child of Cronus would dethrone him. Such prophecy was predicted long ago."

She touched my ring with her fingertip. It began to glow, and she went perfectly still, hardly breathing. Then her open eyes clouded over with a milky film.

"Is she all right?" Theo asked.

"She's having a vision," Helios replied.

My ring glowed softly, the same color as Metis's wise eyes. In that vast, heavenly haze, huge stars shone. They began to shrink, accelerating as more and more of them sped away from me until I could see the whole of the universe from her perspective.

Metis blinked, and her eyes returned to normal. My ring went dim.

"He's watching you," she whispered.

She dropped my hand and looked down, mumbling to herself. I wasn't seeking her counsel, but I did want to know who was watching me, for I sensed she knew about the dark figure in the water, the Star Eater.

Metis drank her entire chalice of nectar, her hand shaking. "I've seen what must be done. Cronus must consume a magical draught that will weaken him. The draught comes from a rare violet found only on Crete. Zeus, do you remember my letter? Did you do what I asked?"

"Did I do what you asked?" he demanded lightheartedly. He shoved his hand in his pocket and removed the violet with red-rimmed petals that he had picked from Ida's garden.

Metis took it from him. "I will have the draught made by morning."

"Then what?" I asked.

"Then you, Althea Lambros, will poison Cronus."

Everyone's attention turned to me.

"Her?" Helios asked. "The . . . mortal?"

"I have foreseen the hand by which the Almighty is weakened, and it is hers."

No one spoke. I desperately wanted to know what Zeus and Theo thought, but neither contributed his opinion. I would do whatever necessary to release my sisters, but poisoning the God of Gods? That was a task better suited for a Titan.

"Are you certain? The oracles said . . ." I trailed off as Metis shook her head.

"This is your path," she insisted. "Yours, and your sisters'." The Oceanid's expression welcomed no argument. "For the concoction, I will need hair from all your heads," she said, indicating Theo, Zeus, and me. "You will all play a part. Your mutual allegiance will make the draught stronger."

She plucked a hair from Zeus's head, and he winced. Theo tugged a single strand of his own, and Metis insisted that I pass her three of my hairs. She laid them next to the violet, and her eyes briefly flashed milky white again.

"It has been set in motion," she declared.

"When will this happen?" Zeus asked.

"Tomorrow it begins."

"It is well, then," Helios said with a strained smile.

He may have had quarrels with my role in this plan, but I dared not ask him or the other gods how they felt about bestowing the responsibility of dethroning their ruler to a mortal woman.

Selene pushed her chair back from the table and stood. She bowed her head in farewell, and as she did, a voice filled my mind. *I will watch over your sisters, Althea. Rest well this night.*

This pledge from the goddess of the moon was a kindness I could never repay. I raised my cup and toasted her, just as Bronte always did. "To the moon. May she ever shine."

"To the moon," Zeus echoed cheerfully.

Selene strode into the garden, where a groom waited with a white-winged horse not unlike those that pulled Helios's chariot. A slave draped a shining hooded cloak over Selene's shoulders. She put the hood over her head and mounted the horse sidesaddle. She waved and snapped the reins, and the winged steed launched into the night. They flew out over the pond, then rose steeply into the sky, soaring straight at the moon until they blended into the silver crescent, becoming one with the heavens.

Her departure changed the tone at the supper table. Helios stated he was tired from a long day of travel and excused himself. Zeus began to yawn. He and Metis left the table, him to go to bed and her to concoct the draught. Eos lingered until I had finished eating, then asked if I would like a tour of the mansion. Theo had continued to drink excessively and ignore me, so I decided that the discussion I wanted to have with him about his Titan father could wait, and I accepted her invitation.

We left the table and strolled through a maze of long, torchlit corridors.

"Your arrival is a blessing," Eos said. "This is the most optimistic I've seen Helios in a long while. As the god of the sun, he sees everything, all the sorrows and pains of the world, day after day. It wears on him, and he has many opinions about how our uncle rules."

I had always thought Titans were selfish monsters; I had never considered that any of them would care about the welfare of mortals.

"How does Selene cope with her responsibilities?" I asked.

"She, too, sees much heartache. Mortals use the cover of night to hide many of their misdeeds, but she has a more forgiving nature. Helios can be as harsh as the sun. He cares deeply about what becomes of the world. Everything his light touches has value and worth. He would make a fair ruler, but the intensity of his daily obligation would never leave him proper time to devote to a throne." Eos stared up at the moon, at her sister. "Though I'm the youngest of us, my role is to ensure that both Selene and Helios fulfill the measure of their roles."

"You look after them."

"Just as you look after your older siblings, and now Zeus. You've taken him in as well."

I hadn't thought of him as my responsibility, but that would explain why the Titans' plot to dethrone Cronus left me uneasy. As Zeus's betrothed, Metis was genuinely invested in his becoming the next Almighty, but nothing was stopping Eos, Selene, or Helios—or any Titan, for that matter—from seeking to take his throne.

Eos paused before the door to my chamber. Our tour of the grounds had ended.

"I'm returning home, to my mansion," she said. "Before I go, I must warn you. Not everything you hear about Cronus is true. My uncle keeps counsel with Mnemosyne, the goddess of memory. When he doesn't want others to know what he's doing, he orders her to manipulate others' memories in his favor. My father, Hyperion, protested loudly when my uncle swallowed his firstborn child. He visited the Aeon Palace to try and reason with him, and when he came home, he couldn't remember having gone. Rhea herself refuses to be alone with Mnemosyne. Anyone who works in the palace, or who spends time with Cronus, could have had their recollections altered. Your mother figured out that her memory had been manipulated and went to Oceanus for help. His nourishing waters can restore some memories, but the person must first know their mind has been tampered with, which most never realize."

Changing people's memories was an unthinkable violation. What other truths might Cronus have ordered Mnemosyne to alter?

"Was Oceanus able to heal my mother?"

"In more than one way. He restored some of her memories, and he also helped her move refugees out of Thessaly by providing them safe passage across the sea."

My heart swelled. My mother *had* allied with a Titan, with the one god who had stood up to Cronus. "Did she say which of her memories Cronus had changed?"

"She never said, though I'm certain Oceanus could tell you."

I was more and more intrigued to meet the god of the sea, but seeking him out would have to wait until after my sisters were safe. "Eos, have you had your memory tampered with?"

"That's a tricky question, isn't it?" she replied, her rosy lips turning downward. "For if my memory had been changed, I would likely not remember."

I wrapped my arms around myself to ward off an inner chill. How many truths did I believe that were actually lies planted by the God of Gods to deceive the world?

"You should rest," Eos said. "With the dawn comes new beginnings and new challenges."

Between the revelation of Theo's heritage, the vague magical draught plan, and the possibility that everything my mother had told me about Cronus might have been based on manipulated memories, I had plenty to worry about already. Despite their hospitality, I couldn't quite bring myself to trust these Titans, particularly in regard to the Boy God. My only reassurance was that they could not kill their cousin Zeus, but the discussion of the magical draught made it evident that other tactics could be employed to weaken a Titan. Did these Titans truly wish for the God of Gods to fall and the Boy God to rise? Or was it all a ruse?

Until I knew, I couldn't involve Zeus or Theo any more than I already had. Whatever fate had planned for me, I would go forward alone.

I bid good night to the goddess of the dawn, then went into my bedchamber and sat in the dark until I could no longer stand the torment of my own restless thoughts, and sleep claimed me.

21

A gentle lullaby filled my ears. I stood at the edge of the ravine in the forest, the same one I had fallen into on Crete, only, this time, the gap was filled with water and no rope was stretched across it. The lullaby, the one my mother would sing to me each night, stopped, and a voice called out from the other side.

"Althea."

Mother stood across the ravine. Her figure was partly obscured by the night, but from what I could see of her in the starlight, she was as tall and strong as I remembered.

"My shooting star, you must be tired. Swim across and come rest with me awhile. It's time for sleep."

I dipped a finger in the still, dark water. The frigid temperature would be uncomfortable to swim in, but I hadn't seen my mother in so, so long . . .

The sound of an infant's crying came from across the way. Mother held the bundled baby snugly in her arms. "Althea, your little sister is waiting for you to meet her. I gave her a name. Swim across, and I'll tell it to you."

I could not refuse. I disrobed to my underclothes and slipped into the deep, frigid water. My mother began to sing again as she rocked the babe. I started across the ravine, swimming quickly to warm my muscles.

Something in the water brushed past my leg. I halted and spun in a circle, searching for a sign of what it was. Nothing was there, so I swam harder for the other side, following the sound of my mother's singing. About halfway across, a cold hand wrapped around my ankle. I tried kicking free, but it gripped with bruising force and yanked me under, dragging me down, down, down into the abyss.

Suddenly, I was standing on a beach before a mountain range. Grim and dark, the gray sky roiled with thunderclouds. The side of the closest mountain was pocked with cells, cages that held Cyclopes and monstrous beasts with a thousand hands. In the highest prison, near the pinnacle of the mountain, two burning eyes stared out at me.

Release us, daughter.

I recognized Uranus by his wings. He was bigger now than the shadow I had seen in the sea and pond, but it was him all the same. The Star Eater.

Release us, and we shall conquer Cronus.

Uranus had good cause to destroy the Almighty, but he was trapped in Tartarus, and a mortal couldn't set foot there without perishing.

We are the sky. The sun, moon, and stars are ours. Release us, and command the stars at my side. Touch them, and they will be your weapons to wield.

The hand let go of my ankle. As I kicked toward the surface, my head rang with Uranus's thunderous voice.

I will wait, daughter. I will wait for you to rise . . .

I broke the surface, gasping.

My mother stood on the other side of the ravine, the crying baby in her arms. Her sad gaze peered straight into my soul.

"You have to go, Althea. Your sisters need you."

"No, Mama. I'm coming. Wait for me."

She stepped away from the water's edge and sank into the night, humming. I swam to the embankment and pulled myself out of the water. Pushing to my feet, I sprinted after her. The singing stopped, but the baby's cries surrounded me. Mama and the babe were nowhere in sight. The ache in my chest expanded into a cold gloom of grief. I was lost in the quiet woodland, alone.

"Please don't leave again, Mama. I'll do what I said. I'll look after my sisters."

The babe wailed on.

I woke with tears streaming down my face. Theo sat beside me, perched at the edge of my bed, singing. An all-encompassing calm rested upon my mind, soothing away my cares. My muscles relaxed and my tears dried up. As I started to fall back to sleep, a thought struck me.

"Your voice. It's your Titan strength. I felt its influence before when you sang to me on the boat, and again the first night on the isle when you hummed to me in the tent."

"Shh," Theo said, stroking my hair. "Go back to sleep. You'll have no more nightmares tonight."

I cozied into the balm of his touch. This would be the final night for a while, if not for good, that I could soak in his nearness.

Theo sang again, his melodic voice shushing the turmoil in my heart. My last thought before I fell asleep was how odd it was that he had picked the same lullaby my mother always sang, as though he had also dwelled in my dreams.

I woke alone. Beside me on the bed lay a small green vial—the magical draught with which I would poison Cronus?

I slipped the vial into my pocket and went to find Metis. All of her mystical assurances that I, of all people, would face the Almighty and weaken him seemed preposterous in the light of day. Part of me hoped that impossible task would fall to someone else. I only had two days left to release my sisters before the Erinyes seized me.

The corridors were vacant. No footsteps or voices, not a slave to be seen coming or going. Helios and Eos would be gone to fulfill their duties, and perhaps Selene had her own mansion where she rested during the day, but where was Metis and everyone else?

I meandered up and down corridors and peeked in open doorways. Every room I paused to investigate was unoccupied. Backtracking, I went to the receiving hall where we had congregated the night before. No one was there either, and I still hadn't seen a single slave in the mansion or garden. On the terrace, I found the dining table was set for breakfast. One of the chairs had been knocked to the ground on its side, and all of the cups were filled with wine.

"Theo?" I called. "Zeus? Is anyone here?"

My mind registered the full dishes of now-cold porridge and honey cakes, and the fallen chair, and I began to worry. Zeus would never leave a meal untouched.

Noises came from the garden, footsteps and sounds of men grunting. I glimpsed a familiar sight through the foliage—a soldier's uniform.

Swiping a table knife, I slipped behind a hedge and stayed low. A group of soldiers jogged past. They were leaving the mansion and headed to the coastline. One of the gardeners or slaves had left a shovel nearby. I grabbed it and sneaked down a narrow path to the cliffs.

Helios's private dock was far below in a sheltered cove. There, only one ship was moored—a giant trireme flying the blue-and-white alpha and omega of the First House. The gleaming vessel was the Almighty's flagship, the pride and joy of his vast armada.

I sank low to the ground and watched as sailors loaded countless barrels of wine onto the trireme. They were pillaging Helios's storehouse. I scanned the narrow shoreline for any familiar faces, and my breath caught. The liege men had come not only for spirits.

In plain sight of the working sailors, and guarded by a pair of soldiers, Zeus was tied to a flagpole beside the docks by a thick rope around his middle. His head was drooped so his chin rested against his chest, and his arms and legs sagged. I couldn't see Theo or Metis. I hoped that meant they were in hiding or had escaped. The soldiers had been at the mansion, though, as well as in the storehouse. Where else would Theo and Metis be?

Once I was confident that no additional guards were near Zeus, and the rest of the soldiers and sailors were preoccupied, I tucked the knife and shovel into the sash around my waist and started down the rock face. Holding on to the most secure ridges, I descended to a sheltered position near the flagpole, out of view from the docks.

By the time my feet touched the beach, my arms and legs shook from exertion. The pair of guards near Zeus stood opposite each other, their attention on the sailors who were almost finished loading the wine barrels onto the trireme.

I crept up behind the closest one and smashed the shovel over his head, knocking him out. The second guard turned at the sound. I jabbed him in the gut with the end of the shaft, then smacked him in the face with the broad side of the shovel. With both guards disabled, I tossed the shovel aside and ran to Zeus.

"Wake up," I whispered hoarsely, cutting at his bindings with the dull table knife.

He slumped forward against the rope, his eyes half-closed, his head lolling. Though he appeared awake, he was far from lucid. After more vigorous sawing, the rope finally dropped to his feet, and he fell forward onto his knees.

"Ow," he said, somewhat belatedly.

I slung his arm over my shoulders and tried lifting him. He might have been on the thin side for someone of his height, but he was still heavy as deadweight.

"Come on, Zeus," I said, grunting. "You have to help me."

"Althea?" he slurred. "I cannot feel my legs."

"Did they drug you?"

"The last thing I remember is drinking wine at breakfast." He tried rising and stumbled. I toppled over with him onto the sand, landing on his chest. His lips curved lazily. "Finally, I have you where I want you."

"This is no time to regale me with stories of your virility, Zeus."

He groaned, a genuine show of discomfort, as I tried lifting him again. At last, he got his feet beneath him, and we distributed his weight between us.

From where they had been hiding in the rock pilings, a dozen soldiers stepped into the open and obstructed our escape routes. Even the ledges above were guarded by archers. Decimus stepped forward, and a wintry frost coated my insides. I rejected the inner tug to go to him, and pain flared from the tag at the back of my neck.

"Althea," he said, his tone like a disapproving father's. "I've been waiting for you."

Zeus rolled his slumped head back. "Who's this bastard?"

I couldn't support his weight any longer. Lowering him to the ground, I whispered, "Stay down." Then louder: "Release him, Decimus. It's me you want."

The general wore an amused smirk. "I don't have to choose. I have you both."

"You never had me." Every muscle in my body, down to the finest sinew, quivered in protest as I raised the table knife to my throat.

Decimus's expression hardened, even as he scoffed. "You bluff."

"You don't know what I'm capable of." I drew the blade closer and pricked my skin. The blood was immediate, a warm trickle. My hand shook harder. I could have passed out from wrestling the influence of the curse, but I held firm.

Decimus aimed his sword at me, a poor move considering I already held a blade to my throat. "Althea, quit with this insanity! The Almighty has requested your presence. I'm to bring you to the Aeon Palace."

"Let Zeus go, and I'll come with you." The icy punishment of disobedience began to numb my resolve. Gooseflesh covered me. I couldn't resist the curse much longer.

Decimus chuckled at my trembling. "You'll come, kitten, because I'm telling you to."

Theo appeared above, descending the main pathway to the docks. He walked about freely and wore his colonel's uniform. He would not look at me. Despite the sword in Theo's hand, his arrival elicited no response from the general and his men.

"Colonel Angelos, you were right," Decimus said. "We left Zeus out in the open, and Althea came right to him."

I lowered the knife. "Theo?" I whispered.

He didn't respond or react, not even to cast the briefest of glances in my direction. "The storehouse has been emptied, sir."

"Theo," I said more sharply. "You're Zeus's mentor. You cannot do this."

"He can and did," Decimus replied.

I aimed the knife at Theo, my shock wearing off. "How utterly stupid I am," I breathed. "I knew better than to trust a man, particularly an officer in the Almighty's military."

"I had no choice," Theo said, his tone defensive. "The Erinyes were hunting me too. They came to my bedchamber last night and assigned me an atoning task. After I deliver you and Zeus to the Almighty, I will be released from my oath to the throne, and my mother and I will be free."

"I don't give a damn what they promised you."

"What would you do for your sisters?" Theo retorted. "For your soul?"

I refused to answer that. "I wish you were dead," I snarled.

Theo recoiled, his first genuine sign of remorse.

"Prepare to disembark!" Decimus called.

A soldier disarmed me, but the vial of magical draught was still tucked away in my pocket. Two men seized Zeus and dragged him up to standing. The Boy God was steadier on his feet than before, whatever drug they had put in his breakfast wine wearing off. I was so incensed by Theo's treachery, Zeus and I had been shoved halfway down the dock before I realized we may have been unarmed but we were far from defenseless.

"Zeus," I said. "I think I see a storm coming."

He frowned at the clear blue sky. "A storm . . . ? Oh."

The Boy God tossed one guard into the sea and threw the other into the band of soldiers behind us, knocking Theo on top of Decimus. His excessive strength wasn't a spectacular show of thunder and lightning, but it was effective. I kneed my guard in the groin, then pushed him into the water below.

On the far side of the dock where Zeus stood, Metis steered a smaller watercraft closer, directing the sail, and beckoned for him. Zeus leaped into the water and pulled himself aboard with her.

I stepped to the ledge to jump into the sea, but Decimus locked his arms around me and dragged me back. I kicked and thrashed, elbowing him in his crooked nose. Undaunted, he dragged me farther and threw me onto the deck. My bad ankle turned and popped, sending pain up my leg.

"Get the Boy God!" Decimus bellowed.

Soldiers rushed to the side of the dock just in time to watch a white-capped wave pick up Metis's boat and sweep it out to sea. The Oceanid and the Boy God quickly sped out of range of the archers, propelled by a great, unseen power.

Decimus reeled on Theo. "You should have anticipated this, Colonel."

"Metis is a prophetess, sir. I couldn't have known—"

"You failed to deliver Zeus. I've no more need for you." The general gestured at the soldier nearest Theo and said, "Dispatch him."

Theo rammed the soldier in the gut with the hilt of his sword, then dived off the dock into the water. Archers unleashed arrows after him and waited for his body to float to the top, but he did not resurface.

"Damn him," Decimus growled. "Keep looking!"

I knew they would not find Theo. I was slightly annoyed with myself for caring, but it was satisfying to see Decimus lose.

"Wipe that smile off your face, kitten." Decimus hauled me up and crushed me against his stinky body. "I've thought about this for a long time."

"Throw yourself to the crows."

"Be kind," he warned, his rough hands groping my breasts and pinching my nipples. I suppressed the pain, refusing him any reaction. He nuzzled his sweaty face against my cheek and ear. "Alas, I can go no further until after you meet with the Almighty."

Decimus slapped me hard on the bottom, then passed me off to another soldier while he finished overseeing the crew's preparations to disembark.

My guard led me limping across the gangplank and chained me in plain view of the entire deck, securing me to the mainmast. Sailors came aboard, countless rowers taking their places at the oars, and then, at the direction of the helmsman, the piper called out the rowers' rhythm. Their efforts drove the massive vessel into the briny winds, and we navigated out to sea, sailing closer and closer to the God of Gods seated in his throne atop the world.

22

Our return to Othrys cost me dearly. The trireme moved swiftly, but it was still a day's voyage from the Midnight Mansion to port, and then an additional two hours' trek up the mountain to the city. Less than a day remained until the Erinyes came for me.

The city was cheerless compared with years past. Though the procession of the Titans had been canceled, the Almighty must have permitted the people to continue some of the more subdued practices in his name. Weathered decorations for the First House Festival were everywhere. Strings of flowers hung across alleyways in zigzag patterns, their blossoms tattered by the wind. Alpha and omega flags draped out of windows, and sickles leaned against front doors, a token of allegiance to Cronus.

During the festival, a beggar could knock on any door and be invited in to break the traditional bounty bread with the hosts. At night, families held symposiums, dinner parties that began with a bout of drinking and ended with a large meal. Guests would enjoy entertainment provided by traveling performers, usually slaves, who danced and played instruments. Cleora's favorite were those who performed acrobatic stunts over a hoop rimmed with knives. People usually dressed in traditional ivory woven robes, like the one Cronus wore when castrating his father, but with the theater performances and symposiums canceled, the streets were devoid of merriment.

The wagon halted outside the palace gates, and a sack was placed over my head before we continued. Again, we stopped, and a guard hauled me out. I swayed on my feet, dizzy and weak from hunger. Decimus had refused to feed me anything after I retched up the salted fish he gave me yesterday on our voyage. I hobbled between two soldiers up several stairs. At the top, the flooring was more slippery, and our footsteps echoed around us. A door creaked open, and the sack was yanked off my head, revealing a grand bedchamber.

"You're not here as an honor maiden," Decimus said. "You're a guest. Do not embarrass me. Eat and rest. You must look your best for His Excellency."

Decimus pressed his lips to the side of my head in a slimy kiss, then took his leave.

Dirty and tired from my travels, I was out of place in the elegant chamber. From the furniture to the rugs to the draperies, the room was clean and exquisite. A balcony provided a stunning view of the well-tended gardens in the late-day sun.

A large black vulture landed on the terrace and stared in at me. The menacing bird hopped closer. I grabbed a pillow off the bed and prepared to toss it, but the vulture took off and flew out of sight.

I set down the pillow and feasted. After devouring cheese, olives, grapes, and cured meat—all of my favorite foods had been set out on the sideboard—along with a chalice of watered-down wine, I was pleasantly full and exhausted. I lay down on the bed and covered my face with a pillow to shut out the light.

I faintly heard a door open, then someone jumped on top of me.

"Althea!" Bronte threw the pillow off my face. "I was so worried about you."

"Me? I was worried about *you*." I hugged her so hard she made a funny little strangling sound, so I stopped. "Bronte, where did you come from? How did you get here?"

"I arrived from Crete last night. The slave ship brought me, along with a couple dozen women from the tribe. The warriors mutinied when we arrived at port. Euboea led the crusade, but she couldn't get to me since I wasn't in the cargo hold where they were. I was brought here, and the soldiers put me in a chamber off the solarium. Have you seen Cleora?"

"No, have you?"

The corners of Bronte's mouth slid downward. "No. Where are Zeus and Theo?"

"I don't know. We went to Helios's palace and met with Metis, Zeus's betrothed, and some of Zeus's cousins. Helios, Eos, and Selene all plotted with us about Zeus's overthrow of Cronus, but this morning, Decimus arrived. Theo arranged to exchange Zeus for his mother's freedom. Zeus got away with Metis, and Theo escaped on his own. Decimus caught me and brought me here."

Bronte's frown deepened, and she touched my arm consolingly. "I can scarcely believe Theo betrayed you."

"I should have known better than to trust a soldier." I shrugged from her touch, too raw to accept her comfort or to tell her that Theo was a son of Prometheus. Theo's parentage seemed irrelevant now anyway. I doubted we would meet him again. "Have you seen anyone since you've arrived?"

"Just my guards and the Almighty's councilor, Mnemosyne."

My pulse gathered speed. "Did she tell you anything to make you feel strange?"

"She asked questions about us, such as what we like to eat and how we prefer to spend our time. I told her you dance, and I sing, and other benign things."

I hugged the pillow against my chest, holding it over my thudding heart. "Eos, the goddess of the dawn, told me that Mnemosyne can alter memories. Think hard, Bronte. Is there anything she might have made you forget?"

Bronte pondered for a long moment before answering. "I honestly don't think so. Like I said, everything she asked was about our interests. I doubt she would alter that."

I wasn't as certain, but she seemed her normal self.

Bronte sat with her legs crossed and leaned in, her voice dropping to a whisper. "I've been monitoring the guards in the palace. As Prometheus says, 'Observation is the window to solution.'" She rambled off the number of soldiers she had seen since her arrival—forty-nine—and explained that the guards changed positions every thirty minutes, rotating in new men with fresh eyes and ears and full bellies twice an hour. She led me onto the balcony to show me their movements. We observed two shift changes transpire, and through them, the guards maintained full security around every doorway, gate, and garden pathway. Bronte's observations were succinct and accurate, yet they mostly served to verify what I already knew. No prisoner escaped the God of Gods.

I slipped my hand into my pocket, wary of telling Bronte of the magical draught, in case spies were listening. Deciding it was not worth the risk, I kept it tucked away.

A knock came at the door. Decimus entered, flanked by his brother, Brigadier Orrin—or who I preferred to call Ratface—and three low-ranking soldiers. The general tossed us our velos.

"Put those on," he said.

Bronte donned her snake mask, and I, my winged mask.

"Let's go," Decimus said. "The Almighty is ready to see you."

The rich foods I ate ground in my uneasy stomach. If only I felt ready to see him.

We ascended a tower to the great hall. I lost count of the stairs we climbed, though my bad ankle felt every single one. Every once in a while, an arrowslit provided a glimpse of the outside world—the setting sun or golden-trimmed clouds. Otherwise, I saw nothing but the smooth walls and shiny floors of the tower.

We emerged from the stairwell into a glossy foyer with lofty double doors on which giant knockers hung so high up they seemed frivolous, for no man could reach them. Then again, they were probably ideal for a Titan.

As we approached the doors, they opened of their own accord.

Lyre music carried out, a gentle composition that resembled birdsong. Soldiers stepped aside at the threshold to let Bronte and me enter.

The great hall, constructed of gleaming marble and cool stone, appeared the same as in the vision that the oracles had shown me. Dozens of massive columns held up a towering rotunda that opened onto expansive balconies on three sides. The rectangular room stretched on and on. Our view of the sun setting over Thessaly was partially obscured by gilded clouds.

Another hundred steps or more, and the music stopped.

Cleora strode in from one of the balconies, a silver lyre in hand. "They told me you had arrived," she said.

We hurried to her, and she embraced us lightly. She smelled not quite herself, an odd combination of juniper berries and autumn frost. Her long, rich red hair had been curled—a style she had never worn before—and she was dressed in a yellow chiton, her least flattering color. The thin gold crown upon her head brought me the most confusion.

"What's all this?" Bronte asked. "You look ridiculous."

Cleora overlooked the insult and took each of us by the hand. "I have so much to tell you," she said. "You may remove your velos. You don't need them here."

"I'll leave mine on," I replied. My contrariness was not to vex her. I merely wanted the familiarity of wearing my mother's mask. Bronte left her velo on as well.

"Let them in, Cleora."

The male voice was not loud, yet it filled the hall. I could not see anyone, though, let alone anyone who might have suited this resonant voice.

"Come," Cleora said, beaming.

Nothing struck me as more out of place than her smile.

Bronte and I exchanged side glances as we followed her. Decimus and Ratface trailed behind us, close enough for their presence not to be forgotten. More than halfway across the length of the hall, the other side of the room finally became visible.

There, the God of Gods occupied one of six thrones, three empty on one side and two on the other. The black vulture that had visited my terrace was perched on a mount behind him. The bird stand was crafted from a dead hamadryad, the spirit's face etched into its trunk. In size, the Almighty appeared average in most ways. He was not fifty feet tall like I had been led to believe, but of medium build and height. His trim figure was well proportioned, and as with all gods, he had a handsomeness that could not be denied. I had expected someone of extraordinary magnitude, splendor, and allure, yet his physique was unassuming.

But the rest of Cronus was far from ordinary.

White flames shone from his hair, and his inky eyes sparkled with stars. His skin glowed a comely bronze, and his perfectly red lips were waxy. I became the focal point of his intense, penetrating gaze. Wisdom and intellect flickered across his face as he appraised me.

"Cleora," he said, still focused on me. "Won't you introduce us?"

"Your Excellency. These are my younger sisters, Bronte and Althea."

"Althea," Cronus mused to himself. "What a unique name."

"Our mother chose it." I couldn't stop myself. "You might remember Stavra Lambros?"

"Of course. Cleora and I are pleased to have you in our home. Please forgive all the steps you had to take to get here. We thought you might relish the view."

"It's . . . notable," Bronte admitted, a tad begrudgingly. She sounded as disconcerted as I was.

"Come see the view from the balcony," Cleora suggested.

She led Bronte outside while I remained with the Almighty. The general stationed himself away from the thrones while the brigadier monitored my sisters on the terrace.

"That's an interesting ring you're wearing, Althea," Cronus remarked. "May I see it?"

"No," I replied flatly. "What did you do to Cleora?"

"*Do* to her?" Cronus questioned. "She's perfectly at home in the palace, and she's free to leave at any time."

"She's your prisoner. Her fear of what you did to our mother holds her captive."

"What I did to your mother," Cronus said, repeating my statement with naked opposition. "Stavra Lambros was content here until she grew too big in her pregnancy for comfort, and then I sent her back to you and your sisters."

I nearly flew at him for daring to suggest that our mother would have chosen his company over ours, but pure disgust held me back. "She hated you, just as I hate you."

"Althea," Cleora scolded, returning just in time to hear my vitriol. "You're speaking to the God of Gods."

"A god you have always detested," I rejoined. "What has he done to you, Cleora? He dressed you up like you're a doll."

"Has he made you one of his honor maidens?" Bronte asked.

"No! He would never." Cleora looked to Cronus. "Shall we tell them?"

"Yes, it's time. Let's ease their concerns."

"Tell us," Bronte said, crossing her arms over her chest. I admired her tenacity. Every time Cronus spoke, my stomach spun around like a whirlpool.

He rose from his throne. Standing, he was taller than any of us. He sauntered forward with the utter certainty of his supreme station, reminding me of Zeus's newfound poise.

"As I told Cleora, you three sisters are of noble birthright." Cronus bowed his head as though we were the gods and said reverently, "You are not mortal women. You are goddesses . . . My daughters."

A laugh burst out of me. The absurdity of his claim didn't merit another response.

Cronus rested a solemn hand on my shoulder. "You've always known you were different. The shape of your soul is very familiar to me." As he touched me, my shoulder blades began to burn, and my shadow, cast across the floor in the low-setting sun, sprouted wings. I looked over my shoulder and saw nothing, but a vast power flapped like a caged bird inside me, thrashing to escape.

Cronus moved on to Bronte, touching her shoulder next. "You've always felt steadier when connected with the earth. Your soul grounds you." Her own shadow shrunk and transformed into the shape of a small winged dragon.

She twisted from his grasp. "What trick is this?"

"No trick. You *are* my daughters. Goddesses and Titanesses."

General Decimus snapped straight, his posture rigid. If this was true, which I very much doubted, he had tagged a daughter of the Almighty.

"You devoured your children," Bronte countered.

"A necessary rumor, which I fabricated. Show them, Cleora."

Cleora removed her sandal to show us the mark on the bottom of her heel. "This tiny scar is from Father pricking our feet with the adamant sickle as infants. The power of the adamant divested us of our godly strength so that he could hide us from the Titans seeking his throne."

"Many in our family wish to be my successor," Cronus explained. "The younger Titans are the greatest trouble. Helios, Selene, and Eos have been plotting against me for decades."

My head whirled with countless doubts, yet Cleora believed this folly. I needed to understand what he'd told her so that I could reverse his brainwashing.

"Divested," I said. "So our godly strength is . . . ?"

"Locked away for safekeeping." Cronus returned to his throne and stroked the breast of his black vulture. "I did you a charity, sending you into the world as mortals. It's a simpler, kinder life."

"A charity?" I retorted. "Women in the world you built are so starved for kindness that they will accept it from a monster."

"Your mother used to say the same," Cronus drawled.

"Stavra Lambros taught us well," I shot back.

"I speak of your true mother," he said. "Stavra raised you three, but she did not birth you."

Again, my tongue buckled under a landslide of questions and doubts.

"Those lioness trinkets you wear?" he went on, indicating my arm cuff and Bronte's necklace. "Symbols of my consort, Rhea. She wanted you to have something of hers when she handed you over to be raised by mortals."

Bronte gripped her necklace in both hands. "Our mother is Stavra Lambros."

"Mnemosyne altered Stavra's memory so that she would believe, with her deepest conviction, that she had birthed the three of you. In truth, she fostered you as infants." Cronus smiled sweetly at Cleora. "My dearest daughter, who is your mother?"

"Rhea," she replied without pause.

"And who is Stavra Lambros?" he prompted.

Cleora appeared conflicted for just a moment, then replied, "She's the servant who fostered us."

"That's enough," I said. "I want to go back to my chamber."

"As do I," Bronte snapped.

Cleora put on another forced smile. "You must be tired. You've both traveled far to get here."

"Come with us, Cleora," Bronte said.

Cronus set his elbows on the armrests of his throne and pressed his fingertips together. "Cleora promised to play for me a little longer. Didn't you, daughter?"

Cleora nodded demurely. "Yes, Father."

I could not fathom what I was seeing. After everything Bronte and I had gone through to get here, Cleora was choosing him over us.

"Cleora, how are you over your fear of him?" I asked. "You nearly burned your face with chastity crosses to avoid his attention."

She shook her head sadly as though she wished I could understand. "I was wrong about him, Althea. Father is generous and kind. He promised that I would never have to marry. I have a future in the palace, a real life that doesn't include running a kitchen or swearing allegiance to Gaea, an absentee goddess."

"Is this true?" Bronte asked the Almighty.

"Cleora shall remain a virgin goddess, forever pure and unspoiled," he answered.

"Nothing could ever spoil her," I retorted. "She's perfect no matter what she does or doesn't do with a man. And since when have you thought so little of Gaea, Cleora?"

"Father has been good to me," she answered, her voice small.

"Then why does he keep you from us?" Bronte extended a pleading hand toward her. "You've missed us. I know you have."

I saw it then, Cleora's glimmer of uncertainty. She was inside there somewhere, buried beneath the costume and the timid voice and the fake smile.

The black vulture squawked and ruffled its feathers.

"You're upsetting Sophus with all this talk of leaving, Cleora." Cronus pet the bird's head. "You know how he adores you."

Cleora went to the vulture and began stroking its head.

A smug smile peeled back Cronus's lips, revealing his sharp teeth. "General, return my daughters to their chambers. We'll finish this discussion after they've had time to think about how much better their lives will be once they accept their heritage."

Bronte and I started to leave slowly, then accelerated our pace to get away from him. We were still within earshot when Cleora began to play her lyre again.

Bronte whispered so as not to be heard over the music. "You know what you told me about Mnemosyne? I think she might have altered Cleora's memory."

I loathed to think that was true, yet it was the only possibility I could accept. I did not know who that woman was, but she was not our sister.

23

My request to see Bronte was ignored three times. After leaving the great hall, we were returned to our respective bedchambers with no indication when we would see each other again. I needed to talk to her about Cleora and how we could find a way out of here.

I called through the door to the guard, asking yet again to see Bronte. On a whim, I asserted my supremacy as a Titaness and goddess, which felt like complete nonsense, but this soldier was intimidated enough to seek out a real answer to my petition, rather than ignore it. He returned after gaining approval from his superior—Decimus, no doubt—and escorted me down a grand double stairway to the solarium on the main floor.

Pausing at the doorway, I waited for my eyes to adjust to the dark. With little moonlight shining through the high, open ceilings, I could not see anyone inside, but I could hear my sister singing softly.

"Bronte?" I called.

"Over here."

The air smelled heavily of musky flowers, spicy herbs, sweet almond trees, and freshly tilled earth—all scents I associated with my garden-loving sister.

I rounded the corner of a copse of lemon trees to a lantern-lit area, and pulled up short. Bronte was kneeling on the ground, tending to a garden bed bursting with white and pink peonies. Beside her, also on his knees, with his hands in the dirt, was Cronus.

Bronte grinned. "Althea, come smell these peonies. They're divine. Tell her, Father."

"That they are," Cronus said.

My insides ran cold. "Bronte, what are you doing?"

"I joined Father and Mnemosyne for supper. They served all my favorite foods and wines and desserts. Then he suggested we come here. He knows how much I adore working in the garden."

"You have a tremendous gift," Cronus said. "And she can sing!"

Bronte blushed—she *blushed*—and went back to digging. I had never, in my entire life, seen her blush for a man. Any man.

Something inside me snapped in two. I stomped over to Cronus and loomed. "What did you do to her?"

"Do to me?" Bronte interjected. "Father has been good to me. He let me debate philosophy with him at supper. He's going to arrange for me to meet Prometheus."

"Bronte, he's beguiling you."

"Althea," Cronus said, "I don't understand your continual ire. I had a pleasant feast with Bronte, and now we're enjoying the garden together. Don't be sour."

"She despises you," I snapped.

"Althea," Bronte admonished. "Must you be so mean?"

I grabbed her arm and pulled. "Get up. I'm taking you back to your chamber."

"I'm not done here." She jerked from my grip. "Why are you always telling everyone else what to do?"

"Pardon me?" I asked, aghast. "I do nothing of the sort. Mnemosyne has tampered with your memories, Bronte. I don't know how she does it, but this isn't us."

"Because I disagree with you?" She pushed to her feet. "My apologies, Father. I'm no longer enjoying the solarium. I'm going to bed now."

He rose beside her and ran a gentle hand down her arm, petting her as he had the vulture. "Sleep well, dearest."

And just like that, Bronte stormed out. No apology. Not even a glance back to check that her little sister would be all right, alone, with the Almighty.

"You didn't need to spoil our good time, Althea." Cronus carefully brushed the dirt off his hands. "Bronte was enjoying herself."

The Almighty was not what I had anticipated. I had imagined a monster that could not keep his hands off of women, but he did not look upon my sisters or me with desire. In fact, he seemed to look at us with joy.

"You judge me, Althea," Cronus said.

"Absolutely."

He chuckled. "You look so much like your mother. I've seen that glare from Rhea countless times."

"My mother is Stavra Lambros."

"Stavra was a loyal servant, but she isn't your mother." Cronus waved at two chairs set in a small alcove between cherry trees. I ignored his invitation to sit, but he took a chair himself, crossed his legs, and leaned back, relaxed and self-assured. I wondered if he sat in every chair as though it were a throne. "Rhea often berates me for my treatment of our children. She did not trust that I had your best intentions in mind. I suppose I was so preoccupied with protecting you from the Titans I did not think to consider that life with mankind could also wreak havoc on you. Men's appetites are insatiable."

"You're responsible for them. You're their ruler."

"I am their god, and an imperfect one at that, but mankind is notorious for disobeying and disregarding its deities."

I fell silent, unwilling to offer my opinion. He did not deserve to know my thoughts.

"As ruler of the First House, my position offers me a rare perspective on others," he said. "I can discern the shape of one's soul. Would you like to know yours?"

I almost said no, just to spite him, but I was intrigued.

Cronus sat forward and whispered. "The shape of your soul is one I have never seen before."

He was baiting me, but I would not ask.

"Your soul resembles a winged lion," he said. "Lions are known for their ferocity and majesty. They are the rulers of the animal kingdom, respected for their power, aggression, and might. Your wings are also meaningful. They demonstrate a desire for independence and invincibility. All impressive attributes."

His flattery may have worked on Cleora and Bronte, but he was wasting his time with me. "What did my mother, *Stavra Lambros*, say to you that vexed you? I was told by witnesses that she spoke out of turn in your throne room."

Cronus's demeanor shifted toward sorrowful. "My brother Oceanus had put lies into her head."

"You mean he restored her memories." I was almost afraid to ask my next question, but I couldn't stop myself. "When my mother learned that we weren't her daughters, that you had manipulated her memory, what did she do?"

Cronus rested his chin in his hand, his elbow on the armrest. "She threatened to expose your identities unless I abdicated my throne to Oceanus. When the soldiers came for Stavra that night at the temple, she had planned to tell you and your sisters who you were. I couldn't let that happen."

"So you brought her here and forced yourself upon her."

Cronus shook his head adamantly. "No, I removed those harmful thoughts from her head. Unfortunately, manipulating a memory is a finicky process. Once is harmless. Twice can be tricky. Three times . . . the results can be unfavorable."

"You ruined her," I accused, "and now you're doing the same to my sisters."

"They're happier and more content here with me."

I backed toward the door. "We were going to start over somewhere else, far away from you."

"Happy memories take root in the mind," he said. "They are the strongest and most difficult to replace. If Cleora and Bronte had truly been content with their old lives, they wouldn't have forgotten them so quickly."

My voice shook with rage. "You're a monster."

"I'm your father, and I know what's best for you." Cronus stood and strode over to me. Up close, his penetrating stare was almost immobilizing. "That ring on your hand. Where did you get it?"

"It was a gift from the oracles."

"It is an emblem of my mother. The oracles serve her." He snatched my hand and ripped the ring off. "Nothing of Gaea's is welcome in my house."

Gaea was the cosmic power behind my string ring? I thought back over every time the ring's timely glow had influenced me, reassured me. Had Gaea been guiding me all along?

Cronus crushed the ring in his fist. "Enjoy these final hours with your memories, Althea. Mnemosyne's strength is immense, but she's limited to one session per day. Tomorrow she will visit you. Do not resist. It's much less damaging that way."

My guard clasped me by the arm and tugged. I stumbled after him up the stairs and to my chamber. The shutting and locking of the door snapped me out of my horror. I pounded my fists against it until my knuckles were bruised, then sank to the floor and wept.

The knock came right after the slaves tried to clear away my untouched breakfast plate and wine cup. I had taken the whole night to devise my plan. Before I answered the door, I checked that everything was in place.

Squaring my shoulders, I opened the door.

Little arms shot out and grabbed my waist. Cleora and Bronte stood there with a girl who was no older than seven. The girl hugged me tightly with her cheek pressed to my ribs.

"Althea, it's you!" She grinned up at me. "Do you remember who I am?"

I glanced over her wheat-colored head, at my sisters. They watched me in anticipation, but I was too startled to say anything. I had been expecting Mnemosyne.

"We have the same nose," the girl prompted.

I looked at her then, really looked at her. Still, I had no idea who she was. "I'm sorry, I don't think—"

Bronte rolled her eyes. "This is Danica, our half-Titan sister."

My jaw quite literally fell open.

"Let us in," Cleora said, pushing past me.

They entered and began moving about the room. Bronte went straight to the food. The girl, Danica, plopped down on my bed and swung her feet.

"Is this a good surprise?" she asked.

My mouth bobbed open and shut.

"She's speechless," Bronte said.

"I was too," Cleora added.

Danica giggled. "Yes, but you two didn't make that face." She scrunched her nose and let her mouth fall open, mimicking me.

I shut my jaw. "How . . . ?"

"I've lived here my whole life," Danica said as though she were decades older. "Father took me in, and the nursemaids raised me."

"Father?"

"Cronus." She giggled again, then hopped down and pranced around the chamber.

Cleora reached for the full cup of wine I had poured earlier, but I grabbed it and held it away from her.

"I'm going to drink that." I pretended to press it to my lips. I wanted, deep inside my heart, to believe that our half sister had survived, but something didn't feel right. Cleora and Bronte would not so readily accept a stranger, no matter how adorable she might be, and then sashay in here as though her discovery was just passing news. "Cleora . . . Bronte . . . Do you remember the night Mama died?"

"Died?" Bronte replied. "She's not dead."

My heart gave a painful squeeze. "I mean Stavra."

Danica frowned. "Rhea is your mama."

I looked at the girl more closely now. She bore no resemblance to Stavra, or even to Cronus. Something about her felt out of place. I longed to reunite with my half sister, but everything about this felt too convenient.

"You must have been scared," I said, "when they took you away from us. You were just learning to walk."

"Oh, yes," she said, her eyes big and solemn. "I missed you all terribly. Though, in truth, I don't remember you well. I was very young."

I waited for Bronte or Cleora to correct her, to remind Danica that she had been taken from us on the very night that Mama died giving birth to her. Neither of them said anything. I'd thought—hoped—that their coming here and bossing me around like they normally did might mean that they still had some memories intact, but they were well and truly gone.

Why would Cronus fabricate memories for Bronte or Cleora, creating a false home here, and send us an imposter posing as our half sister? It was beyond manipulative, beyond selfish. It was deranged.

Another rap came at the door. Cleora answered it.

"Oh, Mnemosyne! Come in."

A petite woman floated into the chamber, moving with the grace of a dancer. Fiery-red hair, streaked with ribbons of white, framed her face. Her smoky-gray eyes glided over me, and her tiny rosebud mouth tilted downward. "I thought you were alone," she said.

"We were just leaving," Bronte replied, shoving a handful of nuts into her mouth. She took Danica by the shoulders and guided her toward the door.

Cleora hovered there, tugging on her lower lip. For a moment, I thought she remembered who she was and would step in to protect me, but instead, she reached out and pushed back a strand of my hair.

"You need a better brush," she said, and strolled out.

I gaped again, in utter dismay.

The goddess of memory eyed me with a dissatisfied frown. "So you're the Almighty's third daughter."

"I was informed that's who I am," I replied stiffly.

She shrugged. "We are who we were born to be."

I strode to the wine cask on unsteady knees, my nerves still unsettled from the encounter with my sisters. "Would you like a drink?"

"No, thank you."

"More for me." I poured a second cup and held them both.

"Nervous?"

"Wouldn't you be?" I countered.

Mnemosyne laughed, a short yet genuine sound. "No one has ever asked me that."

"Perhaps you should consider how it feels to have your memories taken away and replaced with lies."

Her eyes glittered. "You remind me of Stavra. She could always take a grim situation and turn it into something bearable."

"Let's make it more bearable, shall we?" I offered Mnemosyne the first cup of wine, the one I had poured earlier before my sisters arrived.

Mnemosyne hesitated, then pursed her lips and accepted the drink. For someone so petite and plump, she had extraordinarily long, slender fingers.

"You have beautiful hands," I said.

Again, a light laugh. "You cannot flatter me out of doing this."

"No? Then I suppose I'll have to get you drunk."

She sipped the wine. "I like you. I do hope this doesn't change you too much."

"Can we toast to that?"

Mnemosyne lifted her cup over her head. "To Althea. Long may she reign."

I bowed my head in appreciation, then we tapped cups and drank deeply. My palms began to sweat as we set down our cups. I rubbed them off on my skirt. "What sort of things did you alter in Stavra's memory?"

"I'm not certain I should tell you that," Mnemosyne replied, then jeered at herself. "What am I saying? I can always remove from your memory whatever I tell you."

I tried for a laugh, but it came out vacant.

"I will tell you one thing." She lowered her voice to a conspiratorial whisper. "Tassos's death wasn't an accident."

The suddenness of this admission caught me off guard. I took pause, and shoving down my rising dread, I asked, "What do you mean it wasn't an accident? Everyone I've spoken to about my father's death told me he drowned."

"A lie," she replied grimly. "Occasionally, I'm unable to alter someone's memories. Their mind is so intertwined with their soul, that to amend it would be to reshape their very essence, which is an ability I do not have. Tassos's was one of the few whose minds I could not change."

My voice shook as I replied. "What really happened to him?"

"To protect the existence and location of you and your sisters, Cronus had him killed, then I changed Stavra's memory of Tassos's death so she wouldn't recall what really happened. She repeated that altered memory to others until the truth was buried." Mnemosyne's attention turned inward. "At times, forgetting the past can be a mercy."

The truth of my father's death nearly collapsed my resolve. Cronus had killed both my parents and convinced my sisters of his innocence.

I pushed down my grief, my panic at becoming his next submissive doll, and refocused.

"Where do you want me?" I asked.

"Sit on that chair," she said.

I did as she requested. Mnemosyne stood behind me and put her hands on either side of my head, her fingers spreading to cover the back of my skull.

"The best thing you can do," she said, "is to clear your mind and breathe."

"Sounds easy enough."

She exhaled over me. In the reflection of the tin mirror glass that faced me, I watched Mnemosyne bow her head and murmur something under her breath. A moment later, her head rose, and her brow furrowed. She raised a hand to her temple.

"Forgive me," she said. "Suddenly, I'm dizzy."

"Sit here." I rose and offered her my chair.

"I don't know what's wrong. Perhaps I should have rested more before our session." She rubbed circles at her temples, her eyes drooping closed.

I grabbed the two cords I had set aside, one long and one short, and tied her torso to the chair with the longer piece. As I tied it off, her head snapped up.

"What are you doing?" she said drowsily.

"I suggest you clear your mind and breathe." I shoved the shorter cord between her lips, gagging her, then pulled an empty sack over her head.

I took the rest of her empty wineglass and dumped it out on the patio. Then, just to be safe, in case I somehow got the two cups confused, I poured out the other. The vial with the remainder of the magical draught was in my pocket. I had put half of it in Mnemosyne's drink, since Metis hadn't told me how much constituted a single dose.

I poured the rest into my waterskin and closed it, hoping it would be enough.

Another knock came at my door.

"Who is it?"

"Cleora," my sister called. "Are you and Mnemosyne finished?"

"We are." I dragged the chair across the room, set the bound goddess of memory in the corner, and rearranged the heavy drapery around her.

"Father has summoned us," Cleora said through the door.

"I'm coming."

I smoothed back my hair, dried my sweaty palms off on my skirt, and opened the door. Cleora looked past me, into the chamber, at the wine stains on the balcony.

"Accident," I said, slipping the strap of my waterskin over my shoulder.

She lifted a slim brow. "Did you enjoy meeting our long-lost sister? I expected more emotion from you."

I had to pretend that my memory had been tampered with. "I suppose I was in shock," I said, adding a profound sigh.

"Yes, it was wonderful of Father to reunite us. Come along. He won't wait forever."

Neither would I.

24

Cronus waited for us in the entry hall and embraced us one at a time, me last.

"Did you appreciate your surprise, Althea?"

"I did. Thank you, Father." It burned to call him that, but I had to convince him that my memory had been altered.

"Then you will like this surprise as well," he said, ushering us out of the entryway.

The guards opened the front gates. Through them, Theo led a donkey pulling a cart. My relief at seeing him safe was swiftly replaced by fury, mostly at myself for still caring about him. He stopped the cart a good distance from us but close enough to see its contents—a body in the back.

Zeus.

How Theo had captured the Boy God, I could not fathom, but once again, Zeus was unconscious.

"Colonel Angelos," Cronus called. "You're right on time."

"Do you have her?" Theo replied.

The Almighty waved, and from around the side of the palace, guards brought an older woman in bindings. She walked, hunched forward but with her chin raised, showing neither fear nor reverence for the God of Gods.

"Your mother is free to go," said Cronus. "Her service to the throne is fulfilled."

The guards untied her. She gave them a squinty-eyed glare and hobbled to her son.

"What have you done, my boy?" she asked.

Theo wrapped an arm around her and led her to the open gates. "I arranged a room for you at the tavern, Mama. Go have a meal and rest."

She patted his cheek and threw our group on the palace steps a glare. "Be careful, son."

Theo waited until she exited the gates, then stepped aside from the cart. General Decimus ordered Brigadier Orrin and two other soldiers to haul Zeus into the palace.

"Who is that, Father?" Cleora whispered.

"Why, that's your younger brother," Cronus replied.

Theo brought a cask of wine and set it down. "A gift, Your Excellency, from Helios's private collection. The soldiers left this one behind."

"A considerate gesture," Cronus replied, "from a traitor."

Decimus closed in on Theo. "Your sword," said the general.

Theo handed it over.

"Bring him in, and the wine." Cronus cast a knowing smirk at the sun. "It will vex Helios to know I have it."

Cronus led the way to the throne room. Bronte linked arms with Cleora, and the two of them walked ahead of me. I ended up by Theo.

"Althea, I—"

"Don't." I doubled my pace to catch up with my sisters.

The main-floor throne room was less grandiose than Cronus's isolated one in the tower in the sky, yet its rounded arches and beams still outshone the grandeur of Helios's mansion. The Almighty's immense throne sat on a dais against the far wall and could have accommodated someone ten times his size.

Zeus was laid on an altar in the center of the room.

"Daughters," Cronus said, "watch from over there."

Cleora and Bronte moved to the outskirts. I stayed close to Zeus. If my disobedience bothered Cronus, he didn't comment on it.

Cronus stood before the altar above Zeus's unconscious body. He studied him closely, expressionless, then raised his attention to the rest of the hall. "Decades ago, an oracle predicted I would fall at the hands of my youngest son just as my father fell by my hand. Many Titans began to question the longevity of my reign. Hunger for power had already divided my family. Much to my regret, centuries have passed since my brother Oceanus and I have spoken. I wanted better for my progeny."

Cronus signaled, and a soldier carried in a tray swathed in red velvet. He removed the cloth, revealing a jagged-toothed sickle. It may have been my imagination, but the tiny mark on the bottom of my right heel panged.

"Adamant can only be mined in the deepest trenches of the underworld," Cronus continued. "When forged into a blade, this raw, indestructible material has the unique capacity to open a soul. To absolve my children of the yearning for my throne and alleviate any urge they might have to compete against each other for power, I divested them of their Titan strength. These children are fortunate; they live unburdened by the competition for power. Among these six are my three daughters. Cleora, please step forward."

She did so.

"Before our daughters were handed off for mortals to raise, Rhea and I gave our oldest another name, a name by which she shall be known again, now and forevermore." Cronus paused and gestured toward Cleora. "That name is Hestia."

Cleora bowed her head and stepped back.

"Bronte, come forward."

She did so.

"Her name," Cronus continued, "is Demeter, chosen by Rhea and me on the day of her birth. Welcome home, daughter."

Bronte stepped back and stood beside Cleora again. My stomach pitched. They both wore untroubled expressions. Neither one appeared distressed by this impromptu renaming ceremony.

"And lastly, our youngest daughter was also given an eternal name. Althea?"

I bowed my head.

"I named you myself," Cronus went on, his voice full of pride. "You, my lioness daughter, are Hera."

Hestia, Demeter, and Hera . . . I had never heard these names before, yet at the mention of "Hera," a force began to unfurl inside me, like feathered wings flapping in my chest, beating against my rib cage.

"Rhea and I were also blessed with three sons," Cronus said, suddenly crestfallen. "But the youngest was kept a secret from me. Rhea didn't share my vision for our family, so she hid him away. Now, what I dreaded has happened at last. This boy—my son—has been turned against me. He was told that his fate was to overthrow his father, but this animosity among kin must end. Only then can my family reunite." Cronus lowered the sickle toward Zeus and, with its tip, cut the string ring off his hand. "Family doesn't abandon family."

The familiarity of his delivery stunned me; it was as though he had repeated it many times before. All this time, I had thought those words originated with my mother, but they were his.

I felt the world flip, my mind dangling to hang on to my reality. Cronus couldn't be our father. My sisters and I were mortal. I could hardly ever sit still. Bronte had a biting tongue. Cleora got after us when we didn't make our beds. We were achingly mortal.

And yet.

Something wild resided inside my bones, something that had always intimidated me. A side of myself so big, so monumental, that I feared what I might shatter should it break away.

Cronus turned Zeus's arm so his wrist faced up. As he lowered the sickle, I noticed five pairs of wings on his forearm—the same artwork I saw in Zeus's cave.

"What are you doing?" I asked.

"A prick on his foot won't suffice like I gave you and your sisters when you were infants. As a grown man, opening his soul requires a larger incision."

"Don't hurt him!" I charged forward, but Decimus and Orrin grabbed me and held me back. "Cronus, don't do this."

Cronus halted, the sickle just above Zeus's skin. "You still have your memories, Hera?"

"Enough of them that I know Danica isn't of my blood. What did you do to our real half sister?"

"I traded her away to Hyperion, with all the half-Titan bastards. She's traveling the world with the nomads from the east, last I was told."

I breathed hard to fight back my rising tears. "Was anything you told us about her true? Even her name?"

"Danica is the daughter of a slave. I paid her and her mother well for the girl to pretend she was your sister. I don't know what Stavra intended to call her half-Titan babe." Cronus tilted his head to the side, feigning sadness. "Bastard children don't belong in our fold. I do what must be done for the good of my family, just as you do, Hera."

"My name is Althea, and I'm nothing like you."

"But you are. Though you had the opportunity, you didn't turn yourself in to save Hestia. Nor did you offer yourself in place of Demeter. You allowed them to be taken. You make difficult decisions that no one else will, for the betterment of everyone. Who else does that emulate?"

He had no idea why I did what I did. All my life, everyone had said I was like my mother. I hadn't believed them until now. Stavra never let anyone know how much she was willing to bleed for those she loved.

"Take me instead," I said.

"You're already divested of your strength." Cronus gave me a pitying look. "You know what must be done. Have faith. When this is finished, your brother will be just like you."

But I wasn't me. I was who Cronus told me I should be. The "me" I was fated to be had been taken away, drained out by a prick on my heel.

He lowered the sickle again, then stopped as flapping noises came from above and shadows fell across the floor. All eyes lifted to the open windows high above the throne room. There, the Erinyes were perched, scourges in hand, glaring down at me.

I had run out of time.

25

Cronus lowered his attention from the Erinyes above to those of us standing around him, his blade stopped over Zeus's arm. "What are they doing here?" he demanded.

"They came to collect me," Theo announced.

"You?" I replied. "But you completed your atoning task."

"I was never given an atoning task." He stared at me intensely. "I was playing dead."

My mind ran circles around itself. None of this made sense. Theo said the Erinyes had promised his mother's freedom in exchange for delivering Zeus to Cronus. And he had done just that. Why tell a different story now?

Unless Zeus wasn't really unconscious . . .

Unless *he* was playing dead.

"Your Excellency," Theo said. "May I have one last drink before I go? I carried that cask of wine all the way from the Midnight Mansion. I'll not be having wine like that in Tartarus."

"I could certainly use a drink," Bronte said, sounding so much like herself I wondered whether she, too, had tricked Mnemosyne. Then again, I had never known her to turn down a cup of wine.

"Yes, Father!" Cleora chimed in. "We could toast to our family reuniting."

"Allowing the colonel one last drink would be the merciful thing to do," I added.

"Father is always merciful," Cleora replied.

Cronus's smile resembled more of a wince. "All right," he agreed. "One celebratory drink, for my daughters—Hestia, Demeter, and Hera—for the return of my son Zeus, and for the colonel's years of service to the First House."

The slaves brought in chalices and opened the cask. They filled a canter and watered it down a little, then half filled the cups. My sisters, Theo, Cronus, and I each took a chalice. I diluted mine further using my own waterskin, which I had emptied the last of the magical draught Metis concocted into.

"Why do you ruin the wine, Hera?" Cronus asked, his shrewd gaze on my chalice.

"She prefers hers more watered down," Bronte explained. Her response was so quick and smooth that I again questioned if her memory was indeed intact.

Cronus gave a skeptical "hmm."

Bronte beamed at him, unconcerned by his suspicion, then the second he looked away from her, she winked at me.

Stars, she *was* herself.

Everyone raised their cups, and I locked gazes with Theo. I didn't know what the magical draught would do to me should I ingest it. I could only hope that I had correctly guessed his hint about playing dead.

"To family," Cronus said.

As he tipped back his head to drink, Zeus launched off the altar and grabbed him around the throat.

"Althea, now!" Zeus cried.

I squeezed Cronus's nose shut and threw the contents of my cup in his face. He sputtered and reared back. It was too late. Some of the magical draught had gone down his throat.

Zeus let him go. Cronus hunched forward, bracing against the altar, and started to gag. Decimus ran forward, but Zeus grabbed him by the throat and lifted him off the ground in one motion. Decimus dangled from his grasp, his hands gripping Zeus's forearms.

Cronus sank to the ground, coughing and grasping at his throat.

I picked up the adamant sickle. "You say you did this for your family, but you weakened us to protect yourself. That isn't sacrifice, that's selfishness."

Cronus lay on his belly, panting, his cheek pressed against the floor. Sweat poured from his face and neck. The wings on his forearm began to flap as though they were moths in a bottle trying to escape. I touched one set with the tip of the sickle, and they flapped harder.

Bronte joined me, standing over Cronus as he writhed on the floor. She sent me a sly grin. "Mnemosyne's brainwashing didn't work on you either?"

"Never got the chance to find out." Mnemosyne had said that some people weren't affected by her, but it had been too much to hope that my sisters would be among them. I peered down at the beating wings on Cronus's arm. "Perhaps the rumor that he ate his children wasn't a complete lie. Maybe he consumed their Titan strength."

Bronte raised an eyebrow. "Could it be that simple?"

Cronus groaned. Bronte stood on his hand, pinning his arm to the floor. I lowered the pointy end of the sickle and punctured the first set of wings. They fluttered harder, like a bird caught in a cat's claws. I dragged the blade up his arm, slicing through the other four pairs. The wings flapped so hard they began to peel off his skin and rise. The first two took off, out of the palace. The third sped at Cleora and dived into her chest. She jolted as a golden light burst out of her, then the light dimmed, and she collapsed. Theo caught her as she sank and he laid her on the floor.

Another pair of wings sailed at Bronte. As her flash of golden light went out, she crumpled. I reached out to catch her, but the last pair of wings rushed into me.

My vision filled with luminance. I hit the ground, pain a distant thought, my senses shrouded by the tingling light radiating from me. Through the glimmering, immobilizing fogginess, I saw soldiers file into the throne room and aim their swords at Zeus. He put down the general and backed away. Zeus and Theo were surrounded, my sisters passed out. The Erinyes waited above, watching for the opportune time to swoop down and grab Theo.

Sickle in hand, Cronus started for Zeus. He swung the blade at him, and Zeus ducked. Cronus punched him, and Zeus slammed into the wall, where Cronus pinned him. Thunder boomed overhead.

"There will be none of that, son."

I watched, still numb, as Cronus picked Zeus up and threw him across the room. He crashed through the exterior wall and landed outside in the gardens. He tried to push himself up but slumped back down again. The sky began to clear, and Cronus, still armed with the sickle, went to finish him.

An Erinys swooped down for Theo, her scourges lashing at him. He ducked low over Cleora's unconscious body. The Erinys missed and began circling back.

I needed to get up, but exhaustion dragged me toward a far-off light. Coming into my Titan strength all at once was like trying to drink from a waterfall. My eyes began to close, my body sinking toward the golden glow. A humming filled my head, and within it, the barest of whispers.

Rise.

The voice pierced me to the core.

Rise.

Louder this time, scattering my fogginess. My vision cleared, and I pushed up. Cronus was headed for the opening in the wall, stalking Zeus, who still hadn't gotten up.

I pushed to my feet, woozy and winded. "Cronus!"

He rotated toward me in astonishment. "You shouldn't have the strength to rise yet."

"You should be so lucky."

The God of Gods started for me, blood streaming from the incision on his forearm. A murkiness fringed him, a sort of vapor—the shape of his soul. I couldn't quite make it out. My vision was still fuzzy, as though I had stared into the sun too long.

"Bitch," Cronus growled. "How did you figure out that the sickle could release your strength?"

"Adamant cannot destroy gods; it can only weaken them." In one sense, all mortals resembled gods—their souls could be displaced but not destroyed. Death was circumstantial. The soul lived forever.

Across the throne room, the Erinyes swooped down at Theo. He stood over Cleora, warding them off with his sword.

Cronus swiped at me with the sickle. I evaded and punched him in the chest. It felt instinctual, like a long-time dream fulfilled. He flew backward across the room, landing on the steps of the dais.

I gaped at my hands. I had *strength*.

The soldiers cowered. None of them, not even Decimus, dared to come forward and test my new abilities.

An Erinys picked Theo off the ground and began carrying him out of the palace. I leaped higher than I had ever imagined I could and knocked us all into the wall. The Erinys let go of Theo, and we fell to the floor in a heap.

He groaned, out of breath but lucid.

I pushed to my feet as Cronus rose too. Only . . . he was growing, and the sickle grew with him. Cronus's head almost touched the ceiling, but despite his immense size, he floated weightlessly above the floor. The God of Gods roared, sending the Erinyes scattering.

"Do you know the benefits of being a first-generation Titan?" he asked, grinning with his sharp teeth. "Invincible strength."

He flew at me, catching me by the throat with his free hand. We slammed through the wall and rose steeply into the sky. A blur of scenery streamed past. The ground gave way to the sea, and then we rose into the firmament. We passed the clouds and through midheaven until the atmosphere resolved into an inky-blue chasm studded with diamond stars.

"I am the first and the last ruler of the Titans," Cronus snarled, strangling me with one of his huge hands. "I command the heavens and earth. My domain knows no bounds."

"Not. My. God," I rasped. "Not. My. Ruler."

I pried myself from his hold and bit down on his forearm. He howled and loosened his other hand's grip on the sickle. I wrenched it away and flung it out to space. One second, it was hurling toward the far-off moon, and the next, it was gone.

"You witless wretch!" Cronus grabbed me by the shoulders. "That sickle is worth more than your soul!"

"More than two hundred silver pieces?"

Cronus shook me hard.

That's when I saw them—his wings.

They were not physical. They were smoky extensions of his gloomy soul. Black and feathery, they protruded from his back and expanded to twice the width of his Titan form.

"I can see the shape of your soul," I said, hardly believing it myself. "You're like a black vulture, remorseless and vindictive. Menacing and cruel."

"Careful, Hera. You're describing yourself. Just as half my soul came from my father, half of your soul came from me."

According to Cronus, my own soul was a winged lion, part him and part Rhea.

But I was wholly me.

Cronus sneered. "You think you're a goddess? Then bring me the stars."

He tossed me away, spread his horrible wings, and took off for the earth.

I spun, reaching for anything to hold on to, but there was nothing solid in the starry abyss. I neither slowed nor picked up speed, merely tumbled end over end into the void. Earth fell farther away as I entered a forest of stars. Their brightness flooded past me, leaving trails of glittering dust in their wake. Uranus promised I could command the heavens . . . I reached for a single white star and plucked it out of the endless night.

Cradled in my palm, its radiance tingled.

Still spinning out to nowhere, I closed my eyes.

Breathe.

I didn't want to be my mother or my father or anything anyone told me I had to be. I just wanted to be me.

Warmth coursed through my core. The light that had beckoned me earlier returned, its luster outmatching the sun. A pressure inside me unfurled, spread out behind me, and lifted me up. The speed of my free fall slowed, and my body righted itself.

Opening my eyes, I found myself hanging weightless among a constellation of four stars, suspended by golden wings, extensions of my soul, tawny like a lion's coat, but feathery too. I had never seen anything more *me*.

I flapped my wings on instinct and propelled myself forward. Soon, I hovered over the earth. Clutching the star to my chest, I dived with my wings tucked in behind me, dropping through a clear blue sky. Before plummeting into the sea, I threw my wings open and soared over the waves, rising back up the steep mountainside to the city.

As I approached the palace, I spotted the Cretan warriors battling the liege men outside and spilling over into the palace. My chest swelled at seeing the tribe escaped from the slave traders and fighting for their Boy God. Euboea shouted orders at her troops, and the warriors held their ground, their gold velos flickering in the sunlight like flames.

Theo fought with Decimus, their swords clashing. The Erinyes were nowhere in sight.

I soared over the battle into the throne room. Zeus was on his back with Cronus on top of him, crushing his windpipe. I dived down and smashed into the Almighty, throwing him across the room. I landed on the dais with my wings outstretched.

The walls and floors were pockmarked with scorched patches. Fires burned in the corners among piles of rubble, and smoke escaped through new holes in the ceiling. Bronte and Cleora were still passed out. Zeus didn't get up, but Cronus lumbered to his feet.

"I see you've accepted your wings, Hera."

"You could say that." I held up the burning light in my hand. "Here's your star."

I pitched it at him. The star hit the ceiling above him and exploded in a glittering majesty of radiance, brilliant particles of red, pink, blue, and violet. Stone rained down on Cronus while I scooped up my sisters, draping one and then the other over my shoulders. He caught a large piece of the falling ceiling and hurled it at us. I was thrown backward, dropping Bronte and Cleora along the way, and smashed into his throne. He lifted a fallen column and shoved it across my throat, pinning me.

"Stavra said you would be my downfall. She thought too highly of you, of all women. You're weak, every one of you. You think with your hearts."

"We love, and love isn't weak," I wheezed. "She knew you were unworthy."

"Stavra was a whore. She wouldn't weep. It took twenty-three days of bedding her morning and night for her to break. Her tears tasted sweeter than nectar."

I shoved upward against the column as hard as I could, but I was breathless, my strength failing.

"So weak." Cronus tsked.

Darkness crept in. I saw stars again, but these were of no use to me.

A bank of thunderheads roiled overhead. Cronus looked up as a lightning bolt struck the column across my throat, cracking it apart and throwing Cronus off me.

Out of the dust and rubble, Zeus appeared and lifted me to my feet.

"You can fly, Althea? Or is it Hera? I don't know what to call you now."

"That's easy. Just call me 'goddess.'"

He picked up a velo that one of the warriors had dropped, and offered it to me. I put it on and stood. Together, we turned to face the God of Gods.

Cronus hovered, his wings fully extended. He hefted another column, resting it over his shoulder in preparation to swing.

Zeus opened his hand, and a lightning bolt hurtled down to it from the thunderhead. He cast it at Cronus like a spear. The Almighty struck the lightning bolt with the column, redirecting it back at us and flinging us sideways. Zeus and I crashed through columns and landed in a heap on opposite sides of the room from each other.

Cronus laughed, a darkly delighted sound. "Is that the best my children have to offer? Neither of you is worthy of my throne."

I started to get up, but he slammed me across the back with the column. Jagged fragments of lightning bolts sizzled around me. I tried reaching for one, but my fingertips fell shy.

Another voice spoke nearby. "Father?"

Cleora stood to his side, fists raised. Gossamer insectile wings spread from her back, their iridescent sheen threaded with comblike veins. She launched off the floor in a mighty leap and punched Cronus across the chin.

"That's for hitting Althea."

The Almighty spun from the impact, only to find Bronte waiting on his other side. Her wings were reptilian, with leathery skin, well-defined veins, and talons at the widest tips. Dragon wings. She smacked Cronus's face with the sharp end of one, producing an ear-splitting crack.

"That's for making Cleora wear yellow," she said.

Cronus stumbled to the side, gripping his jaw.

"Yellow really is my worst color," Cleora agreed.

Cronus glared at her. "Your loyalty is fickle, Hestia." He picked up a sharp shaving of lightning bolt and slammed it into her chest. Cleora crumpled over, the spike of light protruding from her torso. Bronte fell to her knees beside her in horror.

Alighting, I sped at Cronus and slammed into him, hurtling us through the wall of windows. Holding him, I shot us upward, far above the city and the sea, higher and higher, past midheaven, until we were back in the vault of stars. He grappled with me for control, the two of us spinning as I shoved back, aiming us for the sun. The increasing heat began to singe my wings as I propelled us closer, as close as I dared.

Cronus twisted around, forcing my back toward the solar flares. "Do you really think you can overpower me, Hera? The whole world trembles at my name. You will be known only for the gods you align with and the Titans who take you into their bed."

"There's one other thing I'll be known for." I plucked a star from the firmament; its brilliance fit perfectly in my palm. "Don't ever cross me."

I shoved the star into Cronus's mouth, then thrust him around and pushed with all my might. He tumbled backward, toward the sun, plummeting into the blinding light.

As swiftly as possible, I dashed back to the palace. The throne room was a disaster, the structure crumbling. The highest tower that housed the great hall teetered. The warriors and soldiers paused upon my arrival. When Cronus did not also return, Euboea called for the soldiers' surrender.

Theo held a disarmed Decimus at sword point. I landed, ripped off my velo, and grabbed Decimus by the front of his shirt.

"Revoke the curse," I growled.

Decimus tried to tear free, but I gripped him harder and lifted him off the ground, locking him in the same hold he had used to capture my mother all those years ago.

"Revoke it," I repeated. "Or I will abandon your worthless hide on the moon, and you will die a slow, agonizing death alone."

"I revoke my curse," he sputtered.

The scar on the back of my neck burned so hot it turned icy, then the sensation abated. I touched it, and the skin had become smooth, his tag gone.

I let go. Decimus fell to the ground, coughing, his armor clanging. Blood spilled from his lips and trickled down his chin. The harder he tried to breathe, the more he choked. He rolled onto his side, gurgling, and stared up at me. Bloody tears trailed from his empty eyes. The curse had claimed him.

The lower palace began to crumble, and the tower wobbled precariously. Everyone began to run for shelter. Bronte and Cleora half stumbled, half flew out of the throne room, Cleora injured but upright.

Bronte shouted at me as they fled. "Zeus is still inside!"

The base of the tower cracked, and it began to drop in on itself, right on top of the lower floors. I flew inside and found Zeus trapped under a wall. Together, we lifted it off him, then I grabbed him up and we shot through the falling rubble, landing in the roadway outside the palace gates. The raining debris spread out into the city in clouds of stone and dust.

"I think," Zeus panted, "I think I landed more hits than you."

"Not this time, Boy God."

Cronus's black vulture landed nearby and hopped over to Decimus's body.

I searched the sky for the Almighty, but instead, I spotted the fleeing Erinyes, with Theo caught in their scourges. I flew up to them, blocking their path.

"Put him down, you shadowy plagues," I ordered.

The Erinyes hissed at me in chorus.

The sky around us darkened. Storm clouds rumbled. On the ground below, Zeus summoned a bolt of lightning with a colossal boom.

"Theo Angelos honored his oath to the throne," I said. "*Our* thrones. Release him."

The Erinyes hissed louder.

Zeus raised his jagged spear of lightning threateningly. The Erinyes lowered Theo to the ground and recalled their scourges, hissing the whole way. Theo collapsed to his knees, breathing hard. I helped him up as they took off into the sky.

Across the way, the warriors rounded up the liege men, and Euboea dictated the terms of surrender to Brigadier Orrin.

Bronte and Cleora supported each other, standing among the rubble. Cleora's chest wound was a bloody mess, but she would heal. With the two of them safe, I leaned against Theo, and he wrapped an arm around me. At our feet was the fallen palace gate, the section with the alpha and omega symbols.

"This isn't finished," I said warily, resting my head against his shoulder. "Cronus will be back."

"Then he will have you to deal with."

"Us," I corrected, my gaze jumping from my sisters to Zeus and then up at Theo.

His other arm came around me, embracing me tightly. "Yes, us."

26

The late-day sun descended behind the far-off hills, casting a glow across the rolling fields of wheat and transforming the earth into a sea of gold. I soared over the plowlands of tares, ruffling the fields of wheat below me. Ahead, dark specks appeared in the expanse of golden straw. Bronte swooped down beside me, pacing my speed.

"Do you think that's them?" she asked.

Cleora banked and joined us. "Helios is expecting us back for dinner soon. I think Eos and Selene are coming."

I squinted at the low-hanging sun to the west. "We have time to question one more group before sundown."

Bronte sang to herself and dived lower, brushing her fingertips across the silky heads of wheat. I flapped my feathery wings harder, reclaiming the lead. My sisters hung back, our V formation improving each time we flew. Though we were making progress with our Titan strengths, we couldn't get used to our new names. We were reluctant to accept anything given to us by Cronus, but that might yet change. We were still new Titanesses with optimism for the future, yet we had much to learn.

Two white-winged horses glided down to join us. Theo waved from his steed, borrowed from Helios, and Zeus waved from his, an early wedding gift from Metis.

"Race you!" I cried.

I zipped ahead, my hair and clothes billowing, my face stinging from the force of my speed. Theo and Zeus quickly fell behind, but Bronte and Cleora raced neck and neck at my flanks. Soon we were circling a group of laborers harvesting the fields of wheat.

I slowed, descended to the ground, and jogged to a stop. My chest pumped as I drew in and tucked away my wings. My sisters landed and folded their wings away too. The laborers were frightened, crowding together and holding their sickles defensively. Nomadic laborers traveled with their families, bringing their children with them into the fields as soon as they were able to walk. Their long robes, high collars, and wide-brimmed hats shielded them from the scorching sun but made them difficult to identify individually.

"We don't wish to keep you from your work," I said. "We're looking for someone. A girl, no older than seven. She might have dark hair."

"Or red hair," Cleora added.

"Or blonde," said Bronte. She pointed at me. "But definitely with a big nose, like hers. Has anyone seen this girl?"

As with the other people we had questioned for weeks, this group's children were too old. The adults were clearly intimidated, and they must have been eager to finish their day's work. I decided to bid them farewell just as Zeus and Theo caught up to us.

And then I saw her.

A girl playing with a straw-stuffed doll, alone and half-hidden in the high wheat. Her dark, curly hair framed her suntanned face. I padded closer and saw that she was cradling the doll and singing it a lullaby that I heard whenever I awoke from a nightmare and Theo sang me back to sleep.

I walked over to the girl and crouched down. A woman I presumed to be her mother from her look of concern watched while she worked. The girl looked up. Except for the two missing front teeth, she fit our description, big nose and all.

"Divine day," I said. "I like your doll. What's her name?"

"Ismena."

"Ismena is a pretty name. I'm Althea. Some people call me Hera. What do they call you?"

"Delphine."

I kept my voice neutral, even as my throat sealed shut. It was another pretty name. A name my mother might have chosen for her. "Delphine, has anyone ever told you that you have a lovely singing voice?"

"My mama."

"Your mama is right." I glanced at the woman who had adopted her and smiled, then returned my attention to the girl. "May I show you a secret, Delphine? It might frighten you."

"No, it won't," she said, lifting her chin high.

"Even adults find it scary sometimes. Do you promise you won't shy away?"

Delphine thought carefully, then nodded. I had been wrong. She did look more like me than she did my sisters, but she resembled Stavra most.

"All right, Delphine. Remember, you don't have to be afraid." I straightened my back and then spread my wings to their full width. Delphine's eyes grew big, and she clutched her doll closer, shielding its face. "Am I scaring you?"

"No."

"Is Ismena afraid?"

Delphine pulled the doll away from her chest and looked into its painted face. Her lips lifted in a smile. "Ismena thinks your wings are beautiful."

Hot tears gathered in my eyes. I could feel her then, Stavra's soul, whispering through the rippling rows of wheat and warming my back like the afternoon sunshine.

"May I introduce you to my sisters?" I asked, adding a secretive whisper. "And if your mama says it's all right, we can take a ride on one of the winged horses."

"Mama?" Delphine asked.

The woman, still watching and listening from close by, gave a succinct dip of her chin.

"Can Ismena come too?" Delphine asked me.

"Do you promise to take care of her?"

She nodded solemnly and slipped her small hand into mine.

A thread of warmth wound around our joined hands, an invincible, invisible link, stronger than spider's silk. It branched out to Cleora, and then to Bronte, weaving us together in a unified tapestry that left me breathless and made my heart soar. Perhaps our connection had always been there, bound by my oath to Stavra, but I knew then, without a doubt, that this constellation of sisters had never been composed of just three stars. It had always had one more.

I squeezed Delphine's little hand, confident that, together, my sisters and I could take on any challenge. Then I stretched my wings wide. "Let's fly."

ACKNOWLEDGMENTS

Warmest thanks to:

Adrienne Procaccini, my savvy acquisitions editor, for taking me on and bringing me into the fold at 47North. Not only do you have the coolest hair colors, but you're the nerdy girl heroine I have always wanted on my side. I look forward to working with you in the years to come.

Jason Kirk, the developmental editor of my dreams. I don't think you have any idea just how much you changed my life for the better. Someday I hope to repay you. Until then, keep brutalizing my manuscripts, and I will keep bringing them back to life. Thank you for believing in me.

Marlene Stringer, agent extraordinaire. No one else quite understands what this mom of four is going through. You "get it," fellow warrior mom.

Clarence Haynes, my truest advisor. Dinners in NYC and chats over email only scratch the surface of just how dearly I cherish your counsel and direction. I will always be in your debt, you brilliant, beautiful man.

Brittany Russell, Kristin King, Michael Jantze, and the rest of the crew at Amazon Publishing, thank you for working tirelessly on my behalf. Your enthusiasm for my stories is a light in my life.

Michael Makara, for pancakes and flowers and desks with monitors. But most of all for being my muse.

Joseph, Julian, Danielle, and Ryan—Mom wrote another book! We all know what that means. Dance party in the kitchen! And John, for continuing to root me on and for picking up the slack.

Mom and Dad, for the endless hours of chats and dinners and hugs. I love you both very much.

My beloved sisters, Stacey, Sarah, and Eve. Thanks for providing me fodder for this story. Guess which Lambros sister is based off of you? Just kidding. Or am I . . . ?

My gang of pals: Kate Coursey, Veeda Bybee, Kathryn Purdie, Sara B. Larson, Tricia Levenseller, Jessie Farr, Rebekah Crane, Ashley and Leslie Saunders, Natalie Barnum, and Lauri Schoenfeld. Your texts and messages and phone calls and memes keep me sane. Relatively.

ABOUT THE AUTHOR

Photo © 2015 Erin Summerill

Emily R. King is the author of the Hundredth Queen series, as well as *Before the Broken Star*, *Into the Hourglass*, and *Everafter Song* in the Evermore Chronicles. Born in Canada and raised in the United States, she is a shark advocate, a consumer of gummy bears, and an islander at heart, but her greatest interests are her children and their three cats. For more information, visit her at www.emilyrking.com.